I0607355

Just who was guiding who?

Hakon growled and pulled his own backpack from the Land Rover, locked the vehicle, then stalked down the trail after her.

It took him all of two seconds to decide he should have been the one walking in front. Faith strode ahead of him, dodging ruts and potholes with sure feet. Her hips swayed with each step in a compelling rhythm that drove his body into a riot. He imagined drawing her back against him, kissing that spot behind her ear where tendrils of golden hair had fallen loose....

She stopped dead and turned around with wide eyes. Damn, had he said something out loud? He thought he'd seen a flash in her eyes just before they saw the truck. There it was again, though before, he could have sworn her eyes had been sil—

"Aren't you supposed to be in front of me?" she asked.

Desire and doubt vanished. "I would have been, if you hadn't bolted off in the first place." He stepped around her and went on without pausing. "Next time, let me go first. Clear?"

"Get up on the wrong side of the bed?"

He didn't bother telling her he hadn't slept at all. Her presence had echoed through the walls of the inn like a resonating bell, one moment consuming him with the need to go to her, and the next, driving him away in a fit of resentment.

She was money. His ticket to freedom, nothing more.

Maybe if he kept telling himself that, he might start to believe it.

Praise for Nicki Greenwood

"Tightly written...tense and fascinating...hot."
~Danica St. Como, author

~*~

THE SERPENT IN THE STONE
won 3rd Place
2006 Barclay Sterling Contest

~*~

FLASHPOINT
won 2nd Place
2006 Golden Pen Contest

Flashpoint

by

Nicki Greenwood

The Gifted Series, Book Two

This is a work of fiction. Names, characters, places, and incidents are either the product of the author's imagination or are used fictitiously, and any resemblance to actual persons living or dead, business establishments, events, or locales, is entirely coincidental.

Flashpoint

COPYRIGHT © 2014 by Nicki Greenwood

All rights reserved. No part of this book may be used or reproduced in any manner whatsoever without written permission of the author or The Wild Rose Press, Inc. except in the case of brief quotations embodied in critical articles or reviews.
Contact Information: info@thewildrosepress.com

Cover Art by *Kim Mendoza*

The Wild Rose Press, Inc.
PO Box 708
Adams Basin, NY 14410-0708
Visit us at www.thewildrosepress.com

Publishing History
First Faery Rose Edition, 2014
Print ISBN 978-1-62830-545-6
Digital ISBN 978-1-62830-546-3

The Gifted Series, Book Two

Dedication

For Bruce

Chapter One

I dreamt of the Viking man again last night, plowing his land while his wife sat outside sewing. I couldn't see her face. I never can. Sometimes I dream that it's me.
—Faith's Journals, age twelve

Faith Markham stepped into The Piper's Keg with no greater intention than to sit down and soothe her aching feet. She'd searched half of the telephone book and most of Sydney's nicer boroughs, and then started on the not-so-nice ones.

Didn't Australia believe in wilderness guides?

Perfect days didn't exist, not even close. But as imperfect ones went, this one took the cake.

On the recommendation of a guy who knew a guy, who knew a guy, she'd shuffled off to this pub. Which, to be charitable, looked a bit less like a hole in the earth than...well, a hole in the earth. She doubted she'd find a guide to lead her into the mountains here, either. She had almost resolved to turn right back around and head home, and damn all the trouble.

But the boy needed her.

It had been months before she could find reasonable excuses to get away from her archaeology lectures at New York City's Whitehall University. With a holiday break coming on, the department director had granted her a reprieve. She hoped it would be long enough to help her find the boy before someone else did. All her good intentions of offering her help with his paranormal gift would be for nothing if he ran into the wrong sort of people first.

She sat at the end of the bar, away from the noise of a rugby game on the pub's one television. A row of afternoon patrons crowded the bar's other end, shouting at the referee as if he could hear them.

The barman approached her. "What can I get you, love?"

"Just a cup of tea, please."

He shrugged and beckoned a passing waitress to fill the order. Faith sighed and stretched her long legs out in front of the barstool. She lifted her ponytail and fanned the back of her neck; while New York prepared for winter, Australia had just settled in for the summer. Already it was warm, and warmer still in the stuffy pub.

"Blondie. Oi, blondie. What do you think of the game?"

She looked up. A red-haired young man grinned at her from two seats away. At thirty-one, she guessed herself to be a good five or ten years his senior. Two other men leaned past him to leer in her direction. *Oh, for crying out loud. I've been here two minutes, and already I'm getting the idiot brigade.* "Rugby's not my thing, thanks."

She wished she hadn't spoken the instant the words left her mouth. The first man beamed and slid over to the barstool beside hers. A choking cloud of cologne followed him. "You're a Yank, are you?"

"I'm American, if that's what you're getting at," she answered, trying not to cough.

His two friends plopped down uninvited on adjacent barstools, crowding close to her. "First time in Australia?" asked the redheaded one. "If you need someone to show you some things, I'm your man." He gave her a suggestive grin, and his leg nudged hers.

She drew her legs back and tucked them under her barstool with a smirk. "Actually, I'm looking for a guide."

"There you go, Jeff. She needs a guide," said the brown-haired man sitting on her other side. He waggled his eyebrows at the redhead and sat back. Faith saw a curvy, cartoon woman on his T-shirt. *Stick It Where It's Wet*, read the surfboard strategically placed over the woman's private parts. Groan.

Jeff's smile broadened. "I'll guide you anywhere you want to go, sweetheart."

"Stick It" gave a snorting laugh. The third man hailed the waitress for a basket of fish and chips.

Just great. They were planning to stay. Faith cleared her throat. "I appreciate the offer, but I intend to go hiking in the mountains. Have any of you heard of a man called Goldy? I was told to look for him here."

"Sure, everybody's heard of Goldy," Jeff said, leering. "Goldy's a regular celebrity around here, he is. Isn't that right, mates?"

Jeff's friends nodded with enthusiasm, but offered no further information. All three looked her up and down as though she wore less than the tank top and khaki shorts she'd plucked from her suitcase that morning.

Double groan. She might as well have asked for the Dalai Lama, and gotten the same answer.

The waitress approached with her tea. Faith

accepted it and took a long drink, ignoring the scorch on her tongue. She put a few bills down beside the cup, and stood up. "This has been fun, gentlemen, but I'm serious."

Jeff stood up in a swift, smooth motion, and took her hand. "So are we, sweetheart. Why d'you want to leave so soon? I think the three of us could help you find Goldy, all right."

This had gone far enough. She dropped her casual tone, and gave the young man a calm stare. "I think you have about five seconds to let go of me."

He didn't, tugging her hand in an attempt to draw her closer. "Aw, now, don't be like that."

"Three seconds," she said, and narrowed her eyes.

"*No* seconds," boomed a voice from behind her assailant.

Jeff released her hand with a look of shock, and was lifted clear off his feet. The man behind Jeff set him aside as easily as if he were a sack of feathers.

Faith's gaze drifted to the newcomer's face, and froze there. "Oh my frigging God."

Hakon.

She wondered if her eyesight might be fooling her. The man standing before her couldn't possibly be the thousand-year-old Viking warrior she'd dreamt of during most of her childhood. The same man whose ghost she'd seen—and spoken to—in visions months ago while on a dig in Shetland. She and her team had excavated the buried ruin of Hakon's Viking-era house.

Jeff's friends rallied around him. Encouraged, the redhead wedged himself in front of her once more. "We were talking to the lady, mate. You'll just have to wait your turn."

"You're done talking to the lady, mate," Hakon repeated, emphasizing "lady" with a faint sarcastic bite. His deep, vibrant voice matched his impressive size. The sound echoed down every nerve in her body, so distracting that she almost didn't catch his accent.

Not Scandinavian at all, but Australian. She felt her mouth drop open.

Apparently possessing more bravado than sense, Jeff scoffed. "Find your own girl."

Hakon drew himself up to his full height—much taller than Jeff—and scowled. Jeff lasted about half a beat under that withering stare. He retreated with his friends back to the bar, muttering.

Hakon turned to her at last. Faith could do nothing but gape. The last time she'd seen him, just before leaving Shetland... Hell, she hadn't even really *seen* him—not in waking life—only felt the psychic chill of his ghostly presence.

And here he was. Living. Breathing. Maybe. She wrestled with the urge to touch his broad chest, and see if he was warm.

He looked just as she remembered from her dreams. Strong. Stern. As sharp-featured as though he'd been chiseled from granite. Eyes the mesmerizing turquoise of tropical waters. His copper-gold mane lay loose on his shoulders, longer than most men wore their hair these days. Altogether breathtaking.

And still scowling. "What do you want with me?" he demanded.

She wanted to start with "What the hell are you doing alive, and in Australia?" and segue right into "I want you so badly I can't breathe," but thought better of it. Her mouth seemed to have forgotten how to form words anyway.

His gaze traveled up and down her body, and her skin tingled as though he'd brushed against it. "You are looking for Goldy, right?"

"Yeah," she managed. She *had* to call her sister. Sara would never believe this. Faith's heartbeat surged against her ribs.

"Where are you planning to go?" He crossed his arms over his bright-blue T-shirt.

The motion made his pecs and biceps bulge, and she forgot to answer his question. She tried to raise her stare from his chest, but couldn't budge it.

Hakon bent his knees just enough to bring his gaze level with hers. One eyebrow arched. "You need a guide, yes? Bushwalking, or the rural tour?"

The men at the bar hollered at the television again. Startled out of her daze, she met his sea-blue stare. "Ah... Bushwalking. I guess. I'm... Could we...?" She gestured outside, still reeling. *...run straight to my hotel?*

Without another word, he headed for the door.

She pulled herself together and strode after him, blinking as she emerged into the bright Australian sun. "Wait a minute."

He halted beside a safety-yellow Land Rover parked at the curb.

"I thought we should start with introductions. I'm Doctor Markham." She stuck her hand out.

He shook it. Brief, firm, almost curt. His warm, rough paw engulfed her smaller hand, and then released it. "You can call me Goldy."

"Goldy," she repeated. Her hand still echoed the warmth of his. No frostbite sensations there. Not by a long shot.

He was very much alive.

He must have mistaken her skeptical response to his name for confusion. "It's either the hair, or the earring," he said, putting a finger to his left earlobe. A small gold hoop flashed in the sun. "We're not very formal around here." He fished a set of keys from the pocket of his jeans.

She couldn't help noticing the way the wash-worn denim curved along his muscular thighs and—*ahem*—incredible rear. Wow. No, really. *Wow.* Her dreams had nothing on present-day Hakon. *Goldy, my foot.*

He opened the Land Rover's passenger door, then sifted through a stack of maps on the dashboard. "Where do you want to go bushwalking? There are a lot of good trails in the high country, unless you'd rather check out the—"

She stared at his expansive back as the enormity of her situation came crashing in on top of her. "H-Hakon Ivarsson."

****

He stilled, then turned around with his handful of maps. No one in Sydney ever called him Hakon anymore, not since Lilah. Had the bitch decided to visit some new wrath upon him in the form of one of her conniving friends? Angry suspicion crawled along the back of his neck. "Do I know you?"

The willowy blond in front of him shifted on her feet. "In a manner of speaking," she muttered, though he couldn't be sure she'd meant to address him. She shivered, ponytail bouncing with the motion. "I need to go into the Blue Mountains."

Need to? He wondered what could be so pressing

as to encourage a doctor to trek across the wilderness by herself. But then, maybe she was sick of her day job. He got nutters like that sometimes. "Which part?" He shuffled through his maps for the right one, then tossed the rest back on his dashboard. With a flick of his wrist, the map cascaded open. He rounded the still-open passenger door to spread the map on the hood of the Land Rover.

Her look of uncertainty vanished. She came up beside him, and he caught the faint, flowery scent of perfume. She stretched out a sun-bronzed arm across his map, then dropped her index finger slap in the middle of nowhere. "There. I need to get there."

He took a step back and looked her over once more. The top of her head came just about to his chin. Her snug-fitting white tank top skimmed just low enough for him to glimpse the curving hollow between her breasts. He lingered longer than necessary on her shapely legs.

Bloody gorgeous. This woman was a doctor? Gran had always warned him not to judge a book by its cover, but even she couldn't have denied that Doctor Markham looked more runway model than rural muckabout.

She noticed him looking, and her gaze flashed up and down his body. Something flitted through their ocean-colored depths, and his groin stirred in response. He snatched up the map. "Exactly how much hiking do you do?"

Faint lines appeared between her brows. "I can hold my own. Can you get me there?"

"Doctor Markham, 'there' is officially the back of beyond. Are you sure you want that much 'wild' in your wilderness?"

"I'm sure."

Something in her tone sparked a grudging admiration of her nerve. Coupled with his not-so-grudging admiration of her body, it set off warning bells in his head. He would have turned around and gone right back into the pub, if it hadn't been for the money. A few more payments to his damned divorce lawyer, and he was a free man. Sweet, sweet liberty.

"Right, then," he said. "Half up front, and half when we get back to Sydney. I don't take checks or credit cards. Cash is in Australian bills, and you provide your own food. Have you got camping gear?"

"Yes," she said. "It's back at my hotel."

"Did you drive here, or take a cab?"

"Cab."

He rubbed his chin, then added, "And when do you want to leave?"

"As soon as possible," she said at once. He detected a faint, tense undertone.

An awful hurry for a pleasure hike. "How many are in your hiking party, Doctor?"

"Just me."

Oh, hell, no. A group hike was one thing. Mucking around in the mountains alone with a woman who had a body like that? Completely another.

Besides, she'd called him by his given name. Everyone who knew him knew he went by Goldy now. If this was one of Lilah's little minions, she could find herself another guide. He'd had enough of his ex-wife's cat-and-mousing to last several lifetimes. But then, why would Lilah send an American woman to torment him, when she could do it herself, and likely get more pleasure out of it?

Not like he had anything else that Lilah could take away. She already had his house and everything that went in it. Hakon folded up his map and started to close the passenger door. "I don't do private hikes," he lied.

The blond's hand settled on his arm, cool and feather-light, but the touch froze him in place. "I need a guide, and I've been told you're the one to ask. Please, Hakon."

His name again, spoken with a soft, hesitant tone. She lifted her hand away and looked at him with a searching intensity. He got the feeling he should have known her from somewhere, but couldn't put his finger on it. He drifted in her indigo eyes for several seconds before asking, "What's your given name, Doctor?"

"Faith."

Part of him wanted to laugh at the irony. He hadn't had faith in women for many months now.

But then he looked into her eyes again, and his resolve slipped. He made a last-ditch effort to dissuade her. "The wild trails up there aren't for first-timers. You need to be able to keep up, and there are a lot of dangerous spots."

"I don't scare easily," she shot back.

No help for it, then. He held open his passenger door. "Shall we talk business?"

On the way to her hotel, they discussed payment details further. Taking a single hiker would normally have put a crimp in his budget, but business had been slow the past couple of weeks, and he couldn't afford to be picky. Neither was he in a position to argue about her bizarre choice of destination. Most of his hikers wanted to stay at one of the lodges along the major town route, and sprinkle day hikes in between. If she wanted to trek into the middle of nowhere, and intended to pay for the privilege, who was he to argue?

Still, his conscience kicked him at the thought of letting her take on more than she could handle, and risk injury. "I need to know before we sign any paperwork. Exactly how much of this sort of thing have you done, Faith?"

He didn't think he'd said anything unusual, but she stared at him for a long minute at the mention of her name. At last, she smiled. "I'm an archaeologist. I'm familiar with roughing it in all sorts of terrain."

"An archaeologist? You looking for someone's old silverware out there, or what?"

She stiffened. "What if I was?"

"Are you?"

"Not that it's any of your business, but no."

Oh, this would be a great couple of weeks. He bit his tongue for a full, cautionary five seconds before continuing. "The closest town to where you want to go is Bowen Mountain. We can stop there for a day and pick up rations, then head out into the bush the next morning...if you're sure about this."

"I am," she said.

He offered nothing more until they arrived at her hotel room. She opened her door and beckoned him in. He stepped inside, trying not to dwell on the fact that a beautiful woman and a large bed were both within reaching distance.

But hell if the mental picture wasn't tempting.

Then he took a closer look at the bed, and felt his eyebrows shoot up. A single suitcase lay at the foot of the bed beside a worn but serviceable hiking backpack.

Hakon had never in his life seen a woman pack so few things for a trip. Lilah herself used to bring an entire entourage of baggage for a single weekend somewhere. "Is this all you have?"

"Just the essentials. Do you mind waiting a few minutes while I make a phone call and get ready to check out?"

Ah, there it was. The obligatory one-hour wait before going out, one of Lilah's favorite annoyances. He plopped on the edge of the bed, in spite of the fact that a chair stood a few steps away. "Give it a go."

She opened the suitcase, snatched a cell phone, and then hurried to the bathroom.

He sighed. Probably be Doomsday by the time she came out.

****

"Come on, come on, pick up. I don't care if it *is* the middle of the night in New York," Faith muttered. She clamped the cell phone between her ear and shoulder while she scraped brushes and facial cream into her makeup kit.

On the fourth ring, someone picked up. "'Lo?" mumbled a sleepy male voice.

"Ian. Thank God. Put my sister on the phone."

She heard shifting. "What's wrong?" Sara's husband asked, sounding more alert.

"I'm fine, just put Sara on, okay?"

She waited a few seconds, then her sister's voice came on the line. "Do you know what time it is here? Not to mention, you're disturbing a very pregnant woman's sleep."

Faith danced impatiently on the balls of her feet. "Hakon. Ivarsson. Is here. In Sydney."

"Wha-a-a-t?"

"That's what I said, myself, only with a few more four-letter words. He is alive, and kicking, and *he's-my-frigging-trail-guide*!"

"Does he know who you are? Does he know that you're psychic?"

"*No*, he doesn't know I'm psychic. You think I'm just going to blurt it out to him? I don't even think he knows who *he* is. Was. Whatever. I'm freaking out here, Sara."

"All right, all right. Just give me a minute to get my head on straight." More shuffling, then Sara came back to the phone. "All right, I'm awake now. Listen— do not do *anything*. Don't say a word, and I mean not one syllable. If he doesn't recognize you, you are to leave it that way. Just keep it simple. Or better yet, try to find another guide."

After the Herculean effort it had taken to find Hakon? Doubtful in the extreme. Faith fumed. "Simple? How many Viking ghosts have you conversed with, only to come across them in present-day incarnations?"

Sara made an incoherent noise. "I don't understand how this could happen. Hakon was a ghost only a matter of months ago. You said his soul was trapped in Shetland because he hadn't avenged the murder of his wife."

"Who, may I remind you, is the long-dead version of me?" Faith snapped. "And which, may I further remind you, we already took care of? We solved the murder. We freed his soul. And he. Is now. *Here*."

"Then how? Why doesn't he recognize you?"

"I don't know!" Faith hollered. She cast a nervous

look at the closed bathroom door, then lowered her voice. "Look. I have no idea what he's doing here. All I know is I want to come home as fast as I possibly can." Which wasn't quite the truth, but Sara didn't need to know that. Ha. Simple. Riiiight.

"Did you find the boy yet?"

"Yes. No. He's in the mountains. Hakon's supposed to help me get there."

"Do you need me or Ian to come to Sydney?"

"Don't you dare, either of you. You're about five minutes from having that baby as it is. I'll call you when I find the boy. Just sit tight, because I'm panicking enough for both of us."

She hung up the phone before Sara could argue, and slumped against the bathroom door. Maybe it had been a bad idea to let Sara in on the disaster *du jour*, after all. It was a bad idea to stress a pregnant woman out. Not much Sara could do from New York, anyway.

That settled it. Faith was on her own.

She glared at her reflection in the mirror over the sink. "Hi, Hakon. I'm Faith Markham, and I look just like your thousand-years-dead wife Aesa. Did I mention you're a Viking, and that I'm psychic? Just in case that isn't enough to send you running, I'm also pyrokinetic, and I can astral project. Boo."

So screwed. So very, very screwed.

She groaned, then moved to the sink to snatch up her makeup bag. She gave her reflection a last, annoyed stare. "If we get through this," she promised it, "our next vacation will be on a deserted island."

But then she pictured the very real, very sexy man sitting out there on her bed, and she wasn't so sure she wanted that.

Chapter Two

I left something in Shetland. I've never had a problem dating, but since those visions of Hakon, I haven't wanted anyone else. I feel like part of me will always be missing.
—Faith's Journals, age thirty

Faith emerged from the bathroom with a big smile and—she hoped—plenty of composure.

Hakon still sat on the edge of the bed. She doubted he'd moved an inch. "That was quick," he said.

"I told you I would only be a few minutes."

He shrugged, and his attention came to rest on her suitcase. It lay open beside him the way she'd left it. *Beardsley's Compendium* sat on top of its contents, a thick, much-read leather book on the occult and supernatural. She'd grown to think of it as a good-luck charm since bringing it to Shetland in the past year.

"A little light reading?" he asked, lifting the volume from her suitcase.

"Yes." She scooped it out of his grasp. "Do you always touch other people's things without asking?"

He held up his hands in an innocent gesture, then craned his neck to look at the book's cover. "Sorry. A book with a pentagram on the front tends to get my attention. You're not one of those people who dance naked on the solstices, are you?"

She shouldn't have felt so insulted by the question—obviously meant to pique her temper—but his smirk rattled her. She dropped the book and her makeup kit in the suitcase, then zipped the suitcase shut. As mildly as possible, she asked, "Would it matter to you if I were?"

"Don't get me wrong. I'm all for dancing naked anytime, depending on the company." He raised a brow.

"I'll just bet you are." She hefted her backpack onto one shoulder.

He stood up, so close that she had to arch backward to meet his gaze. An insolent half-smile toyed at his lips, and sinful thoughts of other naked activities flitted through her mind. He leaned closer. His body heat drifted across the scant space between them, teasing her skin. How much like the Hakon of her dreams—protective and fierce when she dreamed him as a child, and much more sensual when she dreamed him as an adult—was this present-day Hakon?

She held her breath, wondering if he'd kiss her. And partly—okay, a little more than partly—wishing for it.

His smile broadened. "Would you like me to get your suitcase, Doctor Markham?"

She deflated and forced the calm, collected Faith back into place. She just managed to keep the annoyance out of her voice. "Yes, that would be helpful."

He swept the suitcase up in an easy motion that made the thing look empty, then headed out the door ahead of her.

Laughing.

"I definitely don't remember the original Hakon being such a smartass," she snarled under her breath.

They loaded her things into the Land Rover, then she slid into the passenger seat. He eased in behind the steering wheel, giving her a brief glance before starting the engine. A telltale hum surged in the air between them. Oh, he was aware of their proximity, all right, and she'd been with enough men to recognize attraction when she sensed it.

It was the suspicion underneath that bothered her.

Did he have any idea who she was? Who he was?

No, he couldn't. *This Hakon* had probably never set foot in Shetland. "How long until we get to the mountains?" she asked, just to fill the silence.

He pulled onto the road, and they started away. "About an hour. A bit more until we get into Bowen Mountain. A friend of mine runs an inn there, and we can get a night's rest before heading out."

"I don't really want to wait any more than I have, if we can help it," she said, thinking of the boy, alone out there with his gift and no one to understand it.

"What's your hurry? The mountains aren't going anywhere."

She opened her mouth on a flippant response to his flippant comment, but what came out was, "Hakon's an unusual name. What's it mean?"

"It's a family name. It means 'high-born.'"

"Oh, so you're royalty, are you?"

"Somewhere way back, somebody in my family was probably the grand mucky-muck of something." He shrugged. "I just run bushwalks. How'd you get a name like Faith?"

"What's the matter with my name?"

"It's *unusual*." He gave her that smirk again.

She couldn't tell whether he was teasing or mocking her, but she decided to give him the benefit of the doubt. "I guess you'd have to ask my mother where she came up with it. My parents were only planning on one child at the time. I was a surprise bonus."

"What do you mean? Are you a twin?"

"Yeah. Fraternal. Sara's nothing like me. Dark hair, brown eyes, good taste in men..." Whoops. *Mouth, meet foot.*

He laughed, and the sound sent intriguing shivers through her skin. "I see you've been burnt, too."

"What's that supposed to mean?"

"If it makes you feel any better, you're not the only one with an imperfect track record. For a little while, I thought you might be one of my ex-wife's friends, visiting just to make my life miserable."

An irrational pang of jealousy flashed through her at the notion that he had been married. A thousand years had ticked by since her past incarnation and his had been man and wife. *This Hakon* could have her arrested for stalking.

So begins the fibbing.

"Why would I want to make your life miserable?" she asked. "We just met."

"Lilah's the only one in Sydney who calls me Hakon anymore."

"Well, you can rest easy, since I don't know a single Lilah. The only thing I want with you is your guide services, Mister Ivarsson." Hmm. Admirably convincing, for a total fabrication.

"That brings me to my next question," he said. "How did you know who I was?"

18

"That's actually...a very good... A friend of a friend of somebody who knew you," she blurted.

He didn't question that, thank God. He was too busy navigating their way through town. A snarl of traffic had developed around a car stalled in the road, and for a while, she was free to study his stern, handsome features without worry of return perusal. Finally, they were directed through the mess, and on their way again.

For the next several minutes of their trip, the radio did most of the talking. Faith didn't mind. Silence rarely bothered her, but Hakon's quiet had a companionable air to it. Comfortable. Almost familiar. Or maybe it was just her own wistful imaginings.

He had tuned the station to classic rock. When he asked if she preferred something else, she opened her mouth to decline, but she found herself pleased at that small consideration.

Then he ruined it by adding, "Anything but that sappy mainstream love junk."

"What's wrong with love songs?"

"They're completely unrealistic. All they do is suck you into getting tied down. My advice? Run like hell."

"That's rather cynical of you."

He slid a glance in her direction. When he spoke, his voice rang with amusement. "This from the woman with bad taste in men?"

"Not *all* of them." She flew through a mental rundown of her past dates. There was... Well, then there was... And what about...? Damn. She crossed her arms and hunched back into the seat. "Not everyone thinks love is worthless."

"Worthless, no. A figment, yes. No one can live up to that stuff in songs and movies."

She looked at his bare ring finger. "You must have believed in it once, or you wouldn't have gotten married."

He grunted. "Once was enough."

"Do you mind if I ask what happened?"

"Hell if I know," he said, gesturing to the radio. "I learned enough to turn off that lovey-love crap when I hear it. No reality in it."

She fell silent, unable to imagine his disastrous relationships being worse than her own. Her last ex-boyfriend had tried to kill her and her sister. No matter how bad this Lilah had been, Faith was pretty sure Hakon couldn't top *that* one.

During the drive, she asked him numerous questions about the mountains, ranging from climate to geology, to evidence of early habitation.

"That's what you're here for, isn't it?" he asked when she inquired about native settlements. "Aborigine artifacts?"

Brilliant idea. She wished she'd thought of it herself. It'd be a damn sight easier to defend that argument than to tell him she was really searching for a gifted boy. "Actually, yes. I'm doing some research."

"I haven't been up along the north side in a while. Most of my tours tend to be along the southern route, since public access is limited in the north, but I know some people who'll let us in. Not scared of heights, are you?"

"No."

"That's a start."

She got the impression he still didn't believe she'd

be able to keep up with him, and bristled with offended female dignity.

And furthermore, he wasn't flirting with her at all. Not one tiny bit since that "dancing naked" comment, and he hadn't acted on the attraction that buzzed in the air between them. Faith usually considered the absence of male attention a welcome breath of fresh air, since most men started throwing telephone numbers at her once they found out she was available. As far as she could tell, his interest had vanished somewhere around the mention of his ex-wife.

Damn it all.

He caught her staring, and gave her a puzzled look. One dark-gold eyebrow inched up.

She wondered if she had a smudge of dirt on her face. Maybe her clothes were wrinkled. Oh, God, did she have frizzy hair? She patted it down with a furtive hand. Stupid Australian summer heat.

She glanced around the interior of the Land Rover. Not the tidiest man she'd ever seen. Crumpled pieces of paper and some loose change littered the passenger floor. Sitting amongst the maps piled on his dashboard was a small silver ring with a pattern of intertwining bands. Intrigued, she picked it up. "Wow, this is a beautiful—"

The ring sizzled in her fingers. "Ouch!" She dropped it on the floor.

"What happened?" He glanced away from the road as she fumbled through the clutter at her feet for the ring. "What'd you do?"

"I-I dropped something." She shoved a crushed fast food bag aside, then picked up the ring using a stray napkin. Unable to help herself, she stared at the piece with stunned fascination.

The age-dulled, braided silver bands had worn around the edges. Norse, by its distinctive design. Old, for certain, but Faith knew exactly how old.

It was Aesa's wedding ring.

She shook, almost dropping it again. "Holy mother of Pete."

Hakon reached out and snatched the ring. "Do you always touch other people's things without asking?" he mocked, all sarcasm.

"Sorry, I just couldn't help it. It's lovely."

"It's not for public display."

"I was just looking," she said. She fisted her hand around her still-throbbing fingers.

And then a nasty thought occurred to her. Had he given the ring to Lilah when they married? Even the idea made her heart ache. She didn't know if she wanted the answer, but the words left her mouth before she had the chance to stop them. "Was it your ex-wife's?"

"No," he answered at once, and she wilted with relief. "It belonged to my grandmother." He stuffed the ring into his pocket.

"Really? Sort of a...family heirloom?" She bit her tongue, knowing she shouldn't pry, but unable to resist. Her fingertips tingled.

"I guess," he muttered.

"How old is it?"

"Really old. Is this Twenty Questions?"

"Are you always so defensive?"

"Are you always so nosy?"

"You don't think I'm a little concerned, myself, about being on a hike for a couple weeks with a complete stranger?" Boy, she was getting good at this fabrication thing.

She *knew* him. Whatever else Hakon had become in the intervening thousand years, she knew that underneath his gruff standoffishness lay an honorable man. The good looks, however, were right out there for all to see. The only concern she had was how to keep her hands off him.

"All right," he said with a conciliatory shrug. "What do you want to know?"

"Have you always lived in Australia?"

"Yep."

So verbose. What had she been hoping for? *"Why, no, I used to live in Shetland, and we were married. Don't you remember me, sweetheart?"* Not likely.

She tried again. "I have this...side project going. About dream psychology. Any strange ones you'd care to share?"

He snorted. "Hello, change in topic. Do you always ask these kinds of things of total strangers," he asked, "or am I just a special case?"

Boy howdy, are you. "Never mind. Like I said, it's just a side—"

"The answer is no," he said, eyeing her like she'd just escaped from the mental ward. "I don't dream, or if I do, I don't remember them. My turn. Where are you from?"

She glanced at the road. "New York City. Why?"

"See, this is the part where we go back to a normal conversation, and ask each other normal questions. I don't know exactly what you're doing here, or what weird ideas you've cooked up from reading that pentagram book of yours—"

"Beardsley's Compendium."

"—but if there's chanting and burning candles involved anywhere on this trip, you can count me out." He sounded cross, but his mouth quirked upward. "If I have to spend two weeks with you, and I wake to find you in a bed sheet with flowers in your hair..." He stopped speaking, and skimmed her body with every sign that he was picturing that exact thing...and not minding it.

He met her gaze. The look disappeared at once, leaving her with a delicious flutter racing along her skin. Hakon cleared his throat and turned his attention back to the road, where it remained for the rest of their drive.

He insisted on staying the night in Bowen Mountain, since it was so late in the day. She decided that one more night in an actual bed wouldn't put them too far behind her quarry, and settled back into her seat without further argument.

Just before sunset, they arrived at McGowan's Inn, a rustic log building tucked into a grove of eucalyptus trees whose scent spiced the air. Gravel crunched under the tires as they came to a stop in the driveway. Faith got out of the car and inhaled deeply, gazing at the red-gold sunbeams glancing off the inn's corrugated tin roof. Flower boxes lined the porch railing, bursting with blue and white and yellow. "This place is heavenly," she said.

"Nearest thing to it," he agreed, hooking a duffel bag out of the Land Rover's back seat. "Grab your gear, and we'll go inside."

She picked up her suitcase in one hand, and shouldered her hiking pack with the other. They mounted the steps, and then Hakon pushed open the front door. A bell tinkled in their wake.

What the lobby lacked in roominess, it made up in charm. Lace curtains fluttered in the front windows. A long wooden counter graced one side of the cramped room, and a grouping of plushy chairs stood at the other, waiting for someone to sit and rest tired feet. She longed to do just that. Her feet might not forgive her by the end of this trip, unless she bribed them with a morning at Giovanni's Day Spa once she got home.

"Well, aren't you the one for surprises," said a voice.

Faith turned in the speaker's direction. A tiny woman with mist-gray hair rushed out from behind the counter with a broad smile and arms flung wide.

Hakon's stiff demeanor melted away so fast, Faith wondered if it had ever been there. He dropped his bag on the plank floor with a plop, then scooped the older woman into his arms. His big frame almost swallowed her. "Miriam, you're a sight for sore eyes." He kissed her loudly on the cheek.

"Put me down, you devil," said the woman. He set her on her feet and she chuckled, patting her hair down and looking every bit like a contented old hen.

"I brought you business, old girl," he said. "This is Doctor Faith Markham from America. She's here on a research hike, and we'll be staying the night. Faith, this is Miriam McGowan, owner of the inn and maker of the best apple pies anywhere."

The light in his eyes when he talked about Miriam melted Faith's heart. How wonderfully sweet. Maybe there was something to *this Hakon*, after all. "How do you do?" Faith asked, clasping Miriam's warm hand.

"Delighted, dear, delighted. An American, then? You must be tired from all that traveling. Toby, get out here, boy, Hakon's come to visit! I'll tan that boy's hide if he's gone fishing again, I swear I will." Miriam rounded the counter again, clucking in disapproval.

By her tone, Faith expected a young boy to answer the summons, but a man entered the lobby slapping a dusty hat against his thigh. He brushed a hand through his shaggy toffee-brown hair, and looked up. "Hakon!" With a grin, he clapped the hat back on his head. "Where've you been, you sorry piece of work?" He cuffed Hakon on the shoulder, and Faith knew at once that only Toby could have pulled that off without being pounded flat.

"I've been doing trail hikes on the south routes, mostly," Hakon answered him. "Faith, this is Tobias McGowan. Toby, Faith Markham. That's *Doctor* Faith Markham. Be nice."

Toby smiled again and shook her hand. "G'day, Doctor. Welcome to McGowan's. Get your bag for you?" Without waiting for her answer, he pulled the suitcase from her hand. "Everything's open, so we'll put you in the best rooms in the back."

"I thought you ran a good business this time of year," said Hakon, picking up his duffel.

"Yeah, we just sent off a fair mob of blokes this morning, on their way up the mountains. You're the first ones we've had this afternoon."

Hakon took a pair of keys from Miriam, then he and Faith followed Toby down a wide hall and up a set of stairs to the second floor. "Hakon, your usual room." Toby thumped the nearest door. "Faith, yours is the next one down. Private bath. Anything you need, just give a yell, eh? Supper's at six. Don't be late, Hakon, or me mum'll box your ears for you." With a wink, he set Faith's suitcase at her feet, then tromped back down the stairs.

She picked up her suitcase. Hakon didn't move, and they stood staring at each other for a moment. Something did the jitterbug in her belly at the intensity in his eyes. "This place is, er...very nice," she fumbled. Anyone else, anyone but him, and she could've given a two-hour dissertation without thinking twice. Now, her tongue seemed to have worked itself into a knot.

"Yep."

She shifted the backpack on her shoulder. "Could I have my key now?"

He opened his hand, palm up, and offered her the key without saying a word. He stared so hard, she wanted to squirm.

As she reached for the key, her fingertips brushed his callused palm. A zing of tension rushed through her, and she felt the shivery push of her powers craving release. If she didn't get out of there, she knew her eyes would turn silver, and they'd have a whole lot more to talk about. "See you at dinner," she said, grappling with the key and the door and her bags.

His hand closed over hers on the doorknob, warm and firm. "Easy, or you're going to break it."

Whoosh. Gooseflesh swept her skin. Her eyes were silver, she just knew it. She squeezed them shut to stem the flow of power, but the chills didn't stop.

Desire.

Rage.

Loneliness.

His emotions swamped her, overwhelming any

sensation of herself. She heard a woman whisper softly in Old Norse as Hakon's fingers glided through spun-gold strands of hair, glimpsed flashes of skin on skin...

Aesa.

An instant later, the passion and tenderness tore away in a slash of pain so great that Faith almost crumpled to her knees. She saw Hakon clutching Aesa's lifeless form and screaming into the sky.

"Let go of my hand," she whispered, begging him with her whole body.

The door clicked open, and his hand left hers. The thundering storm of emotions ceased at once. "Are you all right?" he asked. "Do you want me to send for Miriam?"

"Jet lag," she blurted. She kept her eyes closed, rushing through the open door with her luggage. She slammed the door shut behind her and burst into tears.

****

Hakon stared at the stained-pine door in bewilderment. He heard her sobbing on its other side as though her life had shattered into a billion pieces. His heart wrenched in his chest, and he braced a hand against the door in surprise.

What had he done to make her cry? He lowered his hand, hesitated, then raised it again to rap his knuckles against the wood. "Faith?"

She quieted at once, possibly realizing he'd heard her shedding tears. "Just go. I'm fine."

And then he understood. She'd come so far from home to look at something as simple as Aborigine artifacts. There had been no ring on her finger, no mention of a man in her life during the long drive from Sydney. He knew the signs of a broken heart well enough. Someone had wronged her, and badly.

And still, she believed in love enough to defend it when he'd criticized it. In spite of his own views on the matter, indignation surged within him. No one deserved to be hurt, and the idea that someone had tried to crush her optimism made him want to wring the ungrateful wretch's neck.

But Hakon could help her with that. She'd need time and space. Lots of both. The mountains would provide the perfect escape from whatever troubled her. He had no intention of adding to her problems, and he sure didn't need the headaches any more than she did.

In spite of the impulses racing through his body, urging him otherwise.

He backed away and went into his own room without another sound. He tossed his duffel on the cedar-log bed, then headed for the shower with a disgruntled stride.

By the time he'd cleaned up and pulled on a new pair of jeans and a T-shirt, the smell of Miriam's roasted chicken and apple stuffing had begun wafting upstairs.

He opened his door to see Faith just leaving her room. She'd changed into a pale-cream sundress, and her hair flowed loose around her shoulders. The scent of lilies followed her to the steps.

So did he. "You look great."

"Thank you." She met his gaze, and he found it hard to breathe. She wore the barest touches of blush and eye shadow. No trace of tears marred her face. If she'd truly had her heart broken, she hid it well.

He stared at her strawberry-red lips as they curved into a smile. She looked better than great. Beside her, he felt like he'd just clambered out of a dirt heap. Uncomfortably, he said, "You didn't get dressed up for Miriam, did you? She's practically family."

"Why shouldn't I wear something nice for dinner?"

"I've been coming here since I was a child. I don't think I've ever seen Miriam dress up on anything but Christmas, and Toby wouldn't touch a suit if—"

"Oh, no. I'm overdressed, aren't I? I should go put something else on." She turned away.

He laid a hand on her arm, then pulled it away, regretting the touch. "You're fine. Let's go grab some grub." He gestured toward the stairs, then followed her down.

They entered the dining room, where Miriam was already bustling over the oak table with hot dishes and silverware. Toby brought a pitcher of lemonade over, then sat down. "Get your elbows off the table, Tobias," she said, swatting him.

Toby grinned and snatched his arms away. He looked up at Faith, and his eyes went round in obvious appreciation.

Hakon gave him a long, steady glare, and Toby's gaze slid to the chicken platter. Hakon felt a flush of satisfaction, and then annoyance that he'd thought it necessary to put Toby in his place. Faith could take care of herself, broken heart or no. She didn't seem any the worse for wear from her earlier upset as she sat beside him.

During supper, the McGowans regaled them with reports of the latest goings-on in Bowen Mountain. So-and-So had gotten married, this or that person had taken a new job, someone had totaled their truck during a car accident...

Hakon listened just enough to nod in the right places. Faith kept distracting him just by being there. When she smiled, his pulse jumped. When she laughed, he wanted to laugh, too, just from hearing it. Once, when she reached for the sugar bowl, her hand brushed his and sent a wave of temptation flashing through him. His entire body exulted at her nearness, even as his thoughts scolded him for welcoming it.

He'd been with her only a few hours, and yet she caused a whirlwind in him that no other woman had come close to creating even once.

He scowled and shoveled a forkful of apple pie into his mouth. Damn women. All they ever did for a man was make him weak. Toward the end of his marriage, he felt like he'd been staked down in the middle of the desert with the heat of Lilah's scorn blazing down on him. She'd never understood him, never even tried. Two people couldn't have been more different.

Truth be told, no one had ever really understood him. Even surrounded by friends and family, he'd been alone with the shapeless hollow in his soul ever since childhood. However it got there, it had followed him his whole life. Nothing ever felt...right. Maybe that was why he and Lilah—he and *anyone*—had never worked out.

And what the hell was this mooning over touchy-feely stuff about? *See?* he berated himself. *Weak.*

"Hey, space cowboy. Your ice cream's melting."

He looked up. Faith smiled at him, and gestured toward the soupy vanilla puddle on his plate. He shrugged and set his fork down.

"Never known you not to finish dessert, Hakon," said Miriam. She chuckled and stood up to gather the dishes.

"Mrs. McGowan, he was right. You make the best apple pies anywhere," Faith declared. "Let me help you with the dishes."

"You stay right there. I wouldn't dream of it."

"Please, I'd like to help."

Miriam gave in to Faith's smile after all. Hakon found it way too easy to sympathize. The women left the room, each carrying a stack of plates.

Toby leaned forward across the table. "Hakon, you have the damnedest luck, mate. That lady's a real looker."

"Look elsewhere," Hakon snapped before he could catch himself.

Toby grinned at him, but moved on to other topics. Hakon responded here and there, listening with half an ear to the clinks and clatters from the kitchen. A while later, Toby bid him goodbye and got up to continue his chores outside.

Miriam came in with an armload of clean plates, and began stacking them in the china cupboard. "That doctor's a very nice young woman," she said.

"She's a client."

"Well, your client is out in the back garden taking a walk. Why don't you join her?"

"I've got maps to look over, and gear to check."

Miriam finished returning her plates to the cupboard, then laid a warm, soft hand on his cheek. "You need to move on, Hakon. As beautiful as they are, those mountains can't ever love you back."

He shot Miriam a disgruntled scowl, but she returned it with that kind look that he could never quite dispute. Feeling awkward, he muttered a farewell, then shoved away from the table and went upstairs.

He reached his room and threw his duffel on the floor. He had no desire to look at maps or gear. He'd checked and rechecked it all three times that morning, plagued with a restless energy that drove him from pub to pub in search of his next clients. Once he took care of his divorce bills, it would be goodbye to Australia, and hello to some other place in the world. It didn't matter where. Somewhere he could get lost. Somewhere that would drown the lonely echo inside him in a flurry of distractions.

He drew aside the lace curtain and stared down into the dimming light of the back garden. Faith wandered along the paths, stopping occasionally to brush a hand through tall grasses, or sniff at a bower of climbing roses.

Somewhere definitely without her.

Chapter Three

The best thing about a dig is the challenge. It isn't living if you stay safely behind your desk and write papers. I want to live while I can, and have no regrets at the end.

—Faith's Journals, age twenty-one

Faith woke at dawn. The moment she opened her eyes, apprehension settled in. She couldn't pinpoint the source, but the sensation followed her downstairs into the dining room, where Hakon and Toby had already started breakfast.

Toby winked as she entered the room. "Morning. Ready to dance with The Devils?"

"What?" she asked, rubbing the last of the grogginess out of her eyes.

"The Devils Wilderness," said Hakon. "That's where we're headed this morning."

Faith sat and chose a muffin from the basket on the table. "Are you trying to scare off your tourists with a name like that?"

Toby laughed. "Parts of The Devils even scare some of the locals. Me, I don't touch the place without Bess, there." He jerked a thumb behind him.

A large red hiking pack sat on a corner chair. It was tricked out with all the bells and whistles, including a loop for an ice axe, which Faith couldn't imagine needing in Australia's summer heat, and a hydration pack, which she could. Muffin forgotten, she stared in envious appreciation. "Where do I get one of those?"

"Well, you'd have to pry it out of me. That little beauty's saved my behind on a number of occasions." Toby scooped a spoonful of wheat flakes into his mouth and crunched away.

Miriam entered the dining room with a pitcher of milk. "You two be careful on your hike. There's been a few summer storms moving through, the last week."

"We'll make do," said Hakon.

After breakfast, they packed for their journey and stowed their gear in the Land Rover. Miriam came down the porch steps, holding a bundle wrapped in kitchen linens. Her eyes crinkled at the corners as she smiled at Faith. "Extra muffins for your trip. You hardly ate, and I don't want you leaving hungry. I do hope we'll see you again."

Hakon kissed Miriam on the cheek. "Bye, old girl."

Miriam clasped his hand, then handed the bundle to Faith. Their fingers touched.

Wham. An image of Miriam collapsed on the porch burst into Faith's mind. Blood trickled on the older woman's forehead, and the air seethed with violence. Faith gasped and stumbled back a step.

Hakon snatched her by the elbow to steady her. "What's the matter?"

"Stone in my shoe," she lied. *We can't leave, we can't leave. She'll be hurt, something will happen.*

Miriam clucked in dismay. "This old driveway is an eyesore. I've been meaning to have it paved."

Faith's mind raced for a way to protect the woman,

any way. Quartz! Quartz was a protective stone. She shoved the bundle of muffins into Hakon's arms, then fished in the neck of her T-shirt for a silver necklace with a quartz teardrop pendant. She took it off and handed it to the older woman. "I want you to have this."

"Oh, I couldn't possibly—"

"Please, Miriam. I'd like you to wear it." She tried for a smile. "As thanks for the good food and hospitality."

Miriam smiled back as Faith pressed the necklace into her hands. "Oh, all right. What a lovely little thing. Thank you, sweetheart."

Hakon gave Faith a probing sidelong look, which she tried her best to ignore. They waved their goodbyes, and departed. As they left town, he said, "That was nice of you, giving her that necklace."

"I like her." That much was true. She'd felt like family the moment she arrived. She clenched her hands in her lap, wishing she could tell him the *other* reason she hadn't wanted to leave.

Miriam was in danger. Or would be. Faith had given her the only protection she could, a quartz pendant infused with the spells of an African shaman whose spirit she'd once freed from a vase. She'd worn it this morning only because of that apprehensive feeling on waking. It would be more useful in Miriam's hands than her own.

She shook out of her distressing thoughts to find Hakon staring at her. "What?" she snapped.

He looked back at the road. "We'll park at the ranger station, then go on foot from there. I've already spoken to the rangers, and gotten us permission to hike and photograph whatever Aborigine sites we find.

You're not allowed to remove anything."

Professional affront reared its head. She snapped out of her worries for Miriam and glowered. "What did you think I would do, mine for treasure? I have a little more respect than that."

"Just checking."

She crossed her arms and stared out the other window at the trees flashing past. Road noise took up some of the awkward silence, but his look—even though she wasn't looking back at him—was as loud as a kettledrum.

"They told me to say so."

She glowered some more.

"It's a regulation. What do you want from me, an apology?" When she didn't answer, he flipped the radio on and punched the buttons, getting static on every station.

Faith watched as he got more and more frustrated, then finally turned the radio off with a swipe of his fingers. She smirked. "If it makes you feel any better, my cell phone doesn't work up here, either."

His hands clenched on the steering wheel. "Would you mind getting the map out so we can navigate?"

"I thought you knew all these roads and trails."

"I haven't memorized every rock, no."

"Are you always this cranky?" she asked.

"You started this."

"How did I—" She rolled her eyes. "All right, look. Before either of us gets any more juvenile, I think we should just concentrate on getting to the...the..."

Pain rushed in behind her eyes, and she recoiled with a gasp. Through the stabbing throb, she noticed a fork in the road. The smaller left path veered off into the woods, pitted and strewn with stones. "Turn left."

"What?"

"Left!"

He veered off onto the gravel path. The Land Rover lurched into a pothole and then bounced out again. He steered around a rut, then continued down the side trail. "So now you're navigating?"

She couldn't answer. The pain sharpened into a hiss of angry voices. She pressed a hand to her forehead. *Sacrilege,* the voices snarled in several languages at once. *Follow. Catch. Punish. Vengeance.* "I'm done taking orders from dead guys," she muttered to the voices, willing them to subside.

"What are you talking about?"

She looked up. When their gazes met, Hakon's jaw dropped open. *Oh, no. They're silver.* She clenched her eyes shut, and the voices stopped at once. When she opened them again, he was still staring.

Desperate to escape that searching, shocked expression, she looked out the front windshield. *"Truck!"*

He slammed on the brakes, pitching them forward until the seatbelts jerked them back. Gravel sprayed from under the tires, pinging off the tailgate of the truck parked right in front of them. He stared out the windshield with a look of alarm and anger. "What moron parks their car in the middle of the...? Are you okay?"

She nodded breathlessly, then threw open the passenger door, ripped off her seatbelt, and lunged out onto the path.

She heard Hakon's door slam behind her. "What the hell are you doing?"

Rounding the truck, she peered through its windows. Empty. Nothing inside to hint at why her head had almost exploded when they neared this side road. She touched the hood, but felt no vibration of spiritual presence. Certainly nothing indicating a reason for some new ghostly grudge. The engine was cold.

The last time she'd helped a ghost bent on revenge...well, the result was leaning against the bumper of his Land Rover.

Oh, God, she'd *spoken* to the ghosts in front of him. What must he think of her? She paced back toward his truck and kept her eyes lowered, feeling like a truant child. "Er...sorry."

"Do you want to tell me what dead guys you're talking about, and why we had to take this sudden side trip? I'm beginning to think hospitals, not hikes."

She didn't reply. Where could she even start? He'd never believe a word of it.

His hand came to rest on her shoulder. Suddenly it was too much. She wanted more than anything to leap into his arms, to have him believe her, to feel like one man in this godforsaken world wanted her for who she was, instead of what they saw.

Her heart squeezed. She whirled away to pull her backpack from the Land Rover, locked her door, and then slammed it. Without looking back, she hurried down the trail. "This is the way we need to go!"

****

Hakon stared after her, wondering what the hell had just happened. Again. For God's sake, the woman switched gears faster than a Formula One race driver.

How the hell did she know which way they needed to go? Just who was guiding who? He growled and pulled his own backpack from the Land Rover, locked the vehicle, then stalked down the trail after her.

It took him all of two seconds to decide he should have been the one walking in front. Faith strode ahead of him, dodging ruts and potholes with sure feet. Her hips swayed with each step in a compelling rhythm that drove his body into a riot. He imagined drawing her back against him, kissing that spot behind her ear where tendrils of golden hair had fallen loose....

She stopped dead and turned around with wide eyes. Damn, had he said something out loud? He thought he'd seen a flash in her eyes just before they saw the truck. There it was again, though before, he could have sworn her eyes had been sil—

"Aren't you supposed to be in front of me?" she asked.

Desire and doubt vanished. "I would have been, if you hadn't bolted off in the first place." He stepped around her and went on without pausing. "Next time, let me go first. Clear?"

"Get up on the wrong side of the bed?"

He didn't bother telling her he hadn't slept at all. Her presence had echoed through the walls of the inn like a resonating bell, one moment consuming him with the need to go to her, and the next, driving him away in a fit of resentment.

She was money. His ticket to freedom, nothing more.

Maybe if he kept telling himself that, he might start to believe it. Sneering, he picked up the pace.

The trail wound upward past bogs and outcroppings of rock on either side. She treaded so lightly that a few times he had to look back to be sure she followed. She stayed right behind him, eyes either on her path, or darting around the woods. A parrot scolded them from its perch. Faith gasped as it flew across their path and away into the trees. "Ooh, I wish I'd had my camera out. Ian would love to get pictures of some of these birds."

"Who's Ian?" Hakon asked, trying not to sound as if he cared.

"My sister's husband. He teaches wildlife classes back at the—Oh, how beautiful!"

He stopped and looked back. She had knelt at the side of the trail to look at a leggy patch of small, purple flowers. He found himself smiling. "That's angel sword."

She stood again, and brushed off her knees. "It's so delicate. How does anything like that survive up here?"

"Same way most things do," he answered, turning back around to continue up the trail. "You adapt, or die trying."

"We are still talking about flowers, right?"

"Flowers, animals, people. What's the difference?"

She *hmph*ed, and came up beside him where the trail widened out. He felt her gaze on him as they walked. "So, do you live in Sydney now?" she asked at last.

"I live wherever I drop my stuff at the end of the night. I'm usually on hikes, and clients pay my room and board at lodges. No point keeping a house."

"And in the off-season?"

"Miriam keeps a spot open for me, and I help her make repairs around the place. Watch the spider web." He pushed aside an overhanging branch draped in the gossamer strands.

She ducked underneath it. "Have you been doing the hikes for long?"

"Long enough. How does a lady like you get to be an archaeologist?"

"I worked my ass off, thank you very much."

He chuckled. "I didn't mean it like that. I meant, why that instead of something else?"

"Why hiking?"

"Gets me out of the city."

"So does archaeology." She grinned.

Hakon's stomach dropped into his feet. *Oh, God, smile like that again.* The moment the thought crossed his mind, he crushed it. He tried walking faster to get ahead of her again, but his feet refused to obey.

Kiss her. Kiss her. She wants you to kiss her. Can't you feel it?

No. He would not be made a fool by another woman. And she had no business looking at him that way when someone had broken her heart. Or had they? Hakon began to wonder if he'd been wrong about her tears yesterday.

What did it matter now? She was there, and so was he, and like it or not, they'd entered into an agreement. He'd guide her to a few Aborigine rock paintings, and she'd pay up when they returned to Sydney. The faster they finished, the better. He hurried on, and this time his feet did as they were told.

They turned off the trail, and put several kilometers behind them before stopping for lunch. They ate a quick meal of sandwiches and lemonade, supplemented with wild berries Hakon found nearby.

Faith popped a handful of plump red berries into her mouth. "Have you always been good at borrowing your lunch from Mother Nature?"

"You can't always rely on your own resources out here. Eating bush tucker helps you travel light."

"Bush tucker?"

"Yeah." He held up a handful of berries. "Fruit, nuts, leaves, lizards, insects. Bush tucker."

She cringed. "You've eaten insects?"

"Get used to it. You're on the Ivarsson Wilderness Tour. The bugs aren't bad, once you get past the crunchy parts."

"Ewww."

He chuckled at her horrified expression. "I'm kidding. If we need extra food, there are plenty of non-insect varieties."

She glared at him and stuffed the last bite of sandwich into her mouth.

He couldn't help it. Teasing her just came too easily. Shaking with laughter, he added, "For an archaeologist, you're awfully squeamish."

"For a trail guide, you're awfully revolting."

He caught the gleam of amusement in her eye, and his body went on full alert. Reckless desire flooded him. He tried to stamp down the reaction, but everything in him gravitated toward her. He scraped up the sandwich wrappers and stuffed them in his backpack. "Time to go."

"You don't let the grass grow under your feet, do you?"

"No point in hanging about when there's still a long way to the first Aborigine site."

She brushed crumbs off her shorts, and got up just as he neared the rock on which she'd sat.

Hakon stopped short. They stood almost nose-to-nose, breathing each other's air. Everything around them blurred out, suddenly far less important.

Her lips parted on a soft, indrawn breath. She leaned a fraction closer. Her gaze flitted to his mouth.

He had only to lean forward to touch his lips to hers. All at once, he longed to tug her ponytail loose and let the golden strands flow through his fingers. To feel her lips under his. To answer the invitation smoldering in her eyes.

Fighting to master his urges, he stepped around her and hitched his backpack onto both shoulders. "Come on." He heard the barest sigh behind him, and it shivered down his spine like a skimming touch.

Too close.

For the rest of the afternoon, he avoided getting any nearer to her than necessary. She didn't comment on any more of the flowers or animals they happened to pass. He found himself listening for her voice. The longer she stayed silent, the more he dangled between relief that he hadn't kissed her, and regret.

How could he think of kissing her when she might be trying to get over a broken heart? He had enough problems without throwing another woman into the mess. Not to mention, she was a client, and he ought to act like a professional. Professionals didn't make moves on their clients.

No matter how much they wanted to.

He checked his compass and turned up the mountain, following a thin ridge of rock. Sweat trickled down the back of his neck. Eventually the trees gave way, and they emerged into a clearing that gave them a panoramic view of the forest canopy on the slopes below. The oily scent of eucalyptus hung heavy on the cooling air. Sunlight gilded the tops of the trees.

"Incredible," said Faith, stopping behind him. She turned in a circle to admire the sweeping scenery. "I've never seen anything so beautiful." The sun flashed off her pale-gold hair. She stretched her arms out as though embracing the view, gave an enraptured sigh, and closed her eyes in an expression of perfect bliss.

Me, neither. He stared at her, envisioning other ways to put a look like that on a woman's face. He took a step toward her, then halted instantly. She was beautiful, sure enough...and more hazardous than anything the mountains could throw at him. With a supreme effort, he dragged his eyes away from her luminous figure.

He glanced at the sky directly above, so blue it almost hurt to look at it, then stared up the winding ridge at a charcoal-gray smudge looming over the mountain's peak.

She opened her eyes and did the same. "Is it storming up there?"

"Yeah. That's the mountains for you. You can see so far from some points that you'll have storms on one ridge, and sunshine on the next. There's an old cabin up ahead. It should do for the night."

"You've been here before? God, how do you tell one rock apart from another? No compass out, no map." She wound her way between a few shrubs, then came toward him.

He laughed. "That's why I'm the trail guide, and you're not. Hey, your pack's crooked."

She checked the fit of the shoulder straps, then took a closer look at the left one. "Damn it, it's fraying. I knew I should have had it fixed before coming to

Sydney." She gave him a sheepish grin. "I've had it since I was an undergrad, and I can't bear to part with it."

He looked at the moody sky again. "Some things are worth being sentimental about. Hiking gear, not one of them. Hopefully, it'll hold until we get to the cabin." He reached under the strap to help her adjust it, and the warmth of her shoulder heated his fingers through her T-shirt. He gritted his teeth, sending vehement pleas to his body. *Ignore, ignore.* The minute he'd tightened the strap, he let go and spun away to cross the clearing.

"Gee, thanks," she called, sounding annoyed.

He hunched his shoulders, feeling guilty for being so terse. He cleared his throat and looked back. "You're welcome."

Her aggravated stare relaxed, and she smiled once more. "That wasn't so hard, was it?"

He bit back a snarky reply, and made what he thought an admirable show of forbearance by picking up the trail again. *You will never know how hard,* he thought, still itching to spar with that self-satisfied look in her eye.

Another half-hour's hike brought them to a shallow river. They continued upstream until finding a narrow point where they could cross without much trouble. He tested the water with a fallen branch and found that, even at its deepest point, it might only reach his knees. "If we hurry, we might make it to that cabin by nightfall." He waded into the river, skirting large boulders sticking out of the sluggish current.

He slipped on a flat stone toward the opposite bank, but righted himself by jumping to another rock. "Watch your step there."

When he reached dry ground, Faith was still in the middle of the river. She'd paused to fumble with the torn strap on her backpack, which had come loose again. "Come on," he urged. "You can tie it off later."

"Damn thing," she growled. "Any chance your friend Toby will sell me that pack of his when we get back to Bowen Mountain? I'm going to get it out of him one way or another." She flashed a startling grin that whipped his insides into a frenzy.

God, she was sexy when she wanted something. He started to smile back, but then he heard an ominous rumble coming from upstream. His heartbeat staggered, then resumed at double speed.

Flash flood.

He jerked the coil of rope off its clip on his belt, then stripped out of his gear and flung it down. "Faith, get out of the water!"

She froze, looking bewildered.

"Faith! Now!"

The rumble became a threatening roar. She shrieked and scrambled toward him, sending up frothy arcs of spray in every direction. He started to swing the rope, lasso-style.

Then she slipped on the same flat stone and went down. He screamed her name just as a wall of water surged down the river. He heard her cry out, and then the roiling waves swept her away.

Hakon threw the coil of rope on his shoulder and bolted downstream along the bank. Leaping over fallen branches and dodging rocks, his breath churning like a steam engine, he scanned the water. He thought he saw a flash of golden hair amongst the boiling waves, and plunged ahead—far enough, he hoped, to outstrip the rushing water.

He skidded to a halt beside a large gum tree, flung one end of the rope around it, then clipped the other to his belt. He had one chance to get her. The water downstream seethed and crashed around larger and larger boulders. She'd be killed if she hit them.

He dove off the bank. The waves gushed over his head and slammed him into a rock. Pain lanced through his ribs and almost stole his breath. Thrusting his feet against the boulder, he pushed outward into the mad current and broke the surface gasping.

There.

He plunged ahead into the middle of the stream and snatched Faith by her backpack. He gripped her with both arms in a bear hug as they swept downstream together. "Hold your breath!" God willing, she'd heard him.

He wheezed in a breath of his own, and the rope sprang taut. Both of them went under.

With one arm around her waist, he groped with his free hand for the knife in his belt. Jerking it from its sheath, he sawed at the straps of her pack. The waterlogged pack sucked them downward until his feet touched the river bottom. Deep here—too deep to stand and get a breath, even if there weren't rapids roaring over their heads. Bugger all. He shoved against the river bottom, and they broke the surface again.

Snap. One strap broke free. They went under again, and smashed into a boulder. He grunted and lost his breath in a surge of bubbles.

They came up once more. Choking, he jerked his knife under her waist strap.

Snap. It broke loose. The pack dragged at her body,

still hung up by its torn strap on her shoulder. She flailed limply in his arms. He dropped his knife and tore the backpack free. With one arm around Faith, and the other clinging to his rope, he angled toward the bank. Waves plowed over them, and they bashed into another rock. He spun underwater, putting her body upstream from his, and strove for dry land with his lungs shrieking for air.

They reached the shallows at last. He lifted her into his arms, coughing and half-blinded as he stumbled out of the swirling water. Bruised, aching, he dropped to his knees and laid her on the silty bank. She remained mute, her eyes closed. He wiped the water from his face, then shook her. She didn't respond. "Don't die. Don't you dare die on me," he sputtered, feeling for a pulse.

Nothing. No pulse, no breath, no movement. For the first time in Hakon's life, real terror kicked him in the gut. His heartbeat slammed into overdrive as if the river had been a mere lap swim. *No!*

He bent and blew his breath into her mouth. Once, twice. No response. He pressed the heel of his hand to her breastbone and started CPR. Still nothing.

Panic surged through him, strangling and burning and stabbing from every angle. The scream burst out of him without thought: *"Aesa!"*

She grunted, and water poured from her mouth and nose. Her chest rose in a gasping breath, and her eyes flew open, staring wide and unseeing.

And silver.

He didn't have time to think about it. The instant she began coughing, he lifted her into a sitting position and flung his arms around her. Relief plowed past the terror. Alive, she was alive.

She heaved for breath and slumped against him. "I heard you...call me," she said, panting.

"Oh, God, I thought you drowned. Holy Jesus. Faith, I thought you drowned." He hugged her close, then arched away to look at her, brushing a lock of sodden hair off her cheek. Her eyes were blue, the same blue he'd seen all day. "Are you all right?"

She nodded and fisted a hand on her chest, rubbing at it as she gasped for air. She stared at him with a look of awe. "You called me...Aesa."

"Aesa?" He glanced around the woods in a perfunctory search for shelter. "Are you all right? Is anything broken?" He made to reach for her leg, to test the bones.

She laid a stalling hand on his, and shook her head. "I'm fine. You said 'Aesa,' Hakon." Her voice cracked. River water, or something else?

He remembered yelling at her just before she regained consciousness, but only that he'd spoken. Something, anything to drive away the tearing horror that she might have died. "What does it matter what I said? You're alive." He swiped a hand through his dripping hair, then helped her to her feet.

When he tried to tug her away from the riverbank, she didn't follow. He pivoted back.

She pulled him closer and stared so hard he felt like a science project. "You know me." She poked his chest. "*This body* knows me, even if you don't."

Chapter Four

I found out what the voices are. They're ghosts. I hear them talking when I'm supposed to be asleep. I told Sara, but I'm scared she doesn't believe me. What if no one will?
—Faith's Journals, age ten

"What in hell are you talking about?" Hakon dropped her hand as if she'd burned him, then unclipped the rope from his belt.

"You know who I am!" Her heart raced. Not quite hope, yet. She didn't dare.

He took her hand again, looking worried. "Did you hit your head on the way downriver?"

"I'm fine. I swear I'm fine." Was it possible she'd gone from heartache to heartache only because she and Hakon were fated to find each other again, after a thousand years apart? Was this their chance?

She heaved a difficult breath. "Hakon, I—I need you to know some things about me."

Thunder boomed overhead, and rain began pattering down. He glanced up. "Shouldn't we do this after we find a dry place to stay?"

"Wait, please—"

"We'll have time to talk when we're not both freezing and soaked through. Let's go," he said, sliding an arm around her shoulders.

He found a shallow cave, mercifully unoccupied by wild animals, but pitch-dark from the gloom of the storm outside. She shivered and huddled against the far wall, chilled after the warmth of his nearness.

"I'm going back for my gear," he said. "I'll try to find some dry wood, and come back as soon as I can." He slipped out through the narrow mouth of the cave, and disappeared into the storm.

Faith wrung her ponytail out, then tried to squeeze the water from her clothes. "Everything I own is probably at the bottom of the river." She groaned. "Including my cell phone." Sara would have a fit when she couldn't reach Faith. Even if Sara *could* reach her, up here in the boonies.

Faith thought about calling in a favor from one of the ghosts she'd helped over the years, just to get a message to her sister, but she doubted they'd be able to travel such distances even if they wanted to. They wouldn't just be hovering around to hear her request, anyway, and it took hard effort to summon a ghost. She had too little energy left for that.

A quick search of the cave yielded no dry fuel for a fire, unless she counted a few crumbling leaves. "Well, I'm not going to sit here and freeze to death while I wait." Summoning her resolve, she headed back out into the storm.

She found enough fallen branches to provide a night's firewood, then arranged the pieces just inside the mouth of the cave. Touching the damp wood, she called on her pyrokinesis. A shiver fluttered down her back, adding to the chill of being soaked to the skin. "Burn, baby, burn."

A stream of heat flowed from her fingertips into

the wet wood. The kindling steamed in the cool air. It took her a good fifteen minutes of concentrated effort to dry the woodpile until flame caught and blossomed in its center. "Finally!" She snatched her hand away and sat back with a smug smile, basking in the fire's warmth.

Sometimes it paid to be different.

She dried out another pile of wood, then pushed it into the back of the cave. Hakon returned just as she'd finished, with his backpack over his shoulder and an armload of soaked wood. He blinked when he saw the fire, then looked past it at her with his jaw hanging open. "How'd you get that going?"

"Actually, that's what I want to talk to you about." Now that she'd reached the verge of telling him everything, her stomach somersaulted. "You, ah... You might want to sit down for this."

He set the pile of wood down and spread it out to air dry, then twisted water out of his copper-gold hair and tied it into a ponytail with a band from his pocket. "Right now, I'm thinking about getting these wet clothes off before we get sick."

"And change into what? I don't exactly have a lot of spare garments lying around."

"Look, we're both adults. Being naked is better than catching your death waiting for your body heat to dry out your clothing, isn't it?" He stripped off his shirt and dropped it.

She gaped. The firelight flickered on his damp skin, caressing each contoured muscle of his broad chest as though taunting her. He seemed not to mind the scrapes and bruises he'd earned in the river. Her mouth went dry at the way the water molded his jeans to his burly legs. Raw power drifted off him in palpable waves. Delicious chills sped up her arms. She forgot all about being sore and weary.

He bent to rummage in his backpack, pulled a wool blanket from its recesses, and then came toward her. The waves of power sharpened, and she took an instinctive step back. His gaze flashed up and down her body. She sensed a change underneath his air of intensity.

He wanted her. She'd never felt such a visceral aura in her life. The waves of his desire splashed against her skin, and she trembled with longing—partly the echo of his, and partly her own.

He shook out the blanket, then draped it around her shoulders. "I have an extra sweatshirt and a pair of jogging pants. You can have them until your stuff dries." He pulled the blanket closed around her, and their hands came together. His Bermuda-blue eyes glowed with reflected firelight...and much more. Her shivers multiplied.

He tugged her closer and slid his arm around her. Even drenched with rain and river water, he exuded heat. "Come closer to the fire and get your clothes off." He sounded half-strangled as the words left his lips.

She stayed where she was, robbed of breath even to respond. The blanket fell to the ground. Slowly, she spread her palms on his chest. His skin pulsed with warmth. Fine hairs tickled against her fingertips.

So familiar. So wonderfully, devastatingly familiar.

He stilled. His stare blazed into hers. A soft breath escaped him, and in the barest shift, for just an instant, he leaned into her touch.

Faith turned her face up to his and closed her eyes.

And then he was gone, stepping away so fast that a draft of cool air flushed against her in his place. She opened her eyes, bereft and cold.

He had turned away to tear through the contents of his backpack, shoulders rigid, body tense. "Hakon, I—"

"Get this straight," he interrupted, whirling back with a fistful of sweatshirt. "You and me and whatever just happened isn't going to happen any further. I guide, you pay, that's it. Get anything else out of your head." He shoved the shirt at her.

Hurt stabbed her. She caught the shirt before it fell, and watched him turn away to grope through his backpack. "I didn't realize I was so repulsive," she snapped.

He arched around and glared. The air in the cave crackled on her hypersensitive skin. Heat spiraled into the pit of her belly, and she shuddered.

He turned his back once more, then flung an arm out behind him with his jogging pants clutched in his fist. "Get changed."

She wanted to throw something at him. Preferably a large, blunt something. She snatched the pants, forced her gaze away from him, and shimmied out of her clothes. Naked, she stole another glance. He hadn't moved, but her skin sizzled as though he were touching her. She hastened into the borrowed clothing, then threw her wet things down beside the fire to dry. "I'm finished."

He turned back around and detached his bedroll from the backpack, then knelt to arrange it on the cave floor with the wool blanket over the top. "We'll have to share. We can try to find your backpack in the morning, if it hasn't been washed away. Did you have anything in there waterproofed? Bagged, or in containers?"

"Some of it. I wasn't expecting a swim in full gear."

"Me, neither." He gave a quick, wry smile that set her pulse speeding. With his eyes on his work, he added, "Glad you're okay."

Her throat tightened. Somehow, that unfussy remark meant more than any theatrics could have done. She wrapped her arms around herself, her hands lost in the baggy sleeves of his too-big sweatshirt. "Thanks."

He finished, then stood up to pull another pair of jogging pants and a thermal shirt from his bag. He shrugged the shirt over his head, and a pang of disappointment pierced her. Such a magnificent torso ought really to be displayed for the perfection it was, not draped in clothing. By the time he'd poked his arms out through the holes, she still hadn't looked away.

He pitched his boots and socks into the back of the cave, and stood there barefoot. She realized he was glaring again. "Mind if I put my dry pants on, or are you going to stand there and stare at me while I do it?"

So much for their unspoken truce. "You wish," she spat, and turned away to stoke the fire. She heard shifting behind her, and—God help her, she knew she'd burn in hell for it—peeked back over her shoulder.

He shucked his pants off with a motion that was graceful in its economy, then tossed them beside his boots.

Mother of mercy, the man didn't wear underwear.

He had the most incredible ass she'd ever seen. Perfectly molded, eminently male. Her stare traveled down over well-muscled legs, then back up, riveted. A tiny sigh of awe escaped her, and she looked away at once.

If he'd heard it, he didn't respond. A moment later he bent beside the fire, clothed now, and spread out his wet garments. "Are you hungry?"

That depended on his definition of hunger. Food hadn't crossed her mind in hours. "No. Just cold."

"Get in the sleeping bag, then. I'll be there in a few minutes."

Stinging a little, she said, "You just love to order people around, don't you?"

He glared again from the corner of his eye. She could almost see him counting to ten to keep a lid on his temper. Smiling sweetly, she burrowed into the blankets.

As soon as she rolled onto her side, her smile died. The shiver of his nearness compounded the damp chill settling into her bones until she couldn't tell the sensations apart. She had to tell him what she was, had to know if he recognized anything about her, but she couldn't bring herself to speak.

She heard shuffling as he added some wood to the fire, then he turned the blankets back to climb in beside her. The sleeping bag wasn't built for two, and even though she knew he tried not to crowd her, his body brushed against hers. She bit down on her lip to trap the gasp that forced its way into her throat.

Her powers screamed for release, battering around inside her body so hard her teeth ached. With an inward groan, she surrendered to the flow, and opened her eyes.

Vapor trails rose in the fire glow, blurring against the rock wall. Her body hummed where he touched her with an energy almost frightening in its potency.

"Jesus," she whispered, shaking.

"What's the matter?" His arm slid over her shoulder, and his palm pressed against her forehead, scorching against her cool skin. "Faith, you're freezing."

"T-Told you I was cold," she bit out, still begging her powers to be silent.

He shifted and curled against her back. Warmth spread throughout her body and quieted her chills, but it did little to dispel the psychic roar in her head. She cringed, hearing a shout and a clash of sword metal in her mind. She remembered the original Hakon's violent death at the hands of a power-mad rogue druid. So much blood, so much agony.

Hakon pulled his hand away from her forehead. "Better?"

"N-No."

He sighed, and his hand came to rest on her shoulder. His touch finally drove the visions away, real and immediate against the phantom images in her head. Even the sensation of his unwillingness to be this near to her was preferable to envisioning him dying, over and over. She gulped a breath of relief.

"Good night," he said gruffly.

"Good night," she whispered, wondering if she'd sleep.

Wondering if *he'd* sleep.

****

As soon as her breathing steadied out, Hakon pulled his hand away. With his head pillowed on his folded arm, he stared at the cave wall, tracing every crease and imperfection in the stone.

And begging his body not to disobey him.

She had relaxed, soft with slumber. Her shapely rear nestled into the hollow of his thighs as if she belonged there. He'd held still as long as he could, but the pressure of her against his cock drove him wild with need. He tried moving away, but the too-small sleeping bag prevented it. He tried shifting to his back. Not comfortable, either. He tried facing the other direction. At last, he gave in and curled up behind her once more.

Strands of her ponytail fluttered against his arm as he shifted. Unable to resist, he bent his head and took a deep breath.

Lilies. Shampoo or perfume or God knew what, but the smell drugged his senses. He reached up and brushed a tendril of silken hair away from her face. She sighed in her sleep, lost in dreams.

He wondered what she dreamt of. Something good...or some*one*? He gritted his teeth in a silent snarl, moody and hot-tempered for no reason. Without thinking, he arched his body closer around her. His erection brushed her backside, and he stifled a groan.

"Hakon," she murmured.

He froze.

Her eyes remained shut, but faint lines had appeared between her brows. "Please don't go."

She talked in her sleep? How...endearing. He smiled a little. "Where would I go?"

"Please..." Her head jerked. Her next words rushed out in a language he didn't know, but the sound raked along his spine, and somehow he understood.

She was terrified.

Desire forgotten, he laid a hand on her shoulder. "Faith, wake up."

She twisted and moaned. "Don't, they'll kill you!"

"Faith, wake up!" Worried, he tugged her shoulder until she rolled onto her back.

She whimpered, and her eyes flew open. The moment she saw him, her arms shot around his neck, and she hugged him hard. Her body shook.

"Whoa, easy. It was just a dream." He arched away and eased out of her embrace. Her lashes fluttered, and he saw the glitter of tears in the firelight. "Must have been pretty awful."

"Sorry." She wiped at her eyes.

Uncertain what to do about her tears, he tried for a grin. "You didn't tell me you were multilingual."

"Oh, God. Did I talk? What did I say?"

"I couldn't tell, but it didn't bloody sound good. How many languages do you know?"

She hesitated, and he could track the return from her nightmare to reality on her face. Her eyes, wild with fear before, calmed. "Ten."

"*Ten?* Gran would have loved you, all right." He crawled out of the sleeping bag to add wood to the lowering fire.

"Your grandmother?"

"Yeah. Bit of a language buff, herself, but she never got past three before she died."

Faith rolled onto her belly and propped herself up on her elbows. "What did she speak?"

"Well, English, obviously, but she also had Scottish family, so she knew a bit of the Gaelic, and also some Norwegian." Thunder rumbled outside, and the fire guttered in a gust of cool wind. "Sounds like the rain's picking up again."

"Norwegian?"

"Yeah. Gran gave me my name. Guess she knew

royalty when she saw it." He chuckled.

She burst into an answering smile that stirred his malehood again, and reminded him what he'd been about to do before she spoke in her sleep.

Kiss her. Wrap himself around her body as if he had the right to do so, and press his lips to the soft skin of her cheek. Slide his hand around her waist, and pull her closer.

Her eyebrows arched, and she sat up. Her smile broadened into a grin. Damn it, how did she do that? Every time he loosened his hold on his self-control, she looked at him like a kid with her hand in the cookie jar. He turned and slapped his hand over her discarded shorts. "Your stuff is dry."

She pushed her shirt sleeves up to the elbows, crawled closer, then took the shorts. "Hmm. Gives new meaning to the term 'wash and wear,' doesn't it?" She reached for the shirt laid out beside it, and when she picked it up, he saw a lacy purple bra and thong panties lying underneath.

He shut his eyes, praying for a distraction. Any distraction. "You were supposed to tell me something earlier?"

"It's not that important right now."

"Seemed important enough then," he pressed. *Please, say something to get me off this mad train of thought, because all I can think of is you wearing those skimpy little things...or taking them off for you. This hike is taking an express train straight to hell.*

"Which way is the first Aborigine site?" she asked.

He opened his eyes and stared at her. "You aren't seriously thinking about going on when you just got half-drowned, are you?"

"I have to."

"With what gear? It isn't like this trip can't wait."

"It can't," she insisted.

He sat back on his heels. "What are you after up here?"

"Why can't you just help me?"

"Oh, no. We aren't going another step until you tell me what's behind all this, Doctor Markham. I have a right to know why I'm guiding you."

Shivering, she climbed back into the sleeping bag and knelt there, then wrapped the wool blanket around her shoulders. "I'm looking for a lost boy."

He felt his mouth drop open. Whatever he'd been expecting, it hadn't been that. "I'm not a search-and-rescue. What the hell do you think you're doing, dragging me out here when it's the rangers who should be looking for this kid?"

"Because this is a very special boy."

All sorts of wild guesses flew through his head. "Yours?"

"No. But he's going to need me."

Hakon chucked another branch into the fire. Sparks flew upward. "What makes you think he needs you more than the rangers...or his parents? You're out of your goddamned mind, if you think I'm taking you through these mountains now. You women all think you own the world—"

"I need you to help me find him, Hakon."

"And I told you I'm bloody well not doing it," he snarled.

"He could get hurt out there!"

"All the more reason you should have told me why you wanted to come up here in the first place." He snatched up his backpack, and then began rummaging through its contents for his map and electric torch. "Damned fool, you could have killed yourself today, and now there's a boy lost—"

"What are you doing?" she demanded.

"Finding the fastest route out of here. You're going back to Bowen Mountain first thing in the morning."

"No."

He looked up. "What do you mean, 'no'?"

"Just what I said. If I have to find that boy myself, I'll do it. He's in trouble."

Hakon narrowed his eyes. "What kind of trouble?"

"I'd love to tell you, but I don't know."

He shifted until he knelt right in front of her, then gripped her by the arms. "Woman, I'm about a hair's breadth from wringing your neck, so you'd better tell me what's going on, and I mean now."

"Back off."

"No way."

"I mean it, Hakon."

"So do I."

She squeezed her eyes shut, looking pained, and squirmed. "*Please* back off."

Suspicion crawled along the back of his neck, and he loosened his grip. "What's the matter with you?"

"You! Let go!" She flung his arms off and fisted her hands on the sides of her head, panting.

"Faith—" Worried now, he reached for her again.

"Don't touch me!" She scrambled backward so fast, he snatched his hands away in surprise. She threw off the wool blanket and brushed her hair away from her face.

Silver eyes flashed in the fire glow. No mistaking it

this time. For an instant, Hakon lost the thread of reality. Instead of seeing Faith sitting on his bedroll in his shirt and pants, he saw her in a plain brown dress, reclining among furs with those same quicksilver eyes. He blinked and shook his head. The image was gone as if it had never happened.

"What are you staring at?"

"You and your silver eyes." He couldn't believe he said it even as the words left his mouth.

"Oh, God." She shut her eyes, then opened them again.

He watched them—*watched* them—fade from silver to blue in the firelight. Slowly, he backed away.

"I'm not going to hurt you." She spread her hands out in a pleading gesture.

He laid one hand on the steel barrel of his electric torch. He surprised himself with the calm in his voice as he asked, "Want to tell me what the hell you are, then?"

Her shoulders slumped. "I'm a psychic."

"Yeah, right." He burst into laughter.

"I am! You wouldn't find it so funny if you woke up hearing ghosts every other night. You'd find it even less funny if you knew what I know about you."

"Don't tell me. I'm going to meet a strange woman, and acquire wealth and fame."

"What do you think my eye color is? A parlor trick?" She did it again. Her eyes melted into silver in an instant.

"All right," he said, "you can quit that any time, because it's really bugging me."

She huffed and snatched the wool blanket around her shoulders again. "You wanted to know what's going on, so I'm telling you. I'm psychic. I hear the little voices that go 'Boo' in the night. I'm also pyrokinetic, which means I can start fires just by thinking about it. And before you get all weirded out about that one, let me just make it clear that we'd be freezing to death tonight if it weren't for me." She jerked her chin in the direction of the campfire.

He looked at the fire from the corner of his eye, half expecting flames to leap out of the kindling at him. They didn't. "Next, you're going to tell me you can fly," he snapped. "Have you got a broomstick stashed somewhere, or did it get lost in the river?"

"I can astral project, too. If you're going to laugh at me, I might as well fully earn it."

"You do realize you're raving bonkers, don't you? What the hell is astral projecting?"

"Wait, you haven't heard the best part yet. You're not even Australian."

"Oh, I'm not?" He crossed his arms and gave her an expectant stare. How the hell had he managed to get himself on a hike—alone—with a madwoman? He really needed to interview his clients better.

She hunched deeper into the blanket. "You're Australian *now*. But a thousand years ago, you were a Viking warrior who was very much in love with his wife...a woman named Aesa."

He stared, teetering on the edge between disbelief and worry for Faith's sanity. If it weren't for being stuck in a cave with her in the middle of nowhere, the whole thing might have been downright entertaining. Thunder growled outside as if putting the exclamation point to his entrapment. Helpless to convey any other emotion, he smiled. "Was I rich?"

She threw her dry T-shirt at him. "Make fun of me all you want, but just so you know, I don't plan on leaving these mountains until I find that boy. If you want to go home, you do it without me."

"What's so special about this kid that he needs you?"

"He's gifted. Do you want that kind of power in the wrong hands, or do you want him to learn from someone who knows what they're doing?"

"I'm not so sure *you* know what you're doing. I damn sure don't know what *I'm* doing up here *with* you."

"That's it." She shoved the blanket off and crawled toward him, then thrust a hand out, palm-upward. Hakon jumped backward into a crouch and came up against the cave wall.

A lick of flame burst into being in her palm, dancing in her half-curled fingers. She glared, flashing those eerie mercury eyes. "Is *this* convincing enough for you?"

Chapter Five

Todd Garrett is a jerk. He picked on me about my breasts, and made me so mad I accidentally started a fire in the girls' bathroom trashcan. The whole school had to evacuate. Oops.
—*Faith's Journals, age sixteen*

"Holy bleeding Christ." Hakon flattened himself against the wall, staring at the flame in her palm as if she were about to attack him.

Faith cringed at his reaction. She'd been a fool. She shouldn't have told him, certainly not this way, but he *infuriated* her. She closed her fist, and the flame winked out. "I told you, I'm not going to hurt you. Give me five minutes to explain."

He skirted around her, looking doubtful. "I don't think five minutes is going to be enough to explain what the bloody hell you are!" He shot across the cave floor and seized his flashlight, holding it like a nightstick.

She bit back a growl of frustration. "Are you going to bludgeon me, or would you rather hear this?"

"Fine. Start talking." He sat down, but didn't let go of the flashlight.

Once she began, the words burst forth. The cave became a confessional, and the firelight, the flickering glow of church candles. She told him how she and Sara had gotten their powers as children, developed them, and learned to control them. She'd always been afraid to reveal her abilities to anyone as a girl, and more so as a young woman—but strangely, explaining to *him* took no effort at all.

Until she came to his part in the tale.

"This past year we went to Shetland, where we excavated the ruin of a Viking house." She hugged herself. "That's where I found you."

He crossed his arms and tucked the flashlight under one elbow. "And I wouldn't remember this because...?"

"Because it was you from a thousand years ago. You vowed to avenge your wife's murder, and when you failed, your soul got trapped in Shetland. My sister and I freed you."

"So my entire life history, and my parents, and their parents, and whoever else on back to bugger-all, is completely false."

"No. You are who you are now. You're also that man, the one whose soul we freed."

"What have I been doing for the past thirty-two years? Walking around Australia without a soul?" He started to laugh again.

"Without some part of you, yes. A piece of you would have been missing until this year." She studied him, searching for telltale signs in his aura, but found no trace of the Viking she'd known in her dreams. Doubt crept in, and she blinked to let her eyes fade back to their normal color. "Don't you feel any different?"

"Right now, I feel I'm making things worse by asking you questions about any of this ludicrous bullshit."

"I pulled flame out of thin air. How can you argue with that?"

"Fine, I saw...whatever I saw. Magic tricks, voodoo, goddamn smoke and mirrors, I don't care. Whatever you are, you go ahead and be that. Don't lump me into it." He glared at her, his eyes flashing with the distrust she felt in the air around him.

"You said 'Aesa' when you thought I was dead. Your wife's name."

"And where's my dear departed wife now?"

Faith bit her lip. The words danced at the tip of her tongue. No. She couldn't tell him, couldn't bear his ridicule if she told him *she* was Aesa. She sighed and crawled back to the blankets.

She couldn't have been wrong. He and the Shetland ghost were one and the same, right down to the aqua-blue eyes. She'd even had a flash of his former life when their hands touched back at the inn.

He had Aesa's wedding ring.

Thunder roared, and the chilly mist of rain gusted into the cave. Lightning flashed and disappeared. Faith shimmied into the sleeping bag and flopped down, regretting that she'd told him anything. "If you want to turn me in," she snapped, "you'll just have to wait until morning."

Seconds stretched out. At last, she heard the rumble of his voice from across the cave. "I wouldn't even know who gets you first—the government, or the tabloids."

Well, his sarcasm was better than outright horror. "The tabloids would try to give me three eyes, and say I came from Mars."

"Where *did* you come from?"

She rolled over and scowled at him.

He held up his hands in a placating gesture. "I'm not saying I believe in all this, but if you were...like that...and your sister, too, what about the rest of your family?"

"You sound like Ian." When he didn't respond, she added, "Big into the genetic theories. He seems to think it's an inherited, mutated gene of some sort. We think our parents were carriers...but no, they weren't gifted."

"You have theories on this sh—stuff?"

She looked away again. "If you were me, wouldn't you want to know what you were, and why you got that way?"

Time passed while she listened to the hiss of the rain. Sleep began stealing up on her, and she bunched up the corner of the sleeping bag under her cheek.

A few minutes later, Hakon seemed to come to a decision, and slipped in beside her. "I don't care if you're the devil himself. I'm freezing my arse off out there." He shifted and let out a long sigh. His warmth spread along her back.

She smiled.

****

Hakon woke to the musty scent of the damp cavern. The rain had stopped at last. Puddles gathered at the mouth of the cave, and he wondered if they'd be able to get Faith's pack from the river bottom.

Then he wondered why he was even contemplating doing so, instead of marching her right back to Miriam's place. And then he remembered.

The boy. God, there was some kid lost and wandering around out here. Hakon frowned. Going back to the inn now would only mean another day spent hiking in the opposite direction while something horrible happened to the kid—if it hadn't already, in yesterday's storm. The thought made him sick to his stomach. Glancing at Faith, he sat up.

She stirred and opened her eyes. "Good morning."

He grunted a response, staring at the gray ash of the dead campfire. "Let me ask you something. How do you know where this boy is?"

"I don't, exactly. I had help tracking him into the mountains, and I just know he's up here somewhere." She seemed to realize how crazy that sounded, because she looked away.

"Does the term 'needle in a haystack' mean anything to you?" he asked.

Sitting up, she yawned and combed her long fingers through sleep-tousled hair. "It's not going to be as hard as you think. In fact, I think the first thing we need to do is find one of those Aborigine sites."

"And how, exactly, is that going to help a lost kid?"

"Ghosts," she said, and a chill crept down his back. "If I find any ghosts, I can ask for help locating him. What, did you think I came up here with no game plan?"

"I think I'm nuts for going along with this."

"So you're going to help me?" She beamed at him again, and his belly lurched in an all-too-familiar manner.

How could he refuse while she looked at him like that? He broke the gaze. "I'd rather keep an eye on you than have you wandering out here lost, yourself. But as soon as we find a ranger station, we're reporting this kid, and that's the end of it."

She stood and picked up her scattered clothes. "I'm not letting that boy go on thinking there's no one out there like him—no one to believe him, or help him with his gifts."

"What is this, some selfless mission?"

She rounded on him. "I had my sister to help me. God knows what kind of person I'd have become if I thought I was all alone."

An ache settled in his gut. He'd become too used to being alone. He wouldn't have wished the feeling on his worst enemy, much less a boy. With a sigh, he climbed out of the sleeping bag and rolled it up, then left the cave so she could change clothes.

He'd stowed a few of Miriam's muffins in his backpack, and after a quick breakfast, they fished Faith's pack from the river where it had snagged on a low branch downstream. She sat on the riverbank to go through the pack. "Lucky break," he murmured when she found most of its contents still protected by their watertight containers.

"Looks like I've only lost a couple of things...oh, damn it all." She pulled a large leather book from the bag. Its wrinkled pages dripped with river water. "*Beardsley*'s shot."

He took the book. "What are you doing, hiking with this thing? It's extra weight."

"It's also the closest thing to a user's manual a gifted person can have."

"So buy another when you get home." He motioned to drop it at the water's edge.

"No!" She shot to her feet and snatched the book from his hands, then hugged it to her chest. "It's out of print. You can't find it anywhere for less than a small fortune."

"Damn shame for the kid when he goes to look for his own copy, then."

"You think you're funny, don't you?"

"Occasionally." He grinned.

She stuffed the book under her arm, then hoisted the pack over her shoulder by a broken strap. She pointed upstream. "Is this the way you were planning to go?"

"Yeah."

"Good." Without another word, she marched past him.

His grin died. "Faith, come on. Give me some of what's in your pack, and I'll carry it in mine."

"Why should I give you the satisfaction?"

"Because I'm trying to do a nice thing. You're going to break your back, carrying your bag the whole trip like that."

She turned so fast, he bumped into her. A smile spread across her face. "Fine. You carry *Beardsley*." She thrust the book into his hands. "And don't bother putting it in your backpack, 'cause it needs to air dry." She spun back around and resumed her march upstream.

He cursed and followed her, skirting fallen branches and uprooted shrubbery close to the soggy riverbank. For the first half of the morning, he berated himself for taking her on in the first place.

For the second half of the morning, he admired the view as she walked ahead of him. Really, she must have spent a lot of time working out to get legs like that. Muscular, but very feminine. She'd probably be a knockout in a bikini.

Hell, he was divorced, not dead. No harm in looking.

And speaking of divorce, if he ended the hike at the next ranger station, he wouldn't get the other half of his promised guide fee. He needed that money to finish paying his lawyer.

Damn it. Stuck with another woman...at least until the end of this hike. A woman claiming to be gifted with superpowers, at that.

He looked at the cover of the tattered book in his hands. *A Comprehensive Guide to the Occult, With Extensive Commentary by the Author, and New Annotated Appendices by H.L. Stillwater, Ph.D.* Hell of a moniker. Sort of matched the hefty book. He raised his eyebrows and opened the cover.

He managed to skim through the first few pages while walking. Some of them stuck together, and he peeled them carefully apart. The introduction rambled on about ancient rituals and astrological signs and man's continual search for cosmic answers. "Fat lot of malarkey, I call it."

But he kept reading, navigating the narrow game trail out of the corner of his eye. A while later, he looked up from the book to double-check their surroundings. She had paused a few strides ahead to stare at the thick growth closing in around their path.

She'd hiked them right into a dead-end on what should have been an obvious trail. He leered. "Good job."

"Hey, you're the expert. Are you going to guide, or should *you* be paying *me*?" she shot back.

He shrugged. "Let's just turn around and go back. We're looking for a squarish rock formation. It'll be on the left. You hungry?"

"Enough to eat bark."

Shrugging out of his pack, he sat on the ground against a nearby boulder, then laid her book aside. "We'll stop for lunch."

She doubled back, then sat beside him with a grimace. "I think I even have a bag of peanuts that might have survived the swim."

He pulled his canteen off his pack and offered it to her.

She drank deeply. "I'm surprised I'm this thirsty after drinking half of Australia's water supply back there."

"Hiking's tough on the body." He bit into a well-stuffed wrap sandwich, then picked up her book, balanced it on his knees, and began reading again.

"Awfully interested in the supernatural for a non-believer, aren't you?" she asked.

"Maybe I'm looking for a way to explain *you*."

"What do you want to know?"

"You never got around to telling me how you astro-whatsit."

"Astral project. And I think you're creeped out enough by all of this for that one, yet."

"If you don't tell me, I'll just look it up," he said, flipping to the back of the book with a smug smile.

"All right, all right." She laughed and laid a hand on his arm. The sensation of her skin on his flashed through him, soaking up his attention, and he almost didn't hear her response. "It's kind of an out-of-body experience where you can walk as a ghost."

He snapped the book shut. "You can't be serious."

"I can, and I am. I rarely ever do it, because the

first time, it scared the crap out of me."

He looked down at her long fingers on his tanned forearm, then back up to her face.

She blushed and let go. He regretted that. They stared at each other for a few minutes over the water-stained book until he offered her half of his sandwich. She grinned and took it, then ate with a gusto most women were too self-conscious to show.

"Wasn't going to let you starve," he mumbled around a bite of sandwich.

"Comforting," she said around her own mouthful. Her eyes crinkled at the corners. "I appreciate that you haven't forced me to bugs, yet."

He smiled, but didn't trust himself to respond to that devilish look on her face.

After lunch, he led them on. They came at last to the rock formation he'd mentioned, a near-square block of sandstone. Undergrowth had almost swallowed it so that they nearly passed it by before noticing. "We'll turn off here. You might want to put a long-sleeved shirt on. We'll be breaking trails from this point."

She found an oxford shirt in her pack and slipped it on over her T-shirt. Hakon used his bulk to break a trail ahead of them. Now and then, a startled bird burst from the undergrowth and flapped away into the forest. They walked perhaps a handful of kilometers before either of them spoke.

"How frequently do people visit these Aborigine sites?" she asked.

"Most of the popular ones have some kind of guided tour, and the trails aren't so overgrown. The one I'm taking you to doesn't get many visitors because it's so far into the back country." He shoved a spreading shrub aside and stepped into the gap.

"I can see why you like it out he—here—son of a bitch!"

He jerked around to find her standing in the middle of the trail, clutching her head. "What's wrong?"

"We're close, aren't we?" she ground out.

"Yeah. Why?"

"The ghosts. They're shouting at me. At somebody. Shut *up*, will you?" She shook her head and rubbed at her temples.

He frowned, not quite sure whether she was talking to him, then shifted on his feet. "Do you...need some help?"

"No. I'm fine, but they're pissed off about something. One at a time, damn it!" She dropped her backpack and pressed the heel of her hand to her forehead as though she had a massive headache.

The whole thing gave him a case of the chills, but she genuinely looked hurt. That tugged him toward her without his conscious thought. He took her by the elbow. "Come on. We're almost there, and you can rest for a while." He picked up her bag and tossed it over his shoulder, then urged her ahead down the trail.

She stumbled along, moaning in discomfort. Still doubtful, but afraid to make things worse, he avoided speaking until they reached the site. It was little more than a small cave with a semicircular apron of bare ground at its mouth. Faith stopped, and her shoulders slumped. "Finally."

He relaxed, not realizing he'd been tense the whole walk. He'd also pressed his hand at the base of her spine to urge her forward. He snatched it away. "What?"

"They shut up," she said, sounding more like herself. She struggled out of the oxford shirt, then tucked it under her arm.

"Do they...yell at you...a lot?"

"Just enough to annoy me at all the worst possible times." She stalked into the cavern.

How much would that suck to hear voices and not have the option of shutting them out? At least he could walk out of the room if he didn't want to hear someone yapping at him. He followed her inside, squinting in the sudden gloom.

Faded, primitive paintings ranged across the yellowish rock. He stared at them in discomfort. "I guess you found your ghosts, then?"

"Yeah. Let's hope one of them avoids ranting long enough to help me find the boy. I'm going to take some notes first. Mind waiting?"

Hakon shrugged and set his pack down. She knelt and withdrew a thin leather book and pencils from her bag. Silence throbbed in his midsection. He nudged at a stone with the toe of his boot. "These paintings are about twenty thousand years old. Next to them, a thousand-year-old Viking should be pretty spry, don't you think?"

"You're a drop in the bucket, chum." She pulled on a pair of leather gloves, then set an electric torch on the pitted floor, adjusting it to shine on the paintings. Balancing the book on her knee, she studied the images on the rock.

"Why do you need gloves just to look at something?"

"Because I don't want to touch it barehanded by mistake. The psychic pull would be too much to withstand."

He laughed. "You've touched me."

She didn't look up from her notes, but he thought he saw a faint blush coloring her cheeks. The jump in his groin took him by surprise. Irritated that she had such an effect on him, he forced a grin and crouched beside her to press a fingertip against her shoulder. "We're touching now."

"Do you mind if I work?"

"Horribly." He stayed put.

She gave him a disgruntled silver stare. "Remove your finger, please."

"Am I distracting you?"

She jerked her shoulder, and he let his hand drop away. "You know, I liked the first Hakon a lot better."

Her prickliness was a hell of a lot easier to take than that look on her face a minute ago. He relaxed and sat back on his heels. "What are we looking for here?"

"Right now, I'm just making the notes to take back to Gemini."

"What's that?"

She poked through her bag for a tape measure, which she used to take down the sizes of the primitive animal and human figures on the wall. "My sister and I run a firm together. Being twins, we thought the name sort of catchy." She flashed an infectious smile.

He returned it. "Aren't you the clever ones."

Finished with her notes, she put the book away, tugged off her gloves, then stood up. "Okay." She held out a hand. "Hold me."

"What?"

She waggled her hand in his face. "Hold me. I'm going to touch the wall, and I need you to be my anchor."

"You just told me you can't touch it...and to quit touching *you*."

"I'll be fine if you anchor me. Are you going to help me, or not?"

He stood. "What's this supposed to accomplish?"

"I'm going to try to contact a ghost for help," she explained. "I need someone from here and now to hang onto me, in case it's too strong for me to come back on my own. Make sense?"

"Not remotely." He glanced, uneasy again, from her to the wall and back, then slipped his hand into hers. A spark of heat shot from his hand to his belly when she threaded her fingers through his.

"Just hang on to me," she said. "If I stumble or collapse, pull me away from the wall. Don't let go, okay?"

He tightened his grip on her. "Are you sure about this?"

She smiled. "You're not going to see anything but me staring at a wall, unless something goes wrong. The minute I'm doing anything but staring, just pull me away." With her hand tucked firmly into his, she turned back to the wall, her mirror-bright eyes flitting over the crude paintings of kangaroos and men. She laid a hand against the rough rock. And then she went still.

His gut went into the same sickening dive as when he'd pulled her from the river. Just for an instant, he wondered what would happen if he couldn't wake her from whatever she was doing. A wave of fear and hostility swamped him so fast, he stepped back in surprise. At the last minute, he remembered to keep hold of her hand, and held tighter. *Don't lose her, don't lose her,* his body screamed.

What the hell was that about?

Shocked at his own reaction, he stared at her as if his very gaze could keep her rooted there with him. Seconds ticked by, or maybe minutes. Maybe a lifetime, he couldn't tell.

She shuddered and tugged at his hand, shifting toward the wall. Alarmed, he planted his feet and pulled her backward. She resisted. Her lips parted, and she stepped closer to the paintings.

The silence burst apart with a ringing *whoosh.* Wind rushed into the cavern, whipping her hair but leaving him strangely untouched. Her knees buckled.

Fear crashed through him. He yanked at her hand, but she didn't budge. With his heartbeat thundering in his ears, he threw his arm around her waist and jerked her bodily away from the wall.

The wind ceased at once. They slammed against the opposite wall, and he wrapped both arms around her. Panting, he stared over her shoulder at the painted rock. "What the bloody hell!"

Her glossy golden head came to rest against his shoulder, and she went limp in his arms. Afraid to let go, he shook her. "Faith, wake up!"

A faint groan escaped her. Her eyelids fluttered. "What...?"

He held her closer. "Are you all right? Say something, damn it." He shook her again.

Blue eyes focused on his face. "Didn't say this would be easy, did I?"

Relief. Almost painful relief. He slumped against the wall, but didn't let go. "Didn't say you were going to scare the shit out of me, either. You okay?"

She nodded. "Just disoriented...but I got what we needed."

"What did they do to you?"

"Talking. All of them...talking. Shouting, whispering, hissing. I saw all these...things. Bowls, tools, mats, spears, art. They came at me so fast...I thought I'd... If you hadn't held me..." She lifted her gaze to his, seeming to realize he still embraced her.

Her heartbeat started pounding against his chest. His every sense jerked awake and focused on her like magnets snapping together. The pressure of her hips and breasts drove him mad. Even his hands couldn't resist her. He spread his fingers, needing to feel as much of her as possible, to know for himself that she was there and breathing and responsive.

Her gaze heated. Her full lips parted on a shivering gasp, and it was all over. He threw caution to the wind and kissed her.

She moaned into his mouth and went molten in his arms. Savage triumph punched a hole in the last of his conscious thought. He thrust his hands into her hair, snapping her ponytail band loose in a cloud of golden mane. Spinning around, he backed her against the wall and lifted her by the hips. Her legs circled his waist. He ground against her with a possessive growl, and nipped at the satiny skin of her neck.

"Hakon... Oh, God, don't stop," she whispered. He bit harder and she cried out, dragging at the back of his shirt. Her legs tightened around him. He pressed his straining manhood against her with a tortured groan. Even through their clothing, she burned like hot coals. He wanted her, all of her. Now. Damn everything else.

Then he heard voices outside.

He jerked his head up, and spun to face the cave entrance even as he reached back to catch Faith and keep her behind him.

"...we don't even know what else we're looking for up here," came a distinctly American male voice. "What's the old geezer want with all this crap?"

"What would *you* want with half a billion dollars?" snapped another voice, also male, and a lot closer to the cave entrance.

"Half a bil—? Why aren't we selling it ourselves?"

"Because we don't have the geezer's connections, moron. Shut up. There's fresh tracks here."

The hairs rose on the back of Hakon's neck. A shadow flitted across the opposite wall, and with the same sense that warned him of a treacherous trail, he knew they were in very real trouble.

Faith yanked on his shirt. When he turned around, she snaked her arms around his neck, and her lips crashed against his again.

Chapter Six

*Chivalry is so dead. I asked Brett to open
a door for me because I was carrying all my
textbooks, and he let it slam on my foot
because he was staring at Gina Delgado.*
— *Faith's Journals, age seventeen*

Faith's heartbeat was in overdrive. She kissed
Hakon for all she was worth, hoping the intruders
would see a couple making out and go away. Their
footsteps came closer and—oh, God, what was Hakon
doing with his tongue? Chills raced down her back, and
she clutched his shirt. He nipped at her lower lip. *Yes,*
she wanted to scream. Shivering, she let her hands slide
down his chest and up under his shirt hem. He growled
again, then swept his tongue along hers in a sensual
dance that left her spinning. This was how it should be.
How *they* should be. How—

"Hello?" came a voice behind them.

Damn it.

Hakon broke the kiss to turn around, blocking her
with his body. She stared breathlessly at his back,
needing more.

Men could actually kiss like that?

"Do you mind? We're a little busy," he rumbled to
the intruder.

"Oh. Sorry, man." The newcomer cleared his

throat. "We didn't know anyone was here."

Faith's skin prickled, and she cringed behind Hakon's back.

She knew that voice.

"Someone *is* here, mate," said Hakon. "Can you do us a favor and be elsewhere?"

"Come on, let's just get on with our business," ordered the other voice. She knew that one, too. Oh, sweet Lord.

Elliott Flintrop's men.

"Right. Sorry." The footsteps shuffled away.

When she could no longer hear them, Hakon turned back to her. "What the hell was that all about?" he whispered.

Spurred into action, she slipped toward the entrance to peek around its corner. The men ambled off down the far trail with low laughter. Yep. David Beck and Carl Mancuso. Bad, bad news. She turned back to Hakon. "Those men work for Flintrop, L.L.C."

"And that would be who?"

"Another archaeology firm." She gathered her pack and turned off the flashlight, hesitated, then added, "The owner's crooked, and he knows what Sara and I are. I'm afraid he might be after the boy."

"What makes you so sure they aren't doing research?"

Avoiding his stare, she stuffed the flashlight in her bag. He deserved to hear the truth, since she'd dragged him into this...especially now that he'd kissed her and blown all the pieces of her apart. Every nerve ending sang, echoing that perfect moment that had been waiting a thousand years to happen.

And she had to ruin it.

She took a shaky breath and gathered her courage. "This past year, Elliott Flintrop's grandson tried to kill Sara and me because we're gifted. We think Elliott's still looking for others like us. If he gets his hands on them, it might very well be a disaster."

Hakon snarled and spun toward the back of the cave. "First, it was a research hike. Next, it was a lost boy. Now, you're talking about attempted murder." He rounded on her again. "I've had enough of this, Faith."

She winced, but stood her ground. "I need to find that boy, and I'm going to do it whether you help me or not. Now that I know exactly what kind of trouble he's in, I'll be damned if I leave this country without him." She threw her bag over her shoulder and stalked out of the cavern.

She heard him curse and jog after her. "Where do you think you're going?"

"East."

He slipped around her and blocked the trail, looking furious.

She tried to step around him, but he shifted again, a wall of solid male ire in her path. "Can you please get out of my way?" she snapped.

He glared at her and drew up to his full height as if daring her to try escaping. His gaze raked her from head to foot. A muscle twitched in his jaw. For a full minute, he just stared her down. Her skin itched with the seething anger in that look.

But the longer he looked at her, the less angry it got. She sensed threads of attraction, and could almost see him thinking of kissing her again, then detected a little anger with himself for thinking it. Part of her wished he'd damn well do it.

At last, he sighed and rubbed the back of his neck. He raised his other arm and gestured back the way they'd come. "There's a faster trail that goes behind the cave and up the rock."

She burst into a grin, sprang up on tiptoe, then kissed his cheek. Turning on her heel, she hurried away before he could change his mind.

She chose not to hear the muttered swearing behind her.

****

Goddamned infuriating, manipulating women. Hakon would have liked to drown the lot of them, except that his blood still boiled from that kiss in the cave. His senses had shot into overload, and hadn't stopped since.

He could still smell her sun-warmed skin, feel her breath feathering his ear, and the soft curves of her in his arms. She felt way too good, like she belonged there. And Jesus, her mouth did things to him that could make a man commit sins just to kiss her.

He tried telling himself that he was only going with her to prevent her getting lost. She'd need someone who knew this country. Definitely someone who could navigate it faster than a mob of Yanks, if she had to rescue the boy before those Flintrop people could get to him.

God, what was he thinking? A week ago, he'd been lounging at a pub with a newspaper and a cold one, deciding where to go once he paid his last divorce bill. Today, he'd agreed to put himself—and her—in danger by following a pack of superpower-seeking, attempted-murdering madmen.

He knew he should have called the rangers...but

what if something happened and they discovered her abilities? He hated the thought of something happening to her out here, with no one around to help.

It would be his fault, if he left her.

They turned up the narrow trail leading behind the cave. "Did your ghosts happen to give you a map for this wild goose chase?" he asked.

"No. I could only get a general idea." She let him pass to lead her up the trail. "It's not easy to separate one voice from twenty thousand years of spirits, you know."

"No, I guess I don't know," he said. "Me, being an ordinary mortal, and you—"

"You're not ordinary."

He chuckled. "Right, I'm a Viking. Shouldn't I have a sword and a funny-looking hat with horns on it?"

"You're a regular comedian. They didn't wear horned helmets. That's a romantic myth."

"No horned helmet? That's too bad. Am I still allowed to pillage and burn?"

"No."

He heard the irritation in her voice and grinned to himself, glad he'd moved ahead of her so she couldn't see. He stifled his laughter to add one more zinger. "How about a secret stash of cash? Can I at least have that?"

"You know what? You might."

That stopped him. He turned around to find her staring at him. "What did you say?"

"Treasure. You—ah, you *then*—might have hidden something on Hvitmar that we didn't find. We never really excavated more than the house itself, because of...well, an earthquake, and now it's a wildlife preserve." She scratched her head, and then a broad smile spread across her face. "You could be filthy rich, actually."

For one brilliant minute, Hakon allowed himself the fantasy. A chest of coins, maybe jewels, buried under a thousand years of earth, just waiting for him to go and get it. He could pay off his lawyer billions of times over with what that kind of hoard could bring today.

If he could prove it belonged to him. If he knew where to look, and could find a way to dig it up without anyone else getting there first. If it even existed.

Shaking his head, he turned back around and continued walking up the trail.

"You don't believe me, do you?" she called.

He grunted. "Every time you open your mouth, your story gets wilder and wilder. I'm just waiting for you to tell me I have family in outer space."

"Very funny." Faith marched abreast of him as the trail widened out onto a plateau. "So far, everything I've told you about me has been the truth."

"So far? Planning to lie to me at some point?"

Her gaze fell to the ground. She studied the rocky trail as though her life depended on it.

The sudden change in her expression brought all his doubts flying back in force. "What are you not telling me?"

"I've told you everything I can tell," she answered, falling behind again.

Her evasiveness bothered him more than he wanted to admit, and not just because she could be keeping important details from him. She'd drawn a curtain around herself with those simple words, shutting him out as effectively as if she'd walked away.

No.

He turned around and took her by the arms. Her lake-blue eyes widened. A flash of desire burst through him, and he stamped it down. "Listen," he growled, "you need to be honest with me from now on, if I'm going to help you find this lost kid."

Hope flickered in her eyes. "Really? You still want—"

"If I go back to Sydney now, not only will I wonder whether you've gotten yourself killed out here, but Miriam will personally hang me."

She responded with a dazzling smile. Desperate to ignore the way his body reacted to it, he glared at her. "I mean it. If there's something else you're not telling me, now is the time to speak up, Faith. And my guide fee just increased."

Her smile shifted at once to a glower that did nothing to prevent his urges. "You can't up your fee. I have a signed contract. I already mailed it back to my office."

"Call it a bonus for risk to life and limb," he shot back.

"Oh, for Pete's sake. All we have to do is find this boy before Elliott's men get to him."

Hakon snorted and crossed his arms. "If a guy's family is willing to attempt murder over you and your sister, and he's now looking for a kid with similar abilities, I think it's safe to say he might use force if his blokes run into trouble."

"I'm not paying you extra."

"I'm fast. I'm quiet. I know these mountains. Do

you?" He gave her a steady stare, though he was anything but calm. He relived their kiss with a disturbing amount of interest in repeating it. Hell, she was only getting more inviting as she glared at him like that.

He could call his motive anything he wanted. Protecting her from her own foolishness, or getting his money out of her, or even curiosity...but he couldn't lie to his own senses. Having sampled her lips, he wanted like hell to find out what the rest of her tasted and felt like.

All over. And once would not be enough.

Faith huffed and threw her hands in the air. "Fine. You get a ten-percent bonus...*if* we get to that boy first."

"Twenty percent."

"Ten."

"Fifteen."

Her eyes flashed with an intriguing mixture of annoyance and humor. "Fifteen, then. You're the biggest pain in the ass I ever met."

He stifled a grin and headed up the trail once more. He didn't really believe they were in any danger from Elliott's crew. He knew this area with his eyes closed, including short cuts and game trails that he doubted ever got used by another human being. They could slip in, get to the boy, and be out of the mountains before the men even knew they had company.

By then, he intended to know a lot more about Faith than he did right now.

****

As afternoon approached, they began finding signs of other hikers. Faith realized they'd come upon

Elliott's crew, and said as much to Hakon. She knelt and pressed her hand over a large footprint in the soft earth of the trail.

"What are you doing?" he asked behind her.

"Shh. Reading for intent," she said, letting loose her psychic gift.

Almost at once, needles of savage glee stabbed at her fingertips. She yelped and withdrew her hand, then shook it. "Whoever the owner of this footprint is, he's *really happy* about something. And I'll bet my degree it's not something good."

"I'd guess that half a billion dollars is enough to make anyone happy." Hakon stared at her hand. "Does it hurt?"

"Yeah, a little." She flexed her fingers. "It happens sometimes, when there's a strong emotion connected to something I read. Love, hate, whatever. Back in Shetland, when we dug up your sword, I touched it and it buzzed with anger. You had used it to kill one of the men responsible for murdering Aesa—" She thought of Aesa's ring, and clamped her mouth shut.

Hakon's sword had been charged with hatred for his wife's murderers. It was the only object she'd ever touched that blazed with its very own emotion...until Aesa's ring. That one vibrated with sorrow, as if it were incomplete.

She knew the feeling.

The air shivered around her, and she caught a faint whisper in the breeze. The spirit voices had returned. *Follow. Catch. Punish,* they hissed again.

She shook her head and blinked to stop the flow of psychic power. "The ghosts are talking. They want us to follow Elliott's crew."

"Which is basically what we've been doing already," Hakon muttered. "I guess we keep following, then." He stood and reached for her hand.

She took it, and grinned as he pulled her onto her feet. His fingertips brushed the sensitive skin of her wrist, and something glimmered in his aquamarine eyes. A bolt of excitement surged through her body. She longed to close the distance between them and kiss him again the way she had in the cave. Just once more.

But then he turned away, and the moment was gone.

She frowned at his broad back. How could he ignore this so easily, when it was eating at her from the inside to be near him and not touching him every chance she got?

I'll just have to try harder, she thought, and then smiled at her own audacity. Hakon Ivarsson would be begging for her by the time she finished with him.

Except that she wasn't sure she'd ever be finished with him.

For most of the afternoon, she stayed silent unless he asked her a question. She allowed herself a private chuckle when she noticed his questions becoming more and more frequent. Didn't like being ignored, did he?

They tracked Elliott's men through an upward-winding mountain pass and down the other side, until they came upon a sprawling meadow. Long grasses waved in the wind, and smoke drifted from a modest clapboard building at the edge of the trees. Her stomach rumbled at the mouth-watering scent of ham. "Oh, God. Real food. No offense to Miriam's muffins."

"None taken," he said. "I know the owner of this house. I'd better check on her to be sure she's all right.

Are Elliott's mates going to go crazy when they find you here?"

"We won't know until we try it." Calling on her psychic senses—it couldn't hurt to be prepared—she started off into the clearing.

He followed, shuffling through the grass with a long sigh. "Have I told you how much I don't like your logic?"

As they neared the aging house, an eerie undercurrent buzzed on her skin. Not spirits. Not with energy like that. She froze in mid-stride, and her powers rushed forth. "Hakon, he's here. The boy, they have the boy," she whispered.

He ducked around her and insinuated himself between her and the door. "I go first. Let me do the talking, okay?"

Too worried about what they might find, she could only nod. He raised his fist and thumped the door. At the last minute, Faith scrambled for a pair of sunglasses from her backpack, then put them on to hide her silver eyes.

The door opened with a teeth-grinding creak, and the tantalizing smell of dinner floated into the yard. A thin, weathered woman stood there chewing on the end of a pipe. Rather than looking at them, she stared at a notebook in her hand. "Help you?"

Hakon grinned. "Not dead yet, eh?"

The woman lowered her notebook and looked up. Her slate-gray eyes narrowed in a squint, and then she let out a wild guffaw. "Goldy Ivarsson, you bloody well better have brought me some tobacco!"

He laughed. "Smelled dinner halfway across the mountain. Got room for two more?"

"If I didn't feed you every time you turned up, you'd as like starve out here." The woman chuckled and fished an ancient pair of spectacles from the pocket of her striped work shirt. She put them on, blinked owlishly, then focused on Faith. "Well-l-l, now. I see your taste has improved."

"Get off it, Liv," he rumbled.

The woman merely smiled wider, staring at Faith in expectation. Faith felt a blush rising in her cheeks. She shifted the pack on her shoulder, unsure whether she ought to say something.

Hakon saved her the trouble by waving a hand between the two of them with a sort of disgruntled motion. "Liv, Faith Markham. Faith, Olivia Harris."

Olivia stepped outside and slid an arm around Faith's waist, ushering her toward the house. "She's a sight better than that hellish Lilah woman ever was, mate, I'll tell you that for free."

Hakon slipped into the doorway and blocked it before the women could enter. "Who's your company?"

"Just some men up from the low country," Olivia said. "Mob of bloody scientists, I'll wager, what with my barn looks like a madman's dungeon." She scoffed and flipped a hand in the direction of the small barn behind the house. "I put them up out there. A couple nights with my girls, and they'll be begging to leave."

Faith's mouth dropped open before she could stop herself. "Your...girls?" Did she run some kind of brothel?

Catching her eye, Hakon laughed. "Cows, Faith. Not friendly ones, either." He rubbed at his ribcage. "Makes our trip downriver look like a paddle boat ride."

Olivia shook with laughter and clapped Faith on the shoulder. "Oh, I like this one, Goldy. What've you been feeding her out there? Get inside, and I'll fix a cuppa." She shooed them both toward the house.

Feeling like she'd just been spat out by a tornado, Faith went inside. The main room encompassed the kitchen, dining, and seating areas. Its furniture might have been second-, third-, or millionth-hand, by the look of it. Beside the fireplace, a plush armchair oozed stuffing from its cushions. A sagging ottoman stood nearby. Faith guessed that the two plank doors at opposite ends of the main room might be bedrooms. She sensed no other presence in the house.

"Did you put one of the men up in the back room?" Hakon asked, echoing her train of thought. He eased out of his pack and left it on the floor.

The door thumped shut behind them. "You're under the impression I let them into the house to begin with," Olivia said. She smiled, dropped her notebook on the table, then snatched a hot pad off the counter to pick up the tea kettle boiling on the stove. "Get the cups down, will you, love?"

Again, Faith didn't know if she should answer, but Hakon went to get the china, so she removed her bag and sat at the rickety kitchen table.

Olivia poured them each a cup of tea and, when they nodded, a generous dollop of cream and sugar. She sat across from them. "What brings you up this way?"

"Well, it's funny you should mention that. We're tracking those men," Hakon replied.

Olivia's eyebrows shot up. "Are they wanted?"

"Not exactly," said Faith. "We just want to talk with the boy who's with them."

"Oh!" Olivia slapped her knee. "You mean that pistol, Reilly. Boy's more trouble than a fox in the chook yard. What's he done?"

"Erm..." Faith thought about asking what a "chook" was, but let that question lie in favor of the bigger one. "Can we see him?"

With a shrug, Olivia waved at the door. "Suit yourself. He's probably out back of the barn, shooting at cans with the rest of them fools." As if on cue, a muffled *bang* split the air outside.

Faith couldn't imagine a small boy wielding a gun. She rose out of her seat, but Hakon's hand descended upon hers. Startled, she looked at him.

"I'll go with you," he said. His apprehension feathered the back of her hand where he touched her.

"I'll be fine," she said.

He stood and loomed over the table. "We'll be right back, Liv."

When they were outside, Faith scowled at him. "I can walk around without a chaperone."

"Not if these blokes are willing to hurt you. They tried once before, didn't they?"

"No. That was Elliott's grandson."

"You're not going without me. Deal with it," he said.

He marched at her side with the single-minded air of a personal bodyguard, and she felt a *pop* of warmth under her breastbone. He *did* care...at least a little.

And apparently, Olivia liked her better than Lilah, which she couldn't help feeling was a plus in her favor. "What's she got against Lilah, anyway?" Faith wondered aloud.

Hakon grunted. "Lilah hates the mountains, and

she hates Olivia."

"So Lilah's a city girl, huh?" Plus number two. Faith loved roughing it. "I don't see what's wrong with Olivia, anyway. I liked her right off." She beamed.

He shot her a dark look that said she'd better quit pressing her luck. Before she could respond, they'd reached the barn.

It was empty, save for some science equipment, a pair of sulky cows, and a few bedrolls scattered in the empty stalls. Periodic shouting, the occasional gunshot, and tinny *ping*s issued from the barn's open back door. She ducked around the back doorjamb and peeked out.

With her sunglasses still on, she searched the air for the pinching waves of satisfaction that she'd felt from the footprint earlier. They radiated from a tall man with saddle-tan skin and sun-bleached brown hair. He leaned against a fencepost, watching four men as one of them shot at beer cans balanced on the fence's top rail. David Beck and Carl Mancuso were among them. *Blam*, went Carl's handgun. A can toppled into the paddock and clinked against its fallen fellows. After the men's cheering subsided, Faith cleared her throat.

The one leaning on the fencepost looked up first. "Faith Markham. I wondered if you'd show up."

So much for the element of surprise. Before she could respond, Hakon slipped out the back door. His gaze swept the group, and she saw him looking for the boy. She did the same.

Behind Carl, she saw a teenager with unruly black hair, champing on a blade of grass and looking bored. Faith stared. When they'd said "boy," she'd thought she would be searching for a chubby-cheeked toddler who might be frightened of his powers and ready to grasp at help.

Here was a young man whose every vibe spoke of resentment and haughtiness. She frowned. *This might be harder than I thought.* She blinked to return her eyes to blue before removing her sunglasses.

The group turned their attention on her. Carl lowered his gun, though she noticed he left it hanging at his side instead of holstering it.

The man on the fencepost came toward her first. Even without using her power, Faith sensed Hakon's distrust. His silent presence reassured her, and she stuck out her hand to the stranger. "And you would be...?"

"Sebastian Hale." An American, by his accent. He left her hand hanging in the air. "What do you say we skip the pleasantries and get right to the point? Go home."

So he wanted to play hardball. Sara had always been better at the game of wills, but Faith was no slouch. She withdrew her hand and lowered her voice so that only Sebastian and Hakon would overhear. "What do you say you and I have a long talk about that kid?"

Sebastian just smiled. "You mean, that kid who's eighteen, who can do what he wants as a legal adult? Why don't you ask him for a long talk?" Without waiting for her answer, he waved a hand toward the men. "Kid, come here a second."

Damn. As an adult, the boy would not only be less inclined to listen to her, but he might already side with Elliott. A lot harder to sway than the child she'd hoped to find. How much had Sebastian told him? How much had been kept from him?

The boy approached, and Sebastian laid a hand on

his shoulder. "Reilly Corcoran, meet Faith Markham."

Reilly crossed his arms, and looked her up and down with a thorough appraisal that made her want to fidget. His pale-honey eyes remained cool. "Yeah. Heard of you." He flicked the blade of grass in his mouth from one corner to the other.

Faith straightened her shoulders. "And I suppose you've heard of Gemini, and that we're a bunch of know-it-alls with nothing better to do than bother Flintrop and company."

The boy cracked a brief, humorless smile. "Something like that." He ambled back to the men without another comment.

Sebastian grinned. "There you have it. That's pretty much a long talk in our Reilly's universe. See you around, babe." He turned to leave.

Babe. Hostility boiled up from her toes. She quivered with the impulse to torch the bigheaded jerk on principle. She hadn't come all this way just to fail and allow Elliott's men to corrupt the boy. "Did you bother to tell Reilly that Elliott's a scheming son of a bitch whose family isn't shy of committing murder?" she asked loudly.

Sebastian swung around with a look of fury and reached for her. Shocked at the sudden violence of his reaction, Faith stayed rooted to the spot.

Hakon shot into the fast-closing gap and seized Sebastian's wrist, stopping it short. "I doubt Olivia wants to see you attacking her guests."

"You're right," said Olivia. Everyone looked around to the barn doorway.

Olivia stood there, pipe still clamped in her teeth, with a rifle balanced casually in her hands. "You boys have about four seconds to hand over your firearms, or you're out of here."

Carl dropped his gun on the ground, and David tossed a shotgun beside it. Relief swept through Faith's body.

This wasn't over yet.

Chapter Seven

Even though Sara's only five minutes older, she's always trying to be the smart big sister. Every time I get in trouble, she knows it...but sometimes I'm glad about that.
—Faith's Journals, age fifteen

Sara Waverly stared out her office window at the New York City skyline, angling her head to compensate for the partial blind spot in her left eye. She'd hoped for some word from Faith by now.

Her sister might be getting along just fine with Hakon. Sure, Faith couldn't tell him she had paranormal powers. Sure, she couldn't say Hakon was really a modern-day reincarnation of a Viking warrior, and she was his long-lost wife.

Oh, hell. Faith needed help.

Sara brushed a lock of russet-brown hair away from her face and lowered herself ponderously into her chair. Being almost nine months pregnant made her feel like Madison Square Garden during a championship wrestling match. All morning, the baby had been kicking and shoving, in spite of what had to be cramped quarters. "Ouch. Quit that," she admonished, pressing a hand to her belly after an enthusiastic *whomp* under her ribcage. Sara picked up the phone and dialed the front desk. "Holly—oof—get me Jack at the Flintrop office."

"Will do." Holly disconnected the line, and a few minutes later, the call beeped through.

"Redmond," said a male voice.

"Jack, it's me. I haven't heard from Faith, and I'm starting to worry. What do you know?"

The background noise grew muffled, and she sensed him bending closer over the mouthpiece. "You'd better get a hold of her, then," he murmured. "Elliott has sent men to Sydney after that boy, with a new guy called Hale. That's all I've got, sorry."

"Thanks, Jack." She hung up the phone with a shiver. Even the baby's kicking subsided, as if she felt Sara's apprehension.

So, Elliott had found his protégé.

She lumbered out of her chair, then went to a large, framed photo on one wall of her office. The photo showed her husband grinning beside a signpost reading *Hvitmar National Nature Reserve*. Thanks to Ian, the tiny island of Hvitmar had become a world-renowned place to study Shetland's coastal wildlife. She smiled at his handsome face before turning back the frame on its hinges.

She unlocked the wall safe behind it, and reached in for a folder labeled *Gifted*. Her assistant Becky had located a few individuals who, like Sara and Faith, had paranormal abilities. Sara and Ian had found the first, a scared young woman named Renata, in Kentucky, and given her a job here at the office. So far, the girl had blossomed under the security and understanding of other gifted people.

As for this boy, though... Who knew what he'd be like? Sara flipped to the page mentioning his whereabouts. They knew only that he was somewhere in the Blue Mountains. Had her sister found him yet?

Had Elliott's protégé found Faith?

With another shiver, Sara plucked a second folder from the safe to rifle through its contents. Faith had mailed Hakon's guide contract back to Gemini with emergency contact numbers on it. Sara felt strange holding a document containing Hakon's signature. She wondered if it might have matched that of his Viking predecessor.

She brought the contract to her desk, then found the number for a Miriam McGowan among its pages. At once, she dialed it. It must be late afternoon or evening by now in Australia.

The phone rang a few times, then a woman picked up. "Hello, McGowan's Inn."

"I'm looking for Miriam McGowan."

"Yes, that's me. Can I help you?"

She twirled the phone cord around her finger. "Ma'am, my name is Sara Waverly. I'm Faith Markham's sister, and I hoped you'd know where I can reach her."

"Oh, she's out with Hakon, dear. They aren't due back at the inn for a couple of weeks, unless they come early."

"Could you tell them I called, and that it's important? Thank you." Sara hung up the phone, stood up, then went to the safe to replace the documents.

Someone thumped at the door. A moment later, it swung open. Ian staggered in, loaded down by an armful of thick books. "Becky sent me in with a pile of references from the library. Said you'd been waiting for them."

She just managed to scoop a glass paperweight and

her apple juice out of the way before he dumped the towering stack on her desk.

Her husband thrust a hand through his short brown hair. "Don't you have assistants for this stuff?"

"Looks like you're chief assistant and pack mule," she teased. She stood up, then winced as the baby jabbed her repeatedly in the ribs. "Oh, God, it's like she knows the minute you're in the room."

Ian's blue eyes sparkled. He came around the desk, then embraced her from behind with his chin on her shoulder. The stubble of his three-day beard tickled her ear. "She knows her daddy. Quit playing kickball on your mother." He pressed a hand over Sara's belly.

The baby mashed an appendage against Ian's hand, and Sara winced again. "Don't antagonize her."

Chuckling, her husband kissed her cheek, then drew away. "I'm on my way back to the college, but I stopped to see how Faith is doing."

Sara sat back down. "That's just my problem. I don't know. She hasn't called since Sydney, and it's bothering me. Ian..."

Frowning, he sat on the desk.

"It looks like Elliott Flintrop has appointed his successor. Someone named Hale." Sara hugged her belly, feeling chilled.

His frown deepened. "What about Hakon?"

"Still out in the mountains with Faith, I think. Her cell isn't in service. I called the emergency number on her contract, and they aren't due back at that number for two weeks. She might not even know they're being followed." She fidgeted with the paperweight. "Should I send someone?"

Ian tugged her hand away from her belly,

enveloping it in the warmth of his. "Faith's tough. She'll be all right, you know that. If she were in real trouble, she'd find a way to contact you."

"God, I hope so," Sara replied. She stared across her office at a graduation picture of herself and Faith on the wall. Faith's grin blazed out of the frame.

Her sister was tough, all right. And stubborn, and temperamental, and a magnet for trouble.

Trouble had come calling, and brought a few uninvited guests.

****

Hakon picked up the men's dropped guns, only now realizing he'd been prepared to get into a brawl in Faith's defense. The notion only spurred his anger on. He glared at Sebastian. "I'm sure Olivia won't mind keeping a safe eye on these until you're on your way...right, Liv?"

"Sure," Olivia responded. "Now, if everyone'll play nice, we can have supper. Goldy, set up the sawhorses and some planks for a table out front of the barn. Faith, is it? Why don't you come inside and help me get the food?"

Hakon handed Faith the guns. Her gaze shifted toward the men, heated with resentment, and then flicked back to him. *What now?* she seemed to ask.

"Take those inside and help Liv," he said. "After supper, we'll talk, all right?" He let his touch linger on her arm—in reassurance, he told himself—but his nerves jangled at the feel of her butter-soft skin.

During the meal, he sat stiffly beside her at the end of the table, shoveling ham and potatoes into his mouth like a trucker. The slanting shadows grew longer and longer, until the sky took on the hues of early sunset.

Olivia sat at the head of the table with amiable calm, now that order had been restored in her barnyard. She kept up a running stream of chatter with Faith about mountain life, until finally she asked why Faith had come to Australia.

The entire table fell silent.

Hakon glanced up from his plate. A couple of the men resumed talking in lowered voices. The boy sat at the opposite end of the table, staring at Faith as if waiting for her reply.

She seemed not to notice the attention. "Well, I had intended to fetch back a new assistant for our New York office, but that seems to have fallen through, so I expect I'll go home...after I've had a look around the mountains, of course."

Hakon paused in mid-chew, but recovered and went on eating. What was she up to now?

"Well," Olivia said, sitting back on an old crate, "I can't think of a better guide than Goldy for that. He knows the high country better than most men know their own backside." She stood up and stretched her back, then began gathering plates.

"Let me help with that," Faith said, getting up. She scooped up an armful of dishes, then accompanied Olivia back to the house.

Hakon watched her go, following the tantalizing swing of her hips. She had the perfect ass. Hell, she had the perfect everything. Her pale-blond hair swung loose to the middle of her back, and for a moment he imagined thrusting his hands into it in a wild frenzy of kissing.

Women are nothing but trouble.

He tore his gaze away from her, only to notice a

few of the men also staring at her departing figure. The one at the boy's end of the table—Eddie or Earl or something—leered after her with no pretense of hiding it. The man's lips curled back from his tobacco-stained teeth in a rat-like grimace of lust. When he caught Hakon's eye, he merely smiled wider and went back to watching Faith walk away.

The boy saw his crewmate looking, and followed the stare with apparent curiosity.

"Some piece of livestock, eh, boy?" Ratface jabbed the kid in the side. "Not your type? Ah, you'll learn."

The kid's expression remained unreadable in the fast-dimming light. His gaze dropped to his plate, and he finished eating.

Ratface laughed, a sound as grating as a rusty door slapping in the wind. "Ain't seen an ass like that in years."

Hakon kept seated by force of will. All at once, he didn't care that he'd been staring at her, too. The idea of driving his fist into the man's face started looking better and better. Hakon appreciated Faith's finer points, himself, but Ratface was about to get a sorely-needed lesson in keeping his mouth shut.

"Don't suppose you know the mountains well enough to tell us where Willson's Pass is," said a voice in his ear.

Hakon glanced up. Sebastian had sat beside him in Faith's chair. The man had the eager look of a hound begging to be let off the leash to chase prey. With a grunt, Hakon scraped up the rest of the potatoes on his plate, then stuffed them into his mouth. "What makes you think I'd tell you where it is?" he muttered around his food.

"A favor," Sebastian replied. He gestured in the direction of the trees. "To, er...speed us on our way, as it were." He glanced in Ratface's direction, then Faith's, and then met Hakon's gaze with a long, meaningful stare. One eyebrow inched up in question.

Damn the bastard.

Hakon straightened his spine, half-consciously bracing his legs to lunge out of his chair in answer to the veiled threat to Faith's safety. "You tell me why you want to know, and I might remember where the pass is."

"A little research, is all." Sebastian toyed with Faith's empty water glass in an attitude of supreme boredom.

Right. Faith had said she'd come to Australia for research, too. And pigs, any day now, would start to fly. "Tell you what, mate," he said, scooping up his dish. "You and your men steer clear of Faith, and you might get lucky and steer clear of me, too. The pass is a day's hike northeast." He turned his back and stalked away toward the house.

Inside, he found Faith drying dishes at the sink. "Talk to you a minute?" he asked, touching her shoulder.

She glanced at Olivia, who was busy washing the last batch of plates. "Go on," Liv said. "I'll just be finishing these up, and sit outside to have a smoke."

Faith shrugged and followed him toward one of the bedrooms.

He pushed open the door, then strode inside. She entered, and he shut the door behind her. "Sebastian's heading up to Willson's Pass. There's another Aborigine site there, and a small town. Which would he be after?"

"Not sure why he'd want the town," she murmured. "I'll have to assume he wants to see the Aborigine site, then. His men did show up at the painted cavern we were at." He saw the wheels turning in her mind, and then her gaze met his. "The spirits are angry. They keep telling me to follow him."

"Not without me, you're not," he said, thinking of the way Sebastian's rat-faced crewman had leered after her.

Her eyebrows shot up. She went to a trunk at the foot of the large bed, where her pack sat waiting. Olivia must have offered her the spare room for the night. She opened a zippered pocket. "You've already stuck to your end of the contract. I'll pay you the other half of your guide fee, but I'm sure you'll agree that since they already have Reilly, the bonus isn't going to hap—"

In one stride, he reached the end of the bed and grabbed her by the arm. Her eyes flashed silver in what might have been a defensive reaction, but she merely frowned. Tendrils of heat seeped into his skin where they touched, and he struggled with the desire to kiss her even now. "You aren't leaving this place without me," he ground out.

"Why not? I'll find my way. My compass is still working, and now that I have their trail, I can follow them."

"It's not a question of 'can you,' Faith. I know you'll bloody do anything you put your mind to, whether it's smart or not—"

"Hey, buster—"

"Listen to me," he snarled, shaking her. "Those men are a bad lot. How can you think you'll be safe tracking them by yourself through mountains you don't know?" He refused to add that the way Ratface had stared at her made his blood ice over. A look like that would have been enough to make him worry for anyone's safety.

But especially hers, and for no fathomable reason.

She shook her head and pulled away from him. "I have to follow them. If I can just get Reilly to listen to me, I might be able to change his mind about accepting my help."

"I'll come with you." He made a last grab for her hand.

Her eyes narrowed, and he felt the full weight of that silver stare looking him over from head to foot. The light seemed to shiver around her, and for a moment, he could have sworn he smelled drying herbs and a smoking fire.

Then the sensation vanished, and her fingers curled around his. She reached her other arm around his waist, and pressed her long, curving body against him.

In an instant, he was hard and aching for her. He grasped for sanity—they couldn't do this, he didn't want to be mired up in another woman—but his body betrayed him in a rush of hunger. He kissed her, and when that wasn't enough, he gripped her hips and crushed himself against her.

Her arms came up around his neck, and she opened her mouth to him. She tugged him forward. He followed, not wanting to break the kiss...until he realized she was pulling him toward the bed. *No,* he told himself.

But his body answered a higher need. Her. Warm and real and alive...and here, in his arms.

When they reached the side of the bed, he held her there, filling his senses with her as though he'd never have enough. She smelled of trail dust and the dark, wild scent of the woods. Thrusting his hands up the back of her shirt, he played his fingertips along the smooth curve of her spine. Her teeth closed on his lip, and he hissed. He withdrew his hands, raised her arms, then swept off her shirt.

She kept her arms up, curled behind her head like a wanton siren offering herself to him. Her eyes smoked with seduction.

Fine, then. If she were flame, he'd be the gasoline, and they would burn each other down.

With a feral growl, he pushed her back onto the bed. She wrapped her arms around him and dug her nails into his back. He hissed again and clamped her wrists in one of his hands, then trapped them over her head against the pillows. Bending his head to one breast, full and curving over the top of her lacy bra, he grazed his teeth along the heated skin. She sighed and arched up to him.

If he had any reservations left about what he was doing, they blasted away. He gripped the front of her bra and shredded it open in one pull.

"I needed that for the hike," she gasped out, wrapping her legs around his.

"Don't care." He bent to his work again, closing his lips on one peaked nipple and suckling hard.

She gave a long, low moan and pulled upward on the back of his shirt, branding his skin with her touch. His body chilled with the cool air, only to warm again as she slid her hands along his sides. One-handed, he reached back to tug the shirt off over his head, and flung it away.

He stretched out along the length of her and—Oh, God, it was like holding heaven—pulled her against his body, then rolled until she was on top. As she straddled him, the last of the sunset filtered through the thin curtains of the one window and gilded her body in fire. "Bloody gorgeous," he whispered, and settled his hands on her waist.

"Bloody right," she echoed, staring at him with those smoking eyes. She traced her fingertips along his torso to the trail of hairs disappearing under his waistband. He caught his breath. Her gaze flicked up to his once more. With a brazen smile, she ground her hips into his. Her heat pressed against his throbbing erection, and he thought he'd burst into flame then and there. So close, so close. He had to have her.

With another growl, he flipped her onto her back and loomed over her. She shook sun-gold hair out of eyes lit with mischief and dangerous invitation.

Hell, she knew exactly what she was doing. "Woman, you are asking for trouble," he warned her.

She smiled again, brash and tempting, and went for the button on his pants.

****

He felt better than her dreams.

Never in any of Faith's visions as Aesa had Hakon been so solid and real...and passionate. His need vibrated from him, singing on her skin, and she knew they'd been made for this.

She pulled at his pants button, and it popped open. She reached for his zipper, and that, too, gave way. Without pause, she slipped her hand inside his pants and closed it around his length.

He groaned and thrust his hips against her touch. His hard belly brushed the back of her hand as he pressed against her. She welcomed the weight of him, curling her legs around his as she stroked him.

A low rumble issued from deep in his chest. He closed his eyes and threw his head back, and she noticed the flash of his earring. "I like that," she murmured, brushing aside his ponytail to look at the small hoop. "Your earring. It's sexy."

His eyes opened again, darkened to shaded aqua that sent shivers of expectation speeding through her body. Moisture gathered between her legs at the mere promise in that look. "Sexy, is it?" he said.

"M-hm." She tightened her fingers around the satin-steel of his manhood. Again, he thrust forward, this time more demanding.

He laid one scorching, work-roughened palm over her breast and splayed his fingers over the curves. Her breath caught on a sigh of pleasure, and then he slid his hand down along her belly to her pants zipper. She released him and raised her hips to help him.

He wasn't gentle. She didn't want him to be. He yanked her zipper open, then jerked her jeans and panties off in one swift motion. He knelt above her as if drinking in the sight of her, with his pants undone and the evidence of his arousal plain. "Yours, too," she whispered.

Hakon pushed his pants off and shoved them onto the floor, then lay back down beside her. She rolled on top of him again and lost herself in the bliss of their bodies molding together, skin-on-skin.

He threaded a hand into the hair at the back of her head and pulled her down for a burning kiss. When he plunged his tongue into her mouth, she moaned, feeling another rush of moisture where she wanted his touch the most. She pressed her hips into his, demanding, needing him.

He growled back and slid a hand between them to cup her in his palm. She gasped and arched against him when he slipped two fingers inside her to stroke once, twice, then retreat again. He thrust his tongue deeper into her mouth as his thumb flicked against her center of pleasure. Spinning higher, she dug her nails into his broad chest. Her heartbeat thudded so hard she could barely catch her breath. "Hakon... Now... Hakon..." she said against his lips.

He lifted her hips and thrust deep into her. Her senses ignited into ecstasy. She gasped out his name, and he swallowed it with a kiss. His chest vibrated with a growl of satisfaction under her fingertips. He rocked against her, urging her waves of pleasure to lengthen and linger as they washed over her.

She went boneless in his arms, panting as the spinning sensation receded.

A chuckle rumbled up from his chest. "I like that," he said. "The way you get all limber. It's sexy." He gave a sly smile and rocked his hips again.

He rolled once more until she lay beneath him, then thrust into her, filling her completely. The growl that tore up from his throat poured shivers of pleasure through her. Faster, deeper. He pressed fiery kisses to the skin of her throat, then her breasts. He teased at her sensitive earlobe with his teeth. Higher, higher.

The world burst into white-hot flame. Electric sparks shot up and down her spine. Everything came together, past and present fusing in one joyful blur.

Hakon cried out, and her cry mingled with his, and they were one at last. Time stopped mattering.

She lay there, trembling a little with awe, hyper-alert and unwilling to miss a single sensation of being with him.

There were no words for this.

He settled with his forehead pressed against her shoulder, his ribs rising and falling with each breath. His heart pounded against hers, and his copper-gold ponytail splayed across his sweaty back. The full, heavy weight of him pressed her into the mattress. She'd never felt so wonderful in her life.

Moments passed, and he didn't move. "Hakon?" she murmured.

He raised his head and stared at her as if seeing her for the first time. "Bloody hell, woman," he breathed out.

She raised an eyebrow. "Is that a good 'bloody,' or a bad one?"

He blew a long breath and rolled away onto his back. She saw the corner of his mouth twitch upward for a moment, and then he grinned at her. "I'm going to go with good."

She beamed and shifted to her side, facing him. "You weren't so bad, yourself."

They sighed in unison, and Faith's blissful afterglow began to fade into drowsiness. She wanted to stay awake, to look at him, to wonder at the way their worlds had crashed together just moments before. Had he felt it?

She wanted to touch him, too, but didn't. None of her boyfriends had ever drawn her close afterward, never tucked her into the hollows of their bodies and made her feel like she'd come home at last.

Hakon closed his eyes. She allowed herself another minute sigh and turned away.

His arm snaked underneath her, and he pulled her against him. He chuckled. "Where do you think you're going?"

Startled, she turned toward him. He'd cracked open one turquoise eye that glittered with amusement.

She smiled, and the corner of his mouth turned up in response. Settling beside him, she laid a hand on his chest. *Home. I hope.*

Chapter Eight

My first job was at a museum. Sara and I would assist the exhibit coordinator, unpacking the artifacts for display. It was there that I learned how humbling human history really is.
        —Faith's Journals, age twenty-three

Faith saw a face, shadowed by a deep hood, eyes cold and staring within its depths. Voices chanted. A hand grabbed her from behind. Terror. She couldn't get away, no matter how she struggled. She screamed for help. No one came. The man clapped his hand over her mouth.

Burn them. Burn them all. *She felt her eyes begin to change in a rush of chills.*

Too slow. A knife flashed in the firelight, and she watched it come toward her in despair.

Then the pain, the horrible, horrible pain as they cut her. Her throat burned. She couldn't breathe, couldn't shout, couldn't even whisper. Her soul tore away, and her last thought fluttered with it....

Hakon, help me.

Faith gave a strangled cry and shot upright in bed, clutching her throat.

A blur of skin bolted sideways over her legs, and Hakon was on his feet beside the bed, blocking the space between her and the door.

She caught her breath, realizing at last that she was awake and unhurt. "I'm okay. It's all right. Just a nightmare," she said, as much to reassure herself as him. Reality settled in, and she allowed herself a long sigh of relief. Her heartbeat drummed in her ears.

Hakon swept the brightening room with a glance— probably making sure they weren't, in fact, being invaded—and then glared back over his shoulder. "Mind not waking me up like that? You just scared ten years off me."

She couldn't help but smile. Even naked and messy-haired, he looked imposing. His scowl only added to the giddy swirl of emotions floundering in her belly. She wanted him all over again.

Once definitely hadn't been enough.

His dark look faded a little. "You all right?"

"Yes. Come back to bed," she invited, patting the rumpled sheets.

Someone thumped the door. "All right in there?" came Olivia's voice.

"We're fine," he answered.

He straightened up and ran his fingers through his hair, making it messier even though it was still in its ponytail. Faith admired the way the rising light caught in the ruddy-gold strands, then followed the lines of his broad back down to the taut curve of his buttocks.

He picked his jeans up from the floor, then turned around. Little shivers sped to every nerve ending in her body. He looked even better from the front. Muscular, built for power. Damn near perfect.

If only he weren't still emanating grouchy vibes. "What?" she demanded.

His belly muscles clenched and rippled as he bent to pull his pants on. "We'd better leave, if we're going to tail those men up to Willson's Pass."

Fascination with his abdomen evaporated. Mouth open, she stared at him in disbelief. Did he have nothing to say to her about last night? "Good morning to you, too, sunshine."

His gaze came up, then wandered down her naked breasts and torso to the wash-worn sheets puddled in her lap. Her body quivered at the way his attention lingered on her bare skin before meeting her gaze again. Something shifted in his expression, then shifted back. Fly still unzipped, he eased a knee onto the bed and reached for his shirt, lying rumpled on the trunk at the foot. When he sat back to put it on, he glanced at her with those aqua-blue eyes, and longing rushed through her.

Oh, how she wanted to kiss him. Thoroughly. One of those kisses that might take weeks. She leaned forward.

He backed away and stood with his mouth set in a hard line. He shrugged the shirt over his head with fast, economical motions. "No way. 'Leave' was the operative word, there."

Angered, she thrust the sheets aside. Was he so unfeeling that he could ignore the passion they'd shared just hours ago? "If you're in such a hurry to get out of here, you shouldn't look at me like that." Frustrated and careless of her nudity, she rose from the bed with the air of a queen.

She strode past him to get a clean pair of pants from her backpack, and felt his stare on her as she went. The distinct hum of his arousal buzzed on her skin, even without her using her psychic gift. After allowing him to gaze his fill, she let the smile burst full across her face. "Yep, that's the look I mean." Smug, she turned away to search her pack for a new bra.

She felt his body heat even before he touched her, a long, hard, hot wall of male pressed against her back. He cupped her breasts and drew her closer, kneading gently with his fingers. She closed her eyes and sighed in bliss. *This* was the Hakon she wanted.

"Was there a man in your life, or wasn't there?" he growled, brushing his lips against her neck.

"What...?" she mumbled, floating.

"I can tell he's in there somewhere. Or he was. The way you act, what you say. What you don't say. You've been doing it the whole hike." His teeth grazed her shoulder.

Her eyes fluttered open. He'd been paying attention.

One burning hand slipped to her belly and he pulled her still closer, pressing kisses along her shoulder. He trailed the fingers of his other hand along the sensitive skin of her temple. "Just be honest with me. Is he still in there, or not?"

He is. It's you. She bit the words back before they could slip out.

She knew he only entertained the idea of his Viking past with a sort of wary amusement. He'd laugh outright if she told him she was Aesa. Or worse, he might think she was trying to rope him into some new scheme, and she'd lose him completely. A man with such a dim view of romance would never believe in soul mates the way she did. "No," she lied. "There's no one." The irony of it squeezed her heart.

The heat and desire flaring from him vanished under his aloof shell once more. And then, just as quickly as he'd embraced her, he pulled away.

She found him slipping on the rest of his clothing as if the moment had never happened. He no longer radiated disgruntlement, but there was a hell of a lot of frustration. Chilled, she hurried into her pants and shirt. She'd tell him soon.

But not yet.

****

After a quick breakfast, Hakon and Faith left Olivia's and picked up the trail of Sebastian's men. The men had left the night before, which meant they were in quite a hurry for a little innocent research. Hakon guessed they couldn't have gotten far at night in the mountains.

"I like your friend Olivia," Faith said, adjusting the newly-repaired straps on her backpack. "Will we see her on our way back through here?"

"Maybe. Depends on where Hale's men go," he grunted, touching an hours-old footprint on the trail. He paused at a fork and checked the brush for broken twigs, then went on down the right-hand path. Sebastian had followed his instructions, then, moving northeast toward the pass. He and Faith had lost a lot of time last night, not following them.

He would almost have been willing to lose a lot more time than that, if it meant spending another day in bed with her. His body still echoed with the sensation of touching her, of being inside her. He'd thought he could burn the ache for her right out of himself, but he hadn't.

His own fault. He glowered and shoved a branch

aside. Even this morning, he'd acted like a jealous teenager. What did he care about other men in her life? Of course there were. A woman like her would have a string of admirers, and she didn't seem the type to be lonely for long.

He glanced back over his shoulder on the pretense of being sure she followed. She glowed this morning, hair loose, humming to herself as she stepped around a root sticking out of the trail. He skimmed down her long, long legs, and recalled the feel of them wrapped around his waist.

He didn't realize he'd stopped walking until she halted as well. "What's the matter with you?"

Nothing a few days in bed with you wouldn't cure, he thought, unable to help letting gaze rove along her curves. Maybe that was all he needed: to get her out of his system and be done with it.

She smiled, and a new gleam appeared in her eye. "A look like that isn't going to catch us up to Sebastian."

Gritting his teeth, he turned back around and stalked up the trail. He wanted to snap that if she thought their night together changed anything, she'd better think again.

Except that it had. He wanted her even more...but Hale was, at that moment, dragging a boy across the mountains after something Hakon would have bet they'd better not find. They had things worth selling, things that would bring a hell of a lot of money and probably weren't legal, if they needed "connections" to unload them.

And, for some bloody insane reason, Faith still believed she could talk this kid into changing his mind and playing nice with the good guys.

Hakon couldn't let her go alone, knowing she'd walk right into their camp as if she owned it, and demand to talk to Reilly. They'd be on her like dogs on a rabbit, or shoot her before she even got the chance to defend herself.

Not to mention, he really wanted to help her kick Sebastian's arse, anyway. Hakon grinned. That bloke needed to be knocked down off his high horse.

They stopped for lunch by the trailside. Faith put together their sandwiches out of leftovers Olivia had given them, and after eating, they leaned back against a pair of tree trunks.

He pored through a bit of *Beardsley*, skimming a passage on pyrokinesis, and its woodcut engraving of a man holding flame in his hand. Even the thought of controlling flame with a whim gave him shivers. What disastrous consequences could such power hold in the wrong hands?

Looking up at Faith, he asked, "So...basically, you just think about starting a fire, and that's that?"

"And that's that," she echoed, pulling a plastic container from her backpack. With a smile, she opened it and withdrew a marshmallow, then stuck it on the end of a twig. "Watch this." She suspended the twig over her open hand. He watched her eyes turn silver, and then a tiny burst of flame appeared in her palm. The marshmallow began to brown, and she twirled the stick to heat it evenly.

He felt his eyebrows shoot up. "What the hell are you doing?"

"What's it look like?"

He jerked his chin at her stick. "This is your idea of

a hiking necessity?"

"You haven't lived until you've had pyrokinesis-toasted marshmallows. Better than campfire. Here." She pushed the twig into his hand, then began toasting another for herself.

With a philosophical sigh, he took a bite. The sticky-sweet confection melted onto his tongue. He shook his head. "I can't believe you have a power like that, and you use it to toast marshmallows."

"Wouldn't you?" She shrugged. "Not everything about being gifted has to be a big weight around your neck. My sister treats it like a curse. I say it's damn handy when you're out of matches." She bit into her marshmallow.

He glanced down at the flame in her palm. "Doesn't that hurt?"

"No. It's not touching my skin. See?" She held up her hand, so close that he almost backed away in surprise, but he saw the inch or two of space between the flame and her palm. Grinning, she waved her fingers, and the flame spun in her hand like a top. "I can hold it, or throw it, or if something's close enough, set it on fire without walking over to it, just by looking. Cool, huh?"

"Yeah. And also very freaky."

She scowled and closed her hand, and the flame extinguished. "I'm not a freak."

"I didn't mean *you*. If I thought that about you, would I have done what I did with you last night?"

"Oh, my God, I thought you'd never acknowledge it," she snapped, her voice dripping with sarcasm. Her scowl faded into a half-dreamy look. "Mmm. It's been forever since I had a toasted marshmallow." Her tongue slipped out to lick a drip of the gooey confection off her lip.

He fantasized about drizzling her body with the stuff, only to lick it all off with long, slow strokes of his own tongue. Blood rushed to his groin, and he bit off a groan. "Please stop doing that."

She pulled the rest of her marshmallow off the twig and stuffed it into her mouth, sucking on the tip of her index finger. "Doing what?" she asked, all innocence, but he caught the gleam of amused self-satisfaction in her silver eyes.

God, she had him wrapped around that finger...that she was still sucking on...and was still watching him with those eyes. Daring him to get closer. He felt like a polarized magnet.

And she was due north.

He started to lean closer, but changed his mind at once and stood up, just to prove that he could.

He needed to be able to walk away from her.

By the time he turned around, she'd gathered up their things and slipped into her backpack. She acted as if nothing had happened, but he thought he saw disappointment flash in her eyes. Something tugged within him, and he stifled a wash of guilt.

"How far are we from the pass?" she asked, saving him with the change of subject.

"A little less than half a day, if we hurry." He grabbed his pack, picked up the men's trail again, then started walking.

She bent before a scatter of footprints in the trail. Her hand hovered over the prints before settling on one of the largest. "Still not getting a good vibe from Sebastian," she said, touching the print. "He's nervous.

I think he knows we're following him."

"If I were him, I'd have counted on it," said Hakon.

By late afternoon, they found fresh signs of Sebastian and his crew, and almost stumbled directly into the camp.

True to Hakon's suspicions, Faith started to march into the clearing, shoulders back, head high. He grabbed her wrist and pulled her back into the slanting shadows of the trees. "Are you out of your mind? They'll use you for target practice first, and ask questions later!"

She stumbled to a halt against his chest and glared into his eyes. "I can handle them. All I want to do is talk."

"Unless you're also bulletproof, we'd better come up with something less foolhardy than that." He sighed and ran a hand through his hair. "We'll wait until the boy's alone, and maybe you can catch him and talk then. Do you have any idea what you're going to say to him?"

"Nope," she said, then plopped her backpack down and sat beside it.

He lowered himself to a grassy spot between the shrubs. "Glad to see you have a plan."

"I'll figure it out." She pulled a tiny pair of binoculars from her pack and scanned the clearing. "There's Sebastian. David and Carl are doing something by the campfire. Ugh, that awful Earl guy is skinning something, I can't tell what. Where's Reilly?"

Hakon, who couldn't see the clearing from where he sat, shrugged and started to respond.

Faith scrambled to her feet and dropped her binoculars in his lap. "Hold those!"

"What are you doing?" he whispered. "Faith!" He caught her by the hand.

"Reilly. I sense him. This is my chance to talk to him."

"Not without me, you don't." Hakon stood, then followed her into the trees.

****

Reilly had given the men the excuse that he needed to take a piss, which, today, was the only way he could get the hell away from them. Sebastian had been nothing but cool since Reilly had met him, even knowing what Reilly could do...but last night he'd overheard Sebastian telling the other blokes not to let him out of their sight.

What the hell? Had Sebastian told them about his power? He'd sworn he wouldn't. He'd said he knew other people like Reilly, and was going to make them all filthy rich.

That wouldn't suck. He had nowhere to go right now, and no money to get there, anyway. With money, it might be different.

Where *would* he go?

Reilly sat on a fallen log and fished his necklace out of his shirt, then slipped it off over his head. The copper, bullet-shaped pendant swung back and forth. He held it up, watching the afternoon sun glance off its shiny surface.

Stupid piece of junk.

He could have made himself rich without the help, except he didn't know where to sell any of the things he found. Whatever. He didn't care if he had to share the money. He could find plenty of that old stuff, if he had the time to look in the right places. And he'd heard

Sebastian talking about the stuff, too. It was worth boatloads of money.

Even part of a boatload was still a lot of cash. Whatever happened to the old stuff after he got his share wasn't his problem. He planned on disappearing right afterward.

"Tag, you're it," said a voice behind him.

Reilly spun so fast he almost toppled off the log, but Faith grabbed his shoulder and steadied him. Rattled, he jerked his shoulder away and snapped, "What are you doing here?" He tucked the necklace into his fist and sneered at her.

She straddled the log beside him. "Guess I'm going to have to make an appointment to talk with you, huh?"

"Forget it. Sebastian told me all about you."

"He did, did he?"

"Yeah. He said you were bitchy, and opinionated, and don't know when to keep your nose out of things."

"I'd say he's got me pegged about right."

Reilly tried not to look surprised. He spotted her friend from the corner of his eye, leaning against a tree at the edge of the clearing. "What do you want to talk to me for, anyway? Thought you'd be after Sebastian, the way he goes on about you," he muttered.

"Yeah, he's a real peach, your buddy Hale. Must be the bracing incentive of half a billion dollars that gives him such a friendly air."

How could she know about the money? She wrinkled her nose, and Reilly thought she looked kind of hot, after all. For a lady who could almost be his mother.

She grimaced as if he'd said something out loud. "Do you mind?" She slid off the log, and started away.

"I could almost be your mother."

How had she heard that? "Hey!" he called as she slipped into the trees. Her friend vanished with her.

"See you later." Faith's voice echoed and faded.

He went from thinking she'd actually heard what he thought, to wondering if it were a coincidence, and then decided the whole thing was just way too weird. She couldn't have known what he was thinking.

Unless she was one of those other gifted people Sebastian had told him about.

Holy cow. He wondered if Sebastian knew.

What could she do? Was she anything like him?

When he returned to camp several minutes later, Faith spotted him from across the clearing and started toward him.

Followed again by that impossibly huge blond man.

Reilly stopped at the edge of the trees with his necklace still dangling from his fist, dreading that he had to go back to being watched over like some toddler. Sebastian and the others were talking over some papers spread out on the ground. He turned his back on them.

A sudden shiver raced up his spine and down his arm. His necklace started swinging, though he had barely moved. The pendant lurched in Faith's direction, or it could have been the blond man's.

They had something. Something really old. A ring. Reilly saw a quick flash of twisting silver bands in his mind, and wondered if he should tell Sebastian he'd located another artifact. One that didn't even have to be dug up.

Yeah. He doubted Sebastian would get anything away·from that blond man without big problems. Reilly put his necklace back on and trudged into camp.

An instant later, Sebastian caught sight of Faith. "What the hell are you doing, following us?"

David, Earl, and Carl grabbed their guns and sprang to their feet at once. God, were they going to shoot her? "Wait," Reilly said, jogging forward.

Carl lowered his gun with a skeptical, disappointed look. Jeez, that bloke needed therapy or something. Trigger-happy nutcase.

Sebastian glowered at him. "What did you do, kid? Invite them?"

"No." Reilly hunched his shoulders.

"We came to talk to him," Faith said, coming to a stop in front of them. "As a legal adult, he's allowed to have a conversation without your help, isn't he?"

Raising an eyebrow, Reilly looked her over. She had guts, for someone facing the wrong end of several guns. Then again, the way her friend glared at everyone, Reilly wondered whether even gunfire would be enough to intimidate her. Tension rippled in the air, and it seemed like everyone was waiting to see what everyone else would do next.

Faith beamed and laid a hand on Reilly's elbow, tugging him away from the group. "Excuse us."

Her friend stayed with the others while she towed Reilly toward the edge of the clearing. Burning with curiosity, but worried about looking too eager, he crossed his arms. "You sure don't seem to mind being around people who want to shoot you."

"You don't seem to mind hanging out with criminals," she shot back. She glanced over his shoulder, then turned so that the men couldn't see her face. Her tone dropped to a quiet murmur. "I'm not going to dance around this with you, so here's how it is. I know you're gifted. I came to help you with that."

He opened his mouth to deny it, but she shushed him by holding up a hand. "Don't bother. I've used every excuse in the book, myself. Let's just cut right ahead of all the bullshit. I'm gifted, too." As she spoke, her eyes turned bright silver.

His skin chilled all over. Guessing had been one thing. Seeing her eyes change, just like his did, left his body crawling with shivers. "Holy sh—"

"Are we on the same page now?" She smirked, and her gaze traveled up and down his figure. "Do they know about your gift, or not?"

He fought the urge to rub his arms. He'd never in his life spoken so casually about his ability. And he'd *never* called it a "gift." A cool trick, maybe. A long time ago, before he found out that cool tricks had consequences. "Sebastian...Sebastian knows."

Faith swore. "Great, that means Elliott knows. What do you do, anyway?"

"What do *you* do?" he snapped.

"Pyrokinesis, astral projection. I'm psychic, too."

The way she talked about it, as if she were discussing the weather, gave him the creeps. He took half a step away from her. "All of that...at once?"

"Multi-gifted." She nodded. "Really rare. Want to learn more, or not?"

He hunched his shoulders again, unsure what to say.

"Look, Reilly, I came from New York specifically to find you. I'm not going to waste time not telling you the important stuff. Those men, the ones you're helping? They're working for a man whose family tried to kill me because I'm gifted. I can help you, if you'll let me."

If she wanted to help him with his so-called gift, she was about four years too late. Feeling sick, he turned to leave.

"What is Sebastian doing to get his hands on that much money?" she asked.

Ouch. Could psychics read minds, too? "I don't know what you're talking about," he hedged.

"Sure you do." She laid her hands on his shoulders, and stared into his face with those crazy silver eyes. "Half a billion dollars. That's what they said. What are they trafficking?"

It occurred to him then that she might be working with some kind of inspector. Gifted or not, he might be seeing the inside of a prison for a long time. Dread began trickling in under his carefully constructed show of confidence.

"I'm not here to bust you," she said.

"Stop doing that!" he hissed. "How the hell do you know what I'm thinking?"

She gave a brief, wry smile. "I don't. I know what you're *feeling*. There's a difference. Now what are they dealing in?"

"Old junk. They dig it up, and then sell it. Who cares?"

"*I* care. And I care what they're going to do with you when they're done getting their money's worth out of you."

"I'm going to be rich as hell, and living far away from anybody," he spat.

Her expression mellowed. She blinked, and her eyes faded back to their normal color. Just like his always did. "Reilly, I know you're worried—"

"The only thing I'm worried about right now is, why am I talking to you when I already know what I'm doing?" He stomped away, back to the men.

He hoped like hell she couldn't detect lies, too.

Chapter Nine

I asked Mom for a dog once. She brought up the goldfish I didn't feed, the hamster I lost, and the bird that flew away. I should just be banned from caring for another life form.
—Faith's Journals, age twenty-two

Faith returned to the camp with doubts weighing on her heart. Would Sara have handled the talk with Reilly better? She'd always been the more diplomatic one. Now, Faith worried that she'd thrown too much at the boy, too fast. He wouldn't even look at her, sulking on the far side of the fire as though she'd chastised him.

Some mother I'd make, she thought. *Probably chase them right out onto the streets to a life of crime.*

"Have a nice chat?" Sebastian asked, then gave her an arrogant smile.

"Very informative," she said in the same cool tone. Glancing at Reilly from the corner of her eye, she added, "We'll be leaving now."

Hakon stiffened, obviously wondering what she was doing, but she turned and began to walk away.

"Why don't you stay for dinner?" Sebastian called.

Oh, sure. He was the picture of hospitality, now that he thought he'd gotten his way. Faith pretended to consider it. "I suppose we can stick around for the night."

"Sure, let's just be careful he doesn't try to poison us," Hakon muttered in her ear. His words rang with cynicism.

She plopped down in a patch of grass, and Hakon sat beside her. "How long do you plan on staying up here?" she asked Sebastian.

The man eyed her, most likely trying to figure out how much Reilly had told her about their questionable activities. "Don't know." He divided a wary glance between her and Hakon.

Faith decided that if she were going to be in it, she might as well be in it up to her neck. She might be able to pass along some warnings for Reilly's benefit, at the same time. "I know you're new to the Flintrop enterprise and all, Sebastian, but how much do you know about treasure trove law?"

Ah, that got a reaction. Sebastian scowled at her as if she'd just confessed to robbing his mother at gunpoint. "What are you getting at, Miss Markham?" he asked in a voice full of dangerous calm.

"*Doctor* Markham. I'm just trying to find out whether you intend on keeping any of the artifacts you're plundering, or if you plan to be a good boy and hand them over to the Australian government. Unless, of course, you can prove that whatever you're digging up actually belongs to you somehow. Can you? I'm not really sure how Australia treats the looting of artifacts on government land. Especially if you find gold or silver." She smiled innocently.

"Faith, I don't think this is a good time to piss them off," Hakon hissed.

She reached over and squeezed his hand, hoping to hush him up, but tendrils of agitation seeped from his fingers into hers, distracting her. Her heart fluttered.

He was worried for her.

She just managed to keep her bland smile pasted on, and looked from face to face. Sebastian, Carl, and David wore stony looks. Reilly avoided her gaze completely.

Earl leered at her with no attempt to hide it. She fought back a grimace of disgust.

Sebastian jerked his chin at Carl, who clapped a hand over his gun. "I think you'd better leave. Doctor."

"Hey, you invited me for dinner. I never said I was a model guest." She shrugged and got to her feet, then snatched an apple from the bag beside the fire before anyone could stop her. "Thanks for the snack, anyway." She sauntered away into the lowering dusk.

Hakon shot to his feet and stalked after her. "Are you trying to get us killed?"

"I'm trying to get Reilly's attention. He needs to know the danger he's in," she said as they entered the woods. Now that they were away from the men, she allowed herself a shiver of revulsion at their collective hostility. Negative vibes had always made her want to brush at her skin as if wiping away ants. Now, she wanted a good scrubbing.

"What about the danger *we're* in, now that you've made them all mad enough to form a lynch mob?"

"Angry people do rash things," she said, picking up her backpack from where she'd left it, then shrugging it on.

He grabbed her by the arm. "So do perfectly smart people who should know better than to stir up trouble. I said I'd help you find that kid. I didn't say I'd help you get yourself killed, and me, along with you."

"They'll make mistakes, Hakon. Now that they know someone could blow them in, they'll lead us right to their hoard. We can take it from them and give it back to its rightful owners, and maybe save Reilly a trip to jail. He's just a kid." She pleaded with her eyes, willing him to understand how much she wanted to spare the boy from making a huge mistake.

Hakon's angry expression didn't waver. "I'm not going to help you throw your life on the line. There are authorities for this kind of stuff. We found the kid, and you warned him. That's going to have to be enough."

"It isn't!" she said, clutching at his shirt. "Don't you understand? I can give him a chance at something my sister and I never had."

"And what's that?"

"Understanding. He'll never get it if he's cut off from the only people who could help him handle his gift." She bit her lip and wondered if he saw how much she wanted Hakon's understanding, herself. "If the authorities do decide to make an issue of all this, we may never see that boy again. This isn't just an isolated case of keeping plundered treasure or artifacts. These are repeated incidents."

"Looks to me like he doesn't want your help."

She let her hands drop to her sides. "He does. He just isn't ready to ask for it. I'm sure of it."

"Yeah, I almost forgot. You being psychic, and all." His mouth quirked in an ironic half-smile.

"No. Hakon, I feel it *here*." She fisted a hand over her heart. "I'm able to pass on what I know about being gifted to others, and I'm damn well going to do it. Please help me?"

His eyes softened, and he rested his hands on her

shoulders. "All right, all right. But I'm not sticking around here to let them form that lynch mob. We'll track them for a while to find out if they do have these artifacts in storage, maybe find out a little more about what they're doing. Then we go to the authorities. You have until then to get through to this kid, however you're going to do it. Agreed?"

She nodded eagerly. Warmth spread throughout her body, pushing aside any doubts. With Hakon's help, she knew she could bring Reilly around. He made her feel like she could succeed at anything.

Even a crash course in mentoring.

****

If he'd been a praying man, Hakon would have dropped to his knees and started begging God to help him get out of this mess.

Right now, he wanted to be as far away as possible from the whole situation. The kid, the stolen goods, the guys with guns, all of it.

Except for Faith. He couldn't leave her here alone to get hurt, or worse—

No. He didn't even want to think about what "worse" might mean.

Frowning, he watched her spread out her bedroll and then slide into it. She seemed determined to thrust herself into the middle of danger. Even with her abilities, he worried that she might take on more than she could handle.

He laid out his own bedroll and sat in it, but didn't bother lying down. He wouldn't sleep tonight, and not only because a mob of criminals was camped a short walk away. *She* was too close. Too close, too tempting, too everything. Especially after last night. She'd felt so good in his arms that he found himself plotting ways to get her back into them. When that happened, he cursed himself for wanting her.

He didn't need her. Didn't need the headaches that came with her. She'd changed her story no fewer than three times in the scant handful of days he'd known her, and he suspected that she still hadn't given him the whole truth. Typical of a woman. Conniving. Shifty. Inconsistent.

And Faith looked far too alluring, with her hair spread out like that and the shadows of evening darkening across the curve of her cheek. He leaned close enough to see that she'd shut her eyes and settled down for sleep, then stared at the perfect Cupid's bow of her lips.

Something ached inside him.

He turned away, groping for a distraction, and remembered *Beardsley's Compendium*, still drying off beside his backpack. He picked it up and found his electric torch, then started to read.

He read page after page, barely registering the passage of time until he heard birds singing. By then, he'd read almost half the book. Some of it was just too crazy to be in any way plausible. Some, like the entries mentioning Faith's abilities, gave him otherworldly chills, even though he'd seen her powers in action.

His torch glow had weakened to a dim circle of light on the page. He clicked it off and put it away. When he laid the book down beside Faith's pack, he heard the rustle of leaves, and froze. He scanned the gray shadows of the woods, and caught the flap of someone's shirttail as they slipped away into the fog. Ears straining, he picked up the muffled, fading footsteps of the intruder. No other sound reached him.

Not wanting to take chances, he reached over and nudged Faith's shoulder. "Hey."

"I know. It was Reilly," she murmured. Her eyes opened, and her lips curved into a smile that set his pulse jumping. She sat up and stretched, long and catlike, then took a closer look at him and frowned. "You didn't sleep, did you?"

"Don't worry about me. Worry about people sneaking up on us in the middle of the night." He climbed out of his sleeping bag and packed it up, still peering into the trees around them.

"He's already gone," she said. She crawled out of her sleeping bag, then rolled it up as fast as possible. "We'd better hurry if we're going to keep up with Sebastian's men."

"Willson's Pass is an hour away at most. They'll probably go through the town afterward, and I'm guessing they'll need to stop for supplies. We've got time to catch up."

In spite of his assurances, they finished gathering up what few items they'd strewn about, then started off after their quarry without breakfast. The early-morning chill seeped into Hakon's bones, enveloping him just as the fog shrouded the trees around them. He couldn't see more than a handful of meters ahead, and found himself relying on his compass to avoid getting turned around in the shapeless mist. Better to follow Sebastian now, and have the time to change direction if they made a mistake in this fog, than lose him completely to a late start.

Somewhere deep in the woods, a kookaburra stirred, and rang in the dawn with its distinctive, laughing call. *Glad you find this funny, mate,* Hakon thought darkly. *Wish I could.* "Faith, do you know if any of the other men are gifted?" he asked, pushing aside an overhanging branch.

"Not that I could sense. Just Reilly. Why?"

"I'm wondering if they know we're tailing them. Either they're getting misdirected as much as we are in this mist, or they're purposely backtracking, hoping to lose us." He paused to check the grass in his path, and saw a rounded area crushed in the shape of a footprint going northeast. Laid over that was another, going in the opposite direction. He paused.

"We're still behind them," she assured him. She bent and touched her hand to the later footprint. Her eyes flared into silver. "This one's Reilly. He's curious...and a little scared. I hope he isn't slipping away to check on us. Sebastian might find out and hurt him."

"I'd be more worried about us than Reilly, if I were you." She glared at him for that, and he grimaced. "I'm not trying to sound like a jerk about it. I meant that I doubt Sebastian would do anything to hurt him when he's valuable to them."

"I hope you're right." She straightened and waved her hand as if to shoo him on. "They're still heading toward the pass."

"Do you have any idea yet what this kid can do?"

"No," she said. "He didn't tell me when I asked."

He started walking again. "Did you tell him what *you* can do?"

"How else was I supposed to get him to trust me?"

Stark dread trickled into Hakon's bones along with the morning chill as he realized they might be walking right into a trap. "How do you know he hasn't brought all that information to Sebastian?"

"I don't know for sure, but judging by the sense I get from his footprint, he hasn't."

"I hate following your hunches." He stalked faster.

She stayed silent so long after that, he had to look back to make sure she was still behind him. The mist had burned off by then. Even the shade of the trees proved a poor match for the growing heat, and as chilled as he'd been earlier, sweat began to bead on his forehead as they hiked.

And still, she didn't speak. After looking back for the dozenth time, he couldn't stand it anymore. She looked tired and worried, lips pursed in a tight expression of hard thought. He stopped walking. "What's the matter now?"

She blinked as if she'd forgotten where she was, and her eyes faded back to blue. "Sorry. Are we lost?"

"No. We're almost at the pass. You look like you're waiting for a bomb to drop."

Her gaze skimmed his body, and something strange flashed through their sea-blue depths. His body reacted to the look without even knowing what had caused it, and he reached automatically for her hand. "What's the matter?" he repeated, gentler this time. His skin hummed where her slender fingers clasped his.

For a moment, she looked as if she wanted to say something, but she shook her head. "I'm all right. It's nothing. We should keep going." She pulled her hand from his, and he fought back a frown of disappointment as he started walking once more.

She'd drawn away again, back into that shell where he couldn't get to her. Unlike all the times Lilah had willfully refused to talk to him, taunting him with her silent anger, Faith had simply brushed her mood off as nothing and gotten on with the business at hand. He knew she hadn't done it out of spite.

She'd done it out of need.

He felt the same need to separate himself from her, as strong as the desire to touch her. All night long, he'd warred with it. How many times had he shifted closer to her slumbering form, only to roll away again? Since she'd come into his life, she'd caused an upheaval that pulled him in two opposite directions. Only during their night at Olivia's had the turmoil inside him quieted. Only then had he been able to see past the deep hollow inside him, and feel peace. He wanted that again.

He wanted *her* again. Damn all this running around the countryside.

"Hakon, wait," she whispered behind him.

He froze as if she'd shouted, and realized he might have stumbled into the open on the ridge above Sebastian and his men. Faith's hand clapped down on his shoulder, and she tugged him back into the trees over Willson's Pass.

Damn it. He'd been too distracted by her to watch where he was going. Resentment flickered within him underneath the warmth of her touch.

As he watched Sebastian's men, his upheaval vanished under tension of a different kind.

Deep in the groove of the pass below, the men dug with pick and spade. Sebastian directed their activities, and Reilly stood watch from a vantage point on a boulder along the opposite slope. The boy scanned the trees, and Hakon fought the urge to duck as his gaze passed right over them. Had Reilly missed them, or ignored them on purpose?

Faith's hand slipped from Hakon's shoulder and gripped his fingers with silent urgency.

Sebastian's men lifted a large chunk of something from the hole they'd made, and by the way the men fussed around it, Hakon assumed they'd found what they sought. "Now what?"

"I guess we trail them to wherever they're planning to stash that find," she answered.

Reilly hopped down from his lookout and trotted toward the ravine on the other side of the pass to peer over its edge. Then he turned toward the men. He wedged his way into the group to look at whatever they had found, until Sebastian turned to him and pointed back to his post. From the set of the boy's shoulders, Hakon concluded he'd been ordered back to his boulder. Typical of most teenagers, rebellion ensued. He and Sebastian began arguing, though from his distance, Hakon couldn't catch what they said.

Faith tensed. "Somebody's going to—"

Carl jumped into the argument when Reilly shoved Sebastian in the chest. Sebastian hollered something, then David jumped in front of Reilly.

A gunshot sliced the air.

Gasping, Faith covered her mouth as David crumpled to the ground. "Oh, God," she whispered, her voice thick with horror. "We have to do something."

But Sebastian had already bent over David's body and pointed imperiously toward the ravine. While Earl and Carl picked up the body and carried it away, Sebastian stood and turned to peer around the pass. For the second time, Hakon fought to keep from ducking deeper into the trees. The motion might only call attention. Sebastian's men dumped David's body over the edge of the ravine.

Faith trembled, and he heard her breath quicken. "We have to tell the police. How far is town?"

"Too far. Another half day's walk. By the time we get there and get back, Hale's men will be gone." Hakon pulled out a pair of binoculars, but even then, he couldn't see the bottom of the shadowy ravine. He remembered it as deep and sheer, and choked with sharp rocks. If the bullet hadn't killed David, the fall certainly had.

"He's dead," Faith murmured, as if confirming his thoughts. Then she gripped his shoulder again. "Hakon. Reilly's gone!"

Chapter Ten

You should never ask a favor of a ghost unless you're prepared to return it, even years later. They have long memories, and their favors can be scary as hell.
                    —Faith's Journals, age twenty-five

Reilly crashed through the undergrowth in headlong flight, adrenaline churning in his veins. Leaves and branches slapped at him and clawed his clothing, but the terror in his heart drove him on all the faster.

David's sightless, shocked eyes burned in his mind, speeding him forward as if he could escape the memory. His heart slammed in his chest, and he lurched aside just in time to avoid plowing into a tree. He slowed only for an instant, listening for his pursuers. He'd left a trail a blind man could follow. Some part of him warned that he should slow down, cover his tracks, do something to keep those murdering bastards as far from him as possible.

Murder. Faith had said Elliott Flintrop's family wasn't afraid to commit murder. And he'd just seen the proof that Elliott's employees couldn't be trusted, either.

Reilly gasped for breath as he plunged on, unable to slow down even to leave a less obvious trail. They'd kill him just as soon as they got their hands on him, he knew it.

As he shot past a spreading gum tree, an arm thrust out and clamped around his midsection. He shouted and flailed in his captor's grip.

"Hold it, dimwit, they'll hear you," boomed a male voice. The man dragged him deeper into the trees and pressed an insistent hand on his shoulder. "Get down."

Reilly gulped for air and crouched. Hakon. Faith and her friend had followed him. Fear surged anew. What would they do to him, now that he'd been involved with a murder?

Faith pounced forward and laid her hands on his arm. "Are you hurt?"

Unable to speak past the knot in his throat, he shook his head.

Her hands flitted over him as if she didn't believe his answer. "Hakon, where can we hide him?"

The huge blond man grunted. "That ravine might have been our best bet. We can try the town, or turn back toward Olivia's."

"They're heading for Bowen Mountain," Reilly croaked at last. "Or they will be, after they find me. The rest of their loot is stashed there."

Hakon grunted again, and his bulk blotted out even the weak light filtering through the trees. "How are we supposed to trust *you*?"

"Shh! Argue later. We have bigger problems," hissed Faith. Her eyes went silver in a flash, and he heard her murmuring something, but couldn't make out the words. "They're coming," she said at last. "Go southeast. *Quietly.*"

Hakon hauled Reilly upright. He planted a paw in

the middle of Reilly's back and shoved him forward. "Walk fast. Don't make noise."

Still scared, and now angry, Reilly fought the urge to start running again.

"Both of you, stay ahead of me," Faith murmured behind them.

Reilly felt Hakon hesitate. "What are you doing now?" the man asked.

"Guarding our back," she said. "I'm asking ghosts to create problems for Hale and his men."

"What are ghosts going to do? Spook them to death?" Hakon growled.

"Would you rather I use pyrokinesis to burn the forest, and us with it? Go!" She shooed them away.

Hakon fisted a hand in Reilly's shirt and pushed him along again. Unwilling to linger, Reilly hurried on. "If she gets caught or hurt, you're paying for it out of your hide," Hakon snarled in his ear.

They walked until Reilly's legs shook with fatigue and dread. At last, when he thought his knees might give out, Hakon dumped him beside a broken tree stump. "If you're thirsty, drink." He dropped a canteen with a *clunk* beside Reilly's feet.

Reilly couldn't avoid a sneer of defiance. Had he escaped one disaster only to leap into another? "Keep your stupid water."

The man turned a full glare on him, and a new tremor of apprehension chilled him. "Listen, you ungrateful brat," he spat, "I'm sick of chasing you around the mountains, and just about willing to hand you over to Sebastian. Disobey me, or piss me off in any way, and your arse will be in a sling for months. Got it?"

Reilly hitched a shoulder and stared at his feet. Only when Hakon turned away did Reilly risk a look back the way they'd come. Faith still hadn't appeared. What if they really had caught her? What if they killed her?

Fresh guilt piled on top of him. *That's it. This is the last time I use my power. Ever.*

Hakon stiffened, maybe hearing something in the woods. Reilly sprang to his feet, ready to run no matter what Hakon did to stop him.

Faith hurried out of the trees. Reilly let himself start breathing again. "The ghosts are doing what they can," she said. "It should buy us twenty minutes, tops."

What can a ghost do to stop living people? Reilly wondered, and then realized he wasn't sure he wanted to find out.

"Let's get moving while we have a head start," said Hakon. Faith jogged past him into the trees on the far side. Hakon picked up his canteen and followed.

Reilly started after them, but his feet dragged like lead in the grass and leaf litter. Picking them up quickly became impossible. Confused, he put his hands up, only to find them arrested in midair as if he'd come upon an invisible wall. He stared after Faith and Hakon's retreating figures, and his heart began thudding in his chest. "Hey!"

Faith peered back around Hakon's body. "What is it?"

Reilly pushed at the air, but it didn't give. "I—I can't move!"

Pushing Hakon aside, Faith came back, and Reilly saw her eyes change to silver again. She waved a hand in the air before his face, then flinched and hissed inward. "Let him go," she demanded, to no one in particular. After a pause, she added, "I said I'd get you your things back. Let him go, damn it."

Tendrils of ice crept across Reilly's skin. "What's happening?"

"You can't *have* him. He's the reason I asked you to stop Sebastian in the first place," Faith said.

Was she...talking to ghosts? There was another, longer pause. Faith pursed her lips, then spoke at last. "Me, then."

Hakon returned to her side. "Me, *what*?"

She snapped out of whatever weird trance she'd been in, and directed her stare at Reilly. "Follow Hakon. Do whatever he says."

"Wha—" Reilly started to ask.

"Without questioning him," she interrupted. To Hakon, she said, "Take him southeast and circle wide around the area, back toward Miriam's place." She shuffled in her backpack and came up with a small notebook. "My sister's number is in here. Call her first thing, and get Reilly on a plane to New York."

New York? Didn't he have a say?

Hakon's eyes blazed so hot Reilly thought he'd hit something. "What do you think you're doing?"

"Please don't argue, Hakon. You only have fifteen minutes to get out of here before they're able to follow. I'm taking Reilly's place." She pressed the notebook into his hands.

"No, you bloody well aren't!" Hakon gripped her shoulders, alarm in his voice.

Reilly felt sick. "Who— Taking my— What do you mean? Aren't you coming?"

Her gaze turned on him again, softening. "No. The

men will catch up to me. I'll be okay. Just do as Hakon says, Reilly. I'm trusting you to go with him." She grasped Hakon's hand. Reilly's face flooded with the heat of discomfort at the urgent look that transformed her features. "I'll be okay, Hakon, I promise. You know the fastest ways out of the mountains. Go, please go. Keep him safe."

Hakon hesitated, his eyes blazing. "You've got four days, and if you don't show up, I'm coming after you," he murmured.

God, she was bargaining herself for him. For *him*, and he was just a worthless kid with a ruined past and no future. As he stared desperately at them both, the invisible wall whooshed away so fast, Reilly staggered forward. "No. Y-You can't..."

Then Hakon kissed her, and Reilly couldn't look. They'd kill her for sure. Misery weighted his shoulders.

From the corner of his eye, he saw her pull away. Hakon released her hand only when she was too far apart from him to touch. Without speaking, he turned and ushered Reilly away, his expression hardening.

Step after plodding step, Reilly went where Hakon directed him, not really seeing the path ahead. He felt like a walking curse. It seemed wherever he went, if anyone came in contact with him using his power, they met with catastrophe.

Yet another person would be dead because of him.

****

Sebastian almost blundered on top of Faith in his obvious hurry to find the boy. "Did you follow us, you meddling bitch?" he roared, coming forward with his hands out, ready to strangle her. "Where's the kid?"

She sidestepped his rush and watched in

satisfaction as he staggered into a tree instead. "What's your hurry, Sebastian? No time for a friendly chat?"

"You won't have much to say when I get finished with you," he said, rubbing at his shoulder. He glanced behind him and nodded once to his men.

Carl raised his gun, and his lips pulled back in an eager sneer.

"Not yet," Sebastian barked. He held up a staying hand, and Carl lowered the gun with a faint scowl. "Blindfold her. She's less dangerous to us if she can't see."

The first tremor of fear skimmed up the back of Faith's neck. He knew. The son of a bitch knew about her gifts, at least enough to know that she'd be crippled without her vision. With an effort, she clamped down on her nerves. She'd be no use to Reilly and Hakon if she panicked now. She had to lead the men away from Reilly. As far away as she could. But how, when she'd be unable to see?

Earl pulled a dirty rag over her eyes, and tied it so tight behind her head that it pinched in her hair. The thing reeked of beer and stale smoke, and so did he. Earl pulled her hands behind her and tied them with chafing rope. He brushed against her backside when he was finished, and she knew it hadn't been an accident. *Stay calm,* she told herself.

Sebastian pressed a hand into the middle of her back and pushed forward. "You'll be taking a little walk with us, if you don't mind."

"Boss," came Carl's voice, "we aren't taking her with us all the way back to—"

"Shut up about that," Sebastian snapped. "Have you gotten the cargo, or not?"

"Yeah, we got it," Carl answered sullenly.

Cargo, was it? Faith wondered just what they had dug up before committing murder in broad daylight. "You aren't going to get away with the smuggling," she said, stepping where he pushed her. "Kidnapping, either. You're in for a storm of headaches when you leave these mountains."

"What makes you think we're leaving the mountains?" Sebastian chuckled.

"What makes you think the police aren't already coming for you?" she shot back.

"Why don't you worry about where you put your feet instead of looking after my welfare?" Sebastian gave her a shove, and she stumbled over a tree root. He laughed, and the sound rang out through the forest. "Now, where are Reilly and that overgrown pal of yours?"

"I wouldn't tell you if you paid me." She forced the words through her teeth, hoping she sounded more confident than she felt. *You ghosts better have a damn good plan for protecting my skin, if you intend me to get your artifacts back.*

Something thudded, and she heard a yelp. "Twisted my goddamned ankle!" Carl growled.

Rough hands pushed her onward. "If you watched where you were going, you wouldn't be stepping into holes," Sebastian snarled beside her. "This fool of a woman's got better vision than you, even with a blindfold on. Pick up the cargo, and let's move."

"When are we meeting up with—" Carl started to say.

"I said *shut up* about our business, you mindless idiot." Sebastian's arm jerked as if he'd taken a swing at Carl. "Wrap your damned ankle, and let's move before we waste more daylight."

They continued on for what seemed hours. Faith's nerves began to get the better of her. She longed to hear Hakon's voice and feel his reassuring presence. She'd had so little time with him. Not enough, not nearly enough to make up for the terrible empty feeling she'd had ever since Shetland. She hoped that he and Reilly were far ahead of them by now.

The air grew cooler as the daylight waned. Through the grimy cloth of the blindfold, she sensed gathering darkness. Could she escape at night?

Doubtful, with her hands tied, even if she managed to remove the blindfold. She wished to God she had Sara's ability to read minds. One peek from under the blindfold and she'd know exactly what they carried, where they were going, and what they planned to do with the cargo once they got there.

Maybe she didn't need to read minds. With a deep breath, she stretched out her psychic senses to the forest around her.

Thin vibrations reached her from somewhere above. She latched on to the sensation and willed the ghost to hear her. *Tell me where they're going,* she begged it.

The ghost answered, not in words, but pictures, blurred and shadowy. Faint pressure settled in behind her eyes. It happened when she came across the ghosts of young children or people whose language she didn't know. Stymied by the language barrier, the ghosts would try to flood her with images instead. She'd never been able to get a handle on that, and usually came away with massive headaches that lasted through the next day.

Well, this was her only shot. She couldn't sense any other spirits in the area. *I need more,* she urged, fighting the sharpening headache. *Which way?*

Other images followed in a rush, slightly more distinct in color and form, and she gritted her teeth against the discomfort. None of it was any more helpful than the first batch of images had been. Frustrated, she cast her senses farther out into the forest. There had to be more ghosts nearby, with so much human history up here.

A sudden, stinging heat blasted across her skin, and she heard vicious roaring inside her head. Cutting off a yelp of pain, Faith yanked back on her power until the furor was only a mild tingle on the edge of her senses. She panted for steadying breath as she realized the perpetrator was the same ghost who had just sent her the blurred images. *Who are you?*

Kill-them-kill-them-kill-them! the ghost snarled, and her skin stung again. She saw the flash of a gun in her mind, followed by a falling body.

The same image she'd just seen a short while ago at Willson's Pass.

Amazement warred with horror in her heart. David's ghost. New as he was to the spirit plane, he couldn't know that he was jamming her with pictures and causing her pain. The murder scene flashed again, and she winced. *Knock it off,* she told him as fiercely as possible. *I'm not going to effing help you if you keep attacking me like that.*

At once, the blazing fury lessened, but she sensed his anger still pulsing on her skin. *Kill them,* he said again.

They'll get their due, but you have to help me, Faith assured him. *Now, where are we headed?*

****

"What the hell are you, kid? Besides trouble," Hakon snapped, marching along behind Reilly and glaring at the back of the boy's sweaty T-shirt. It was the first thing he'd said aside from giving directions in an hour, riddled as he'd been with worry over Faith. He'd had to force every muscle into walking away from her. Sebastian and his men could be cutting her into tiny pieces right now. Only her plea to get Reilly out of the mountains kept him from turning back. She trusted him to make that happen, and so he would.

Reilly hunched his shoulders as if trying to make himself smaller. For a few minutes, it didn't seem as though he'd answer. At last, Hakon heard him take a deep breath. "I find stuff. I use my necklace, and it points me toward stuff that's missing or buried."

Hakon let a few swear words slide past his lips. "They were using you to find treasure." His simmering anger began to boil again, much easier to face than the fear of what might be happening to Faith at that very moment. "What in hell gave you the idea to fall in with that lot? Are you bloody brainless? What you were doing is theft, and now there's a man dead—"

Reilly stopped short and spun to face him, his breath coming in short pants. "I know that! I know, already! I'm a loser. Send me to juvie." His voice fell to a mutter, and his gaze shifted away. "Probably where we're going, anyway."

Seeing the despair on Reilly's face, Hakon fought a pang of sympathy. The boy had to be terrified and guilt-ridden enough without his help. "It's not like you pulled the trigger, kid," he said gruffly. "You were a witness. *That's* why we're getting you out of the mountains."

Reilly turned away and resumed walking, stuffing his hands into his pockets. "What happens if I don't go?"

Angered again, Hakon ground out, "You're gonna get found by Sebastian and his mates, and beaten into a pulp. Faith stayed behind to protect you, and put herself in danger to do it. You might try being thankful."

Reilly said nothing more for the rest of the day's walk, which gave Hakon ample time to start worrying again. Haunting memories of her soft skin and passionate sighs raced through his mind. So help him, if they bruised one tiny little spot on her body...

He clenched and unclenched his fists, wanting to punch something. Some*one*, specifically, but he couldn't turn back toward Sebastian and leave Reilly by himself out here. *Muleheaded, ignorant kid.*

They stopped for the night when it became too dark to see without a light source. Hakon hadn't wanted to use his electric torch and give Sebastian's men a beacon to follow. Even when they built a campfire, he kept it low enough so that it wouldn't be seen through the surrounding brush.

After spreading out his bedroll and an extra blanket for Reilly, Hakon searched his pack and found a few pieces of fruit. "This will have to do for dinner," he said, tossing the boy an apple. Then he saw Faith's copy of *Beardsley* at the bottom of his bag, finally dry but still water-damaged. He pulled it out, and pain slashed through his belly. He closed his eyes. What if she...?

No. She was alive. She had to be, or he'd have

known otherwise. He'd have felt it somehow.

"What's that?" asked Reilly.

Hakon opened his eyes and forced back the distress knotting his insides. "It's hers. She said it was sort of a guide for the gifted."

Reilly leaned closer, eagerness and hesitation evident in the shadowy lines of his figure. "Can I...?"

Tight-lipped, Hakon released the book.

As he opened the book, Reilly's expression hardened into wariness. The pages crinkled as he turned them. He looked up at Hakon, and his face glowed in the low firelight. "There's books on people like us?"

Grunting, Hakon crunched his apple. "That's about as close as you'll get, anyway, so Faith said."

Reilly turned to the back of the book and ran a finger down the page, tipping it toward the fire so that he could read it. Evidently finding what he wanted, he turned to the middle of the book and began to leaf through it. At last, the tension in his face relaxed into surprise. "Here it is. Dowsing. That's what I do. 'The finding of persons, places, or objects by supernatural means, usually by aid of a pointing device.' I'm in here!"

"So you're a bird dog. Congratulations, kid. What are you doing with a mob of crooks, instead of helping people with your gift?"

Reilly shut the book with a crinkly snap. "It's not a gift."

Taking another bite of his apple, Hakon stared into the campfire's dancing flames. "It could be, to a nervous parent who's lost her child in the mountains. D'you know how many hikes I've been on, just to help the rangers search for missing people? They don't always end happily."

Reilly didn't say anything to that, but turned his attention back to the book. Let him read, then. He might learn something about himself...or Faith.

Same as Hakon had.

He believed her about her gifts—hell, he'd seen the proof—but her claim that he had a Viking past, Hakon still couldn't swallow whole. Viking ancestry, maybe, but wouldn't he know it if he'd been a Viking in his own past? He remembered his parents dying in a car accident, and then moving in with Gran. He vaguely recalled his grandfather, a smiling old codger who used to spin wild adventure yarns. He even remembered Gran telling him of her own parents, who had lived in Scotland.

He had a history, and the Vikings weren't in it. Were they? He'd always felt that empty place inside, the part that could never settle anywhere and be at peace. Was that the missing Viking part of him?

He started to deny it—habit, almost, because the idea was just as ridiculous as it had been when she first mentioned it. Then he stopped. Where had that emptiness been since the night at Olivia's place? Had he been too distracted by Faith and Sebastian to notice it...or had it disappeared at last?

Hakon finished his apple and lay down. He let his mind wander, until sleep drew him down into haunting dreams of Faith, and murder, and fire.

Over the next few days, he pushed their progress toward the north entrance of the mountains. Reilly, looking pale and exhausted, spoke little, but underneath the silence Hakon sensed a new resolve. The boy helped make and break camp without his typical sullen attitude, and even used his copper necklace to help find fresh food and water in the forest. Sometimes, Hakon would wake late in the night to find the boy reading Faith's book.

When they got back to Hakon's Land Rover, it felt like ages since he'd last seen it. When he opened the door, he imagined a whiff of lilies, and for a second he just stood there staring at the empty passenger seat.

"What's wrong?" came Reilly's voice.

Hakon shook his head, irritable. He climbed in and started the engine. Reilly sat in the passenger seat, and stayed quiet while they drove back to Bowen Mountain.

Hakon was the first to break the silence. "I want you to be nice to Miriam while you're at this inn, all right? She's a good friend, and she'll take care of you until we arrange to get you to Sydney."

"Where are you going?" Reilly asked.

"Back for Faith."

The boy fisted his hands, then shifted in his seat. "I'm sorry," he said, so quietly that Hakon almost didn't catch it. "Is there... Can I do something to help?"

"You can get to New York safely, and leave a message at Miriam's when you arrive. Faith's sister Sara is gifted, too. Tell her everything that went on here." At that, Hakon saw Reilly's eyes widen. "Yes, even the shooting. She'll help you."

As soon as they arrived at McGowan's Inn, Hakon called Faith's sister and left a message that he'd send the boy to New York on the next morning's flight. He considered calling the inspector about what he, Reilly, and Faith had witnessed at Willson's Pass, but he feared such an action might spur that unhinged son of a bitch who had Faith into another murder.

As to Faith's whereabouts, he relayed to Sara only that Faith would call as soon as they got back down to Sydney.

He tried not to think too much about what might happen if he *didn't* get her back down to Sydney, because when he did think on it, his gut started hurting. Not just guilt for leaving her out there in the mountains, either. Mere guilt wouldn't be twisting his innards into pulp.

This was fear. Why did the thought of harm coming to her whip his senses into such total incomprehension?

Reilly had gone to his room to clean up. Hakon told Toby and Miriam only that Faith had been delayed and he had to go back for her.

Toby met him in his room with fresh supplies. "Can you get the kid to Sydney, Toby? Fast, and quiet. He's in a spot of trouble, and I'm sending him to Faith's family in New York."

"Sure, Hakon." To his credit, Toby didn't ask for details, even though he looked like he wanted to. The two had known each other far too long to need that.

Miriam bustled into the room with a stack of clean bed sheets under one arm, and a string of Christmas lights under the other. "Tobias, take these lights and string them up along the porch, please." She frowned as Hakon began stuffing articles of clothing into his duffel bag. "Aren't you staying the night? It's awfully late to go back into the bush now."

"No," he answered, shouldering his bag.

The doorbell jangled downstairs. "Now, who would that be? I'm not expecting anyone until tomorrow," Miriam said. She handed the Christmas lights to Toby and hurried toward the door.

In three long strides, Hakon had cut in front of her. He descended the stairs and stalked into the lobby, wishing for the cold steel barrel of his electric torch under his fingers. He slid the duffel bag off his shoulder and grabbed it by the straps. It might be hefty enough to swing at an attacker, he decided. He laid his other hand on the doorknob, then jerked it open.

A slender, leggy woman with long, burgundy hair and a crisp gray business suit stood on the porch. She set two suitcases on the worn floorboards and removed her sunglasses. Her agate-green eyes fell on him, and a smile spread across her perfect, heart-shaped face. "Hello, Hakon."

Air rushed out of his lungs, and Hakon added another shock to his steadily growing list of the past week and a half. He glanced behind him and caught the surprised looks on Toby and Miriam's faces, then found his tongue.

"Hello, Lilah."

Chapter Eleven

Once in a while, I get lucky and things go exactly the way I want them to. Most of the time, though, I feel like I'm just winging it and trying to make it look intentional.
—*Faith's Journals, age twenty*

Lilah.

Hakon stared at her for a minute, not wanting to believe his eyes. As usual, she'd shown up at the worst possible time. "What the hell are you doing here? Never mind, I don't care," he said, stepping onto the porch and shouldering his bag again.

She smiled once more, and it seemed as if she hadn't even heard him. "God, you're tan. You look like you've spent weeks up here. Running the trails, I suppose?"

"I have somewhere to be, Lilah, so if you don't mind getting out of my way—"

"This is important. You know it must be, or I wouldn't have come," she said. "I need to talk to you"—she lowered her voice, and sidled just a fraction closer—"about this divorce."

As if he needed more problems right now. He didn't bother to temper the scowl on his face. "It can wait."

Her smile melted away into a frown of what might

have been attempted sincerity. He could never be sure with her. "No, it can't. Really, Hakon."

With an explosive sigh, he glanced behind him to see Toby and Miriam scooting away into the kitchen. He couldn't blame them for wanting to avoid Lilah. Considering the many months of trouble she'd given him before their divorce, she hadn't earned herself any goodwill. He pulled the door open. "You've got ten minutes. Upstairs."

"Just let me run to my car. I brought you some things." Turning on her expensive-looking high heels, she strode back down the steps to the door of *his* Camaro. She opened the door and shuffled around in its tiny back seat for a box, then closed the car door with her heel. He gritted his teeth, imagining the spike raking a gouge right across the pristine cherry-red paint.

With the box in her arms, she jogged back up the porch. He was tempted to leave her bags where they stood, but she looked so earnest that his curiosity won out. He grabbed her suitcases and plopped them inside the door, then set his duffel bag beside them to remind her that he didn't intend to stay long.

He went down the hall and upstairs without waiting for her, but heard her following. Back in his room, he rounded on her. "What's this about?"

She set the box on the bed, then opened it. "Most of this was in the attic. There are some things from the garage, too...and the wedding picture you had on your dresser."

"I left it there for a reason," he said at once, allowing a hard edge into his voice. "Is there something important you wanted to say, or can I get back to my business?"

"I've been doing some thinking, Hakon. I—I don't want the house anymore. Without you in it." Her voice trembled as she said the words. "Actually...I'd like it...if you came home."

"What?" Whatever he'd thought she'd say, he hadn't been prepared for *that*. Hell would freeze over before he went back to Sydney with her. Reeling, he yearned to get back into the mountains and hunt for Faith. Lilah's sudden reappearance was a buzzing gnat, a stalling annoyance in the midst of his worry. "I have no time for this."

She blocked him at the door, wide-eyed. "I told you. I've thought some things out, and I think we could have something left of our marriage, if we try."

He tried to step around her, but she blocked him again. Angry, almost ready to shove her out of the way even if he knocked her over, he stalked back to the bed and ripped the contents out of the box. He sifted through their wedding picture in a silver frame, a few books, a drill missing its bits, and a thick, yellowing envelope. He shook the envelope in the air. "This is the stuff that couldn't wait? Our marriage is over. We have divorce papers, and I remember you being pretty keen to sign them."

"Please, just listen..."

"You listen. You spent four years making my life miserable, and if you think you're getting a chance to do it some more, you're—"

"Things are different now," she pleaded. "I swear, they are. You have to believe me."

"Why would I have any reason to believe a single word out of your mouth?"

"Because—" She sounded desperate now, breathy

and urgent. "I still... I still love you, Hakon."

He stalked to the door once again. When she didn't move, he stuffed the old envelope in his back pocket. Unearthing some reserve of kindness, he took her by the shoulders and urged her aside. "Go back to Sydney, Lilah. Right now. This is no place for you."

He stepped into the hall and went downstairs, prickling with anger and worry and the haunting image of Faith's body lying at the bottom of some ravine.

Thump-thump-thump-thump. Someone came pounding down the stairs. He turned, expecting it to be Lilah, but Reilly rushed into the lobby instead. "You're not leaving, are you?" the boy panted.

"Yeah, I am." Hakon reached for his duffel bag.

"You're going after her, right? I want to come."

"Kid, you can't. We just came all this way to get you away from this crap. Faith's sister is going to be waiting for you, and when you don't show up, she'll worry."

"She's going to be more worried if Faith doesn't get home, isn't she?" The boy thrust his necklace under Hakon's nose. "I can find her. I'll stay out of trouble. Once I find her, I'll go, I swear. You're the one who told me I can help people."

Toby interrupted their conversation by coming in from the porch. "I don't think you'll be going anywhere for a while, mate. Your tires are flat, and there was a note folded under your wipers." He handed the paper to Hakon.

Willing his breath to stay steady, Hakon unfolded the scrap of paper. Reilly read it over his shoulder.

Don't bother following us. She might get into an accident.

Hakon bolted to the front door and threw it open. If they'd had time to leave the note, at least one of the men might still be in the area. He found no sign of intruders in the driveway, nor were there any other vehicles in the lot. His Land Rover stood at the edge of the parking lot near the trees, resting sadly on its flat tires.

He ducked back inside. "Toby, can I use your truck?"

"Love to let you, but it's been with the mechanic since yesterday. Mum lent her car to the reverend this morning, too. All I've got is the motorbike." Toby gave him a frown that managed to be apologetic and worried. "What kind of trouble are you in, Hakon?"

At that moment, Lilah came into the lobby. With her head high, she crossed the room to her suitcases and picked one up.

Hakon grabbed her arm. "Lilah, I need the Camaro."

Her lips pursed, and she looked him up and down. "You're not taking my car."

"Damn it, woman, I'll buy you two new ones. Just let me borrow it," he growled, trying not to sound as desperate as he felt.

Something flashed through her glittering green eyes. "I'll drive." Before he could argue, she held up a hand. "That's the only way you're using it, Hakon."

Damn the woman! Arguing with her would only waste precious time they didn't have, and there were no other options. "Give me the keys." He reached for them, but she jerked them away with an icy stare. Almost frantic now, he grabbed her shoulder and hurried her out the door. "Fine, it's your funeral. Let's just go."

He glanced over his shoulder. "Toby, don't open the door for anyone you don't recognize. Reilly, if you want to help me, you're gonna have to do it fast. Come on."

The boy sprang after them as if he'd been waiting for the invitation all his life.

When they reached the car, Lilah slid into the driver's seat. Hakon waved Reilly into the back, then sat in the passenger seat and slammed the door. "The necklace, kid. Do whatever it is you've got to do," he said.

"What about her?" the boy asked, gesturing toward Lilah.

"What *about* me?" she echoed. She frowned over her shoulder at Reilly.

"Never mind her. Lilah, you drive wherever he tells us to go. And when we stop, you're to take Reilly and go back to Sydney, and let him off at the airport. What do you need, kid?"

"Uh... A map, have you got a map?"

Hakon yanked open the glove compartment, then shuffled through a mess of lipstick tubes, receipts, and booklets until he found his old map of the Blue Mountains. He handed it back to Reilly.

The boy unfolded the map in his lap, then dangled his necklace over it. Hakon saw a flash of gold as the boy's eyes changed color. After a few moments, Lilah turned around, opening her mouth as if to say something more. "Eyes front," he told her. "Just start the engine, and don't worry about what he's doing."

With a mutinous scowl, she did so. The engine rumbled into the silence. Seconds ticked by, each of them like an hour.

"It's not working," Reilly said at last.

A fist of panic drove into Hakon's gut. He spun around in his seat and forced calm into his voice. "What do you mean, it's not working?"

The boy gave him a frustrated, anxious look. "What I said!" He cast about the car as if something there could help him. "Uh, your—your ring. You've got a silver ring. Let me have it."

"What do you know about that?" he demanded. "Have you been going through my stuff?"

"No, no! It's my gift. And the ring will lead us to *her*," the boy insisted.

"'Her,' who?" Lilah cut in, angling a sharp green eye at Hakon.

Ignoring her, he thrust a hand into his pocket and pulled out the ring Gran had given him, wondering how it would help them find Faith. But what did it matter, as long as they found her? Every moment that ticked by, he knew he came closer to losing her. What a fool he'd been to leave her. He couldn't remember an instant in his life where he'd felt such tearing dread, and desperation to stop the feeling flooded him. He slapped the ring into Reilly's outstretched palm.

The boy strung the ring onto his necklace, and it chimed against the copper pendant. He lowered the necklace until it swung just centimeters above the map. Immediately, the pendant began to swing faster than Hakon could have credited only to Reilly's hand movements. "Left. Left on the road out of here. I'm getting a—a dark place. Lots of dirt, split logs."

Hope surged. Hakon seized it like a drowning man. "Go left," he said to Lilah.

Glaring at him, she put it in drive and stomped on the gas. The Camaro peeled out of the lot, spewing gravel that pelted up under the wheel wells like birdshot, and probably scuffed the paint job some more. It didn't matter.

Nothing mattered but getting to Faith before something unthinkable happened to her.

****

Faith wondered bleakly what time it was. David's ghost had flickered and faded out days ago. She knew she shouldn't have expected him to stay. Even ghosts that were hundreds of years old couldn't last more than a few hours at a time in communication with the living.

She had no idea where they'd dumped her. Carl had been watching her for a while, sulky and hostile at having been left with her while the others did whatever they came here to do. Then he left as well, and she was alone at last. Thank God.

She shifted where she sat, stiff and uncomfortable, still blindfolded with her hands tied behind her. Someone had stuffed an oily cloth into her mouth to shut her up. The taste made her gag and pine for water.

An earthen wall stood at her back. She twisted, groaning with the effort, and pressed her forehead against the cool dirt. It did little to ease the throbbing in her skull. Talking with David's ghost, trying to decipher his muddled images and words, had all but tapped her power and given her an agonizing, days-long migraine. Even without it, she doubted she'd have the strength to muster an astral projection. Her arms felt like ship anchors, dragging her toward the bottom of a sea of oblivion.

Rest. She needed rest to gather what strength she

could. *As soon as I get my power back, you're all going to be kindling,* she vowed. With a long, slow breath, she concentrated on finding her center, some quiet corner of herself where the migraine still hadn't reached.

And in that silent center, she found Hakon. She saw him in a worn tunic, hazy and indistinct. He crossed a firelit room, then took her face in his hands, kissing her as if his life depended on it. He spoke, too, whispered words that she didn't quite catch, then took her hand, and they rushed out the door of the room. Fear clawed at her heart in the dream, and she knew they were running from something.

Other voices rang out behind them, angry, shouting, but they, too, were indistinct. From the corner of her eye, she caught the tiny, bright dots of torches waving in the night.

Hakon pulled her along, but she felt strangely faint and weak. He swept her up in his arms and hurried on. A few strides more, and a shape appeared in the darkness, large and warm and smelling of horse. He lifted her astride the horse's back, then swung up behind her. His arms came around her, and she knew without doubt that no matter what happened, she'd be safe with him.

A shout in the mine yanked her back from the vision. She shook her head. The slow trickle of returning power tickled the base of her spine. Encouraged, she got her legs underneath her.

"Don't bother to get up on my account, girlie," came Earl's voice. "I like you better when you're on your knees."

Repulsive pervert. She longed to tear the gag out of her mouth, just to shred him with a scathing reply.

Better not to waste her breath on him, anyway. Her head hurt enough without entering into a pointless argument, even if she could speak.

Instead of letting her be, however, Earl bent in front of her, smelling like a moonshine still. "You don't honestly think your friend will be coming after you, I hope. Girl like you, looks like you've got. Ain't much but a piece of meat, you ain't. He could get that anywhere."

His hand slid over her hair and down her neck, until she grimaced with loathing around the oily gag in her mouth. His fingers hooked in her shirt collar and tugged, groping for skin. "Nice meat though you are. Fancy a tumble?"

Outraged, she braced her back against the earthen wall, drew a leg up, then slammed her booted foot in his direction.

The kick hit home. "Oof!"

Then, *wham!* Stars whirled in her head as his strike landed across her face. She shook her head, fighting to stay conscious, to retaliate. *Bastard! Come on, power, hurry!* She forced her gift to obey and felt only a weak shiver.

Before she could act, Earl pushed her over and she knocked her head against the hard ground. The gag swallowed her yelp of pain. Lying flat with her tied arms pinned underneath her, she could gain no leverage before he was on her. Hot breath seared her face, reeking of whiskey. She tried to call on her power, but it wouldn't come.

The man tore at her shirt. She heard the collar stitches popping and tried to kick, to jam her shoulder in his face, to slam her forehead into his, anything. He countered all of her blows and went on trying to tear her clothes off. She screamed through the gag, and he punched her again. Blood welled in her mouth.

She heard a sudden thud. Earl grunted and rolled off her. "Keep your prick in your pants, old man, or I'll cut it off," Sebastian growled from somewhere overhead.

"Bitch was flaunting herself at me," snapped Earl from a short distance away.

"I have no time for your crap. Do it again, and you'll find yourself without your favorite parts. Now, get down that tunnel and start moving those crates before I knock your head in."

Faith's skin crawled. She hated Sebastian plenty enough, but she felt a faint swell of gratitude toward him for stopping Earl from—God, she couldn't even think it.

She heard the strike of a match, and light flashed under the bandanna over her eyes. Her heart leapt. Earl had knocked her blindfold loose in the struggle. With her blood pounding in her ears, she peered under the blindfold at her surroundings.

Sebastian still crouched across the room, closing up a lantern. Its feeble glow danced in a shivering circle around him. Had they brought her to a cave? Some kind of subterranean room? Shadows loomed in the corners, and she couldn't get an accurate size or layout of the place. Nor could she find an escape route without making her search obvious.

He looked over at her, then, and she froze in terror. Had he seen her watching? *Please, God, don't let me lose the only advantage I've had in days.*

But his gaze passed right over her, and went to

something lost in the dark corners of her prison. He stood, and from that point she saw only his legs. He stalked across the room until he disappeared into the darkness. Minutes later, he emerged again, then walked away in the other direction.

She listened until she could hear nothing but her own shallow breath. Fearing that he might come back for the lantern, Faith struggled to her feet and promptly bumped her head on a low ceiling. A bright arrow of pain lanced through her migraine and she groaned, almost wishing she hadn't stood up after all.

Bracing her feet, she dared a few minutes of waiting until her head stopped spinning, then sidled up against the earthen wall again. She pressed her head against it, and used her leverage to push the loose blindfold up off her eyes.

Success! For the first time since her abduction, hope blossomed.

Next, she tucked a fold of her gag between her shoulder and the wall, and pulled. The gag slipped from her mouth and fell to the floor. She fought against dry heaves at the oily residue on her tongue. Those bastards wouldn't get a second chance to put that in her mouth before she burnt them to a crisp.

Now for her arms. She cast about the room, searching for anything sharp enough to cut her bonds.

They'd put her into a mine of some sort, judging by the split beams supporting the earthen walls, but this area offered more space than the usual tunnels. For storage, maybe. The floor was bare, except for someone's rucksack and the lantern. Striding forward, Faith snatched up the bag, then retreated into the shadows to wrestle into it. *Eat your heart out, Houdini,* she thought wryly, groping for the snap closure behind her back.

Inside the bag—oh, thank heaven—she found a hunting knife. Precious time spilled by as she tried to wrest it out of its case. Any moment, she feared one of the men might come back and overpower her before she had the chance to fight. At last, freeing it from its case, she levered the knife in one hand, then wedged it under her bindings. One of the strands snapped, and the ropes loosened. Frantically, she tore at them until they came away.

Freedom! At once she spread her arms, willing life back into her leaden wrists. Her power trickled in faster now, spreading from the base of her spine along her nerves. It burned along her aching arms, and she gritted her teeth. *Let's see how you sons of bitches do when I'm not so helpless!*

Seizing the lantern, she pulled it back into the shadows, and was about to blow it out when she discovered that she'd been standing beside a large, open crate. "Holy mother of Pete," she whispered, stupefied.

For within the crate, snug in their nest of packing materials, lay a fortune in artifacts.

On top sat what appeared to be an Aborigine bark painting of inconceivable beauty. It must have been priceless by itself, though she saw two others like it underneath.

Faith longed to trace her finger along each perfect contour of the stylized work, with its teeming animals and swaths of trees. She'd never seen anything so unique. At once, she realized she'd discovered part of Sebastian's plunder.

Snatching up her dropped blindfold from across the

room, she wrapped it around her hand and came back to the crate. Heart thumping, she pushed aside a handful of packing material. Under the painting, she saw a few ancient weapons that looked Aboriginal, too. *Reilly helped find these things,* she thought grimly.

"Like what you see?"

Damn it! She'd overstayed her welcome, and her power still hadn't reached a usable strength.

But Sebastian didn't know that.

Gooseflesh sped across her arms. She grabbed up the hunting knife and faced him. "Come any closer, and you'll regret it."

Sebastian reached into his back pocket for a handgun, then twirled it lazily on one finger. "You're outnumbered, sweetheart. Your boyfriend's deserted you, and I assume—if you're smart—that you sent that punk kid as far from Australia as you could get him."

I could use a little help, here! Faith thought, fiercely searching for any sign of ghosts in the air. The ends of her hair drifted in what could have been an errant breeze.

Sebastian took a step forward. "Drop the knife, Faith. I'm not in the business of keeping hostages. It's messy. As soon as you give me what I want, you can go, and everybody's happy."

He was lying, and she knew it. "What do I have that you'd want?" she countered, stalling for time. She backed up until the crate bumped against her legs.

Waving the gun toward the crate, he said, "You're going to figure out the map on our little works of art, there."

"What?" She risked a look at the brilliant painting.

The first flash of anger skimmed across his face.

"Don't play stupid. We both know you're this legendary historian. Elliott didn't send me out here without me doing my homework first. The maps, please."

"You're Elliott's goon. You figure them out," she said, trying for bravado while her power seeped back into her bones. She divided a look between him and the shadows behind him, wondering if she could hedge her chances of escape.

"I'm not the academic. You are."

Underneath her fear, she seethed with outrage. These artifacts belonged in a museum, not some crate in a dank underground hole. "What were you going to do with these if I didn't show up?"

"I knew you'd show up. You and your sister are on some noble quest to find other gifted people, and save them from a life of corruption."

"Yeah," she said, inching sideways. "I'm sure Elliott's going to be real happy with you when he finds out you're kidnapping people on his behalf, and murdering his employees."

"Why would Elliott find out?" Sebastian leered, and fear stabbed at her. "Did you think I planned on crawling back to him with all that loot? No, darling. I'm keeping the proceeds. The old sucker just financed my search."

The vague memory of an overheard conversation brushed the surface of her consciousness. David and Carl had said they didn't have the connections to sell the artifacts. Blood pumping, she dared another step around Sebastian. "You can't dump this stuff for a red cent without Elliott's help."

"I don't give a damn about any of that junk. I can

pawn it off on private buyers. Sure, I'll get less than I want, but who cares? The real fun is at the end of those maps. Drop the knife, sweetheart, I know you're stalling me."

Her spine tingled. *Throw it at him,* said a voice in her head.

David's ghost. And her powers had returned.

I can't. I'm not a murderer! she protested.

He is. Do it.

Her heartbeat doubled. Sweating, she flung the knife in Sebastian's direction, purposely sending it wide. While he dodged, she scooped the first bark painting out of the crate and jammed it under her arm. Bolting past Sebastian, she called on her power and flung an arc of flame at him. He screeched, and for a horrible moment she thought the noise would bring the mine down on top of them. She flew past, and down the tunnel behind him.

As she raced along the passages, the lantern light coming from the storage room grew dimmer and dimmer, then faded out. Nothing could be seen in the inky blackness ahead of her, but she couldn't risk using flame to show the way. She forced herself to slow down, for fear of slamming into an unanticipated wall. Panting, she felt her way along, all the while expecting Sebastian to follow with the lantern. He knew these passages. Any moment, he'd catch her, and all she had to bargain with was the single bark painting under her arm.

A side passage emerged under her questing fingers. She took it without hesitation. *How the hell do I get out of here?*

Down, said David's voice.

What do you mean—

Before she could finish the thought, the floor opened under her feet with the crack and rattle of broken wood. She screamed and fell, clutching the painting to her body.

Chapter Twelve

I used to get scared of the dark before I found out I was never really alone in it. The ghosts are almost always there. I just have to listen for them. Weird, huh?
— *Faith's Journals, age fourteen*

Hakon stared out the front windshield, gripping his knee to keep from drumming his fingers in an impatient staccato. Reilly's last sense of Faith had been ten minutes ago, on a detour off the main road leading out of Bowen Mountain. Too long. Way too long.

"Right... Take a right down this side road," the boy said after an everlasting agony of silent driving.

Lilah made the turn. "I don't understand what this is all about, Hakon. Who are you looking for?"

Hakon barely registered the question, searching the trees flashing past as if they would somehow reveal Faith's whereabouts. "As soon as I get where I'm going, I want you to take Reilly back to Sydney with you. That's all you need to know."

She fell silent. He knew she was fuming without even looking, and he didn't care. All of their petty little animosities faded into nothing beside the rhythmic chant running through his head: *Don't lose her, don't lose her, don't lose her.*

Reilly wrenched him out of his daze a moment

later. "Stop, stop!"

Lilah stomped on the brakes, and the Camaro fishtailed to a halt. A cloud of road dust billowed up under the tires. She arched around and scowled at the boy. "Do you mind not scaring the life out of me like that?"

"Back up. I saw something," said Reilly, his nose almost pressed against the rear window.

Hakon's heart thudded in his throat. Any minute, he knew his fragile bubble of hope would burst. As Lilah backed the car up, he squinted into thick trees at the roadside.

"There," Reilly said, and pointed.

Hakon saw a yawning mouth of darkness leading into the belly of the earth. A large yellow sign reading *MINE CLOSED* stood beside the entrance, and the boards covering the entrance had been knocked away.

Hakon unbuckled his belt and leapt out of the car before it had come to a full stop, then pounded across the road. Kneeling, he touched the still-crisp ridges of tire tracks leading right up to the mine entrance, and then away. They'd been here, and recently.

God help them if they'd hurt her.

He stalked back to the Camaro, then pulled a small pack from the back seat. Reilly popped out right behind it. "Is she in there?"

To Lilah, Hakon said, "Take him to Sydney. He needs to go to the airport." He pushed the boy into the passenger seat, then tried to force confidence into his tone. "I'll be all right, and so will she. Thanks for your help, kid."

He saw a faint flash of pride in the boy's eyes, swiftly covered. Then Reilly nodded and shut the passenger door.

Lilah leaned across the passenger seat to glare at him out the window. "What about our talk? When will I see you again?"

He bit back a nasty reply. "Later. Get him to Sydney, Lilah." It took effort, but he forced himself to add, "Please."

"Hakon, we're not finished with all this. I'm not just going to be ordered around and—"

Seething, he shouldered his pack and spun away without hearing the rest of Lilah's remark. The mine beckoned, and he couldn't afford to waste any more time.

Inside, he lit his electric torch and swept the tunnel. Footprints led away into the depths. He bent to study them. Relief washed through him when he saw the small, rounded toe print of a woman's shoe in the dirt. Other, bigger tracks crisscrossed over it. It took every last bit of his nerve not to run after her. If the men caught him before he found her, he'd be no use to Faith at all.

He thought only of seeing her face again, and the way she stared at him with worlds of longing in her eyes. The idea of never seeing that look on her face again twisted him in knots he couldn't even comprehend. Why her? What was it about her that made him so crazed with worry?

The drive to find her hurried him on as fast as he dared to go. Faith's footprints disappeared, either because she'd been carried from that point, or her tracks had been smudged out by those of the men. They had to have brought her deeper into the mine, away from the danger of discovery. Hakon continued down the tunnel with only his instincts to guide him.

Long minutes crept by, fraught with the constant dread of being found by Sebastian or his men. Edging along the wall, straining his ears for any sound, Hakon caught the faint *drip-drip-drip* of water. It sounded hollow and lonely, echoing from far away.

Or, perhaps, from far below. He bent at a split in one of the wall's support beams—dangerous, that, the mine could go any time without warning—and listened. *Drip, drip, drip.* A breath of cool, damp air fanned his face through the crack.

Before he could investigate any further, voices warned him of someone's approach. At least two men, and by their tones, they had noticed his torch light. Swearing under his breath, Hakon flicked it off and ran for the closest spur off the main tunnel.

Light flickered along the far wall of the main tunnel. Instinctively, he backed away down the spur, then slipped into another passage. He prayed they wouldn't notice his boot prints among the mess of tracks on the loose-packed earthen floor.

He spun to face forward and hurried on, feeling his way. At last he flicked his torch back on, no longer worried about staying undiscovered. Another spur. Another. His heart raced as he filed away each turn in a mental map to get back out of this rabbit warren once he found her.

And he would find her. Or they'd pay.

Four more turns. At each one, he felt more and more like the mine had swallowed him, never to give him up again to daylight. At last, he stumbled upon a large storage area. Gouges raked the dirt floor, suggesting that someone had dragged a series of large, heavy objects across it. The place was otherwise deserted.

In the corner, he found the shredded remnants of a few ropes. His heart soared into his throat, and he knew somehow that these were Faith's bonds. If they'd had to tie her, she must still have been alive.

At that point.

He darted back down the tunnel the way he'd come, the only possible way out of that storage area. After flashing through his mental map, he took an unused spur and stalked along it. Finally, he saw a stray footprint at the corner of another side passage.

Faith's. He knew it.

He flew down the spur, scanning the darkness just beyond the reach of his torch light.

Crack. The floor gave way under his feet.

His electric torch tumbled away, spinning into the darkness. He snatched for something, anything to break his fall, and his hand closed around a beam of wood. He grunted as his body lurched to a stop. Splinters dug into his palm. When he kicked his legs, searching for somewhere to put his feet, open space seemed to yawn below. He heard his torch clatter at the bottom of the shaft, and looked down.

And down.

And down.

The torch lay in a heap of broken wood and rubble. Its dim glow revealed a high, narrow shaft. If he reached his feet far enough, he could touch the sides of the shaft and chimney himself down, or try to climb back up.

But Faith had come down that passage above. What if she'd fallen down this shaft, too, and hurt herself?

He dropped his free shoulder and let his pack slip off. As it plummeted to the bottom of the shaft, he braced his other hand on the beam overhead. Stretching his legs as far as they would go to the far wall of the shaft, he arched his back to wedge it against the other wall. He just fit.

Carefully, bit by bit, he lowered himself down, wondering how in hell he was supposed to get back up again. A hand here on one shaky hold, a toe there on a stone sticking out, slide, slide.

By the time he'd reached the bottom, he heard voices above. Abandoning all pretense of caution, he dropped the last couple of meters, grabbed his torch and pack, then darted into the shadows. He clicked the torch off just as the voices grew louder overhead.

"If he fell down there, he probably broke his neck," said one man.

"We should be so lucky," came the second voice. A beam of light shone down the shaft. Hakon backed into an alcove just in time to avoid its glare.

"Don't see him," the voice echoed. "He might not have fallen in. Check back the other way. See if there's a way around this hole to the other end of the tunnel, in case he went that way somehow."

The voices faded, and for the second time, Hakon blessed his luck in avoiding capture. As soon as he thought it safe enough, he clicked his torch on again and swept it around the bottom of the mine shaft.

He found a narrow crack between two broken boards, just wide enough to squeeze through if he went sideways. The tight passageway behind it went on for several meters, and then opened to the right.

Damn good thing he wasn't claustrophobic.

Angling his shoulders, he slipped into the crack and started down the passage. A rat scurried away from his boot and out of the beam of light. "Go bite Sebastian," he snapped.

Once the passage veered right, it widened enough for him to walk forward, though the walls just brushed his arms. The *drip-drip-drip* of water reached his ears again, then intensified into a trickle, and then a steady flow. The air cooled and grew musty.

At last, he emerged from the passage and found himself standing beside an underground stream. He spanned his torch light across it. No more than a few meters across, then. He might be able to jump it with a running start, if he needed to.

He heard racing footsteps just before someone tackled him. His torch flew out of his hands, and a pair of arms wrapped around his neck.

Faith. Alive, oh, God.

He hauled her against him and buried his face in her hair. Alive. Alive. She gave a single sob and hugged him hard. "Are you hurt?" he rasped.

She stiffened, and a warning bell clanged in his body. "I'm fine, I'm fine. Come look," she said, pulling away.

He tightened his grip on her hand and turned her back to face him. In the pale glow of his dropped torch, he saw ugly bruises on her cheek, and dried blood at the corner of her lip. Rage flooded him. "Who did it?" he ground out.

Tears sparkled in her eyes, but she didn't answer. For a moment, it seemed they were no longer standing beside an underground river. The air shuddered. As if in a dream, he heard the far-off murmur of an angry mob. Every muscle in his body tightened, and the need to move seized him. He bent to sweep up his torch in one hand, and took her hand again in the other. "Let's get out of here."

Motion seemed to loosen her tongue. "W-Wait, we need to cross the stream." Instead of following him along the bank, she pulled him toward it. "Come on. It's not deep."

He waded in behind her. The water came to mid-shin, sluicing around his legs and into his boots. Her hand slipped in his as she stumbled, but he held on. He'd be damned if he let go of her again. "Faith."

She turned to face him, gazing at him as if she thought she'd never get another chance. His gut twisted, and he pulled her into his arms once more. He didn't say anything, couldn't find a voice for his surge of pain at the idea of her slipping away from him again.

She circled her arms back around his neck and held him close. "I'm okay," she whispered over the murmur of the water.

He pressed his lips to her cheek, still shaken. *I'm not.*

When she drew back and kissed him on the lips, the force of emotion inside him spilled over. He pulled her hard against his body, and kissed her back with everything he couldn't bring himself to say. Her fingers clenched in his ponytail. He swallowed her moan and pulled her still closer. It wasn't enough. It would never be enough, not if they went on like this for the rest of his life.

Too soon, she drew away with regret in her eyes. "Is Reilly all right?"

"Yeah." He didn't add that, lacking any other options, he'd asked his ex-wife to get Reilly safely out of Australia.

Nodding, she said, "We have to keep moving. I need to show you this."

She tugged him across the stream to the opposite bank, and through another passage. It twisted right, then left, then left again, and it seemed like they began climbing upward. "What is it?"

"You'll see," she said.

They emerged into another underground room, small and unfinished, as if the workers had only begun digging here just before they'd closed the mine. A narrow crack in the wall led away to what might have been yet another tunnel. He wondered how the miners ever returned to the surface after being in this endless maze.

In the corner of the room, he saw what looked like a crudely painted board leaning on its end.

"It's a bark painting," she said in answer to his unspoken question. She picked it up and held it for him to see. "This is a map. Or part of it, anyway—there's two others. Sebastian wants what's at the end of them, but we're going to get there first."

"Whoa, whoa. What's this 'we' business? You're safe. Reilly's safe. Let's get the hell out of here and go to the authorities."

She frowned. "You don't understand. Hakon, if they get to the end of these maps, there's going to be trouble."

"There's plenty enough trouble already."

"There will be more." She laid a hand on his arm. "I read this map. There's a carving at the end, a wooden

189

statue infused with the power to control minds. The Aborigine shamans—"

Something splashed far down the corridor behind them, interrupting her. "Tell me later," said Hakon. He planted his hand at the small of her back and urged her toward the crack in the wall.

They slipped into the cleft, and Hakon extinguished his torch once more. With no room to walk abreast, he stayed behind her and eased along with one wall at his back. The splashing noises ceased, and then he heard the thumping of footsteps. "Where are you, you son of a bitch?" roared a voice that could only be Sebastian's.

Faith froze ahead of him, radiating waves of fear. Her breath came harsh and short over the constant, faint gurgle of the underground stream. Hakon laid a steadying hand on her shoulder and pressed her forward, gripping the barrel of his torch in his other hand. A stifling reek assaulted his nose, something he'd smelled before, but couldn't place....

Faith darted forward again, and he hurried after her. It seemed they went on forever. He began to wonder why the men hadn't followed. The acrid stink sharpened, and his eyes began to water with it.

Then he heard the squeaking. And this time, he knew it wasn't rats.

Bat guano.

He snatched a fistful of Faith's shirt and jerked. "Get down!" he whispered, plunging earthward.

Whoosh. Small, dark shapes exploded down on them from overhead. Faith yelped and plummeted to the ground beside him. He threw his arms around her and ducked as the colony of disturbed bats rushed past them. Tiny bodies fluttered by, whipping the ends of his hair. A wing thumped his ear. Faith whimpered underneath him, something between horror and outright disgust.

Far behind, he heard Sebastian and another man yelp as the bats burst out of the tunnel and into the room beyond. The shouts faded as the men retreated from the airborne onslaught. "Come on," Hakon whispered as the last of the colony flapped away.

"I hate those things," she whispered back, shuddering under his arm.

"Well, the good news is, they're keeping Sebastian busy." He took her hand and squeezed around her, leading the way forward down the tunnel. "And there's better news."

She groaned in revulsion, no doubt discovering herself as patched with bat droppings as he was. "Please tell me you have a five-star power shower waiting once we get out of here."

He jammed his torch through a loop in his belt, then stalked on down the tunnel, still holding her hand. "Not quite. But if the bats were overhead, that means—"

Without warning, they emerged into starlight.

"—there's an entrance nearby," he finished, grinning.

"Oh!" she gasped out. She dropped the bark painting in the gravel, and sucked in fresh air as though she hadn't smelled it in years.

He couldn't blame her, but they had no time to savor their escape from the mine. They'd come out on what looked like the backside, but Sebastian's men might already be searching the alternate entrances.

"Come on. The deeper we get into the woods, the better chance we have of losing them."

Faith picked up the painting, then they hurried into the forest. She jogged after him without speaking. He glanced back to be certain she hadn't lagged behind, and saw the moonlit profile of her mouth, set in a dour line. She stared down at the dim trail as she walked, clutching the painting as if someone might tear it away from her. Dirty, grim, and focused on their flight, she had never looked more beautiful.

Gripped with the need to touch her, he slowed down and took her hand once more. "We'll need somewhere to bed down for the night. Miriam's is too far to walk it, but I know another place."

She stopped walking and managed a smile. "Hakon, I..."

Seeing the sheen of tears in her eyes, he found himself drawing still closer to her. "It's all right now. I'm here."

Her breath caught. "I need to tell you something."

"About the painting? It can wait until we're away from here, can't it?"

"Not—Not about the painting."

The sound of breaking branches stopped his reply. Without speaking, he pulled her onward, as fast as he dared without risking too much noise.

"I know you're out here!" Sebastian's roar echoed through the trees. "Bring the painting back, and this will be over, Faith."

"Over, my ass," she muttered, barely audible. "Just as soon as you put us out of your misery, you mean. Money-grubbing, power-starved murderer."

Hakon let a smile spread across his face. Most of

the women he knew would have crumpled with terror in such a situation. Not Faith. He tugged her off their current path and deeper into the woods. Rotting leaf litter muffled their footsteps.

A gunshot blasted in the air. Birds squawked in alarm. Faith gasped and bumped into him, rattling the summer-dry leaves of a nearby shrub.

Afraid to risk speaking, he pulled her still deeper into the woods, squinting to find good footing among tree roots and fallen branches. She hurried after him, stepping where he stepped, with the painting still clutched tight under her arm. He let her pass him, and urged her forward down the game trail.

"Faith Markham!" Sebastian screamed again. "You can't hide forever. Don't forget, I know where you live—you and your stupid sister!"

Faith spun around with her eyes blazing silver in the gloom, and lunged toward the voice. Hakon threw his arm around her waist and hauled her back, his feet dragging in the leaf mold. "No!" he whispered. "He wants you to take the bait!"

"He's threatening Sara," she hissed, scrabbling to free herself from his grip. "I'll kill him, I swear to God I'll kill him. Let me go!"

Hearing footsteps, Hakon shoved Faith down the game trail. Seeming to grasp their danger, she made no further protest, and ran.

He forced them on until his lungs burned and his legs shook, not content to slow down until he was sure Sebastian had given up pursuit. Even then, he marched them along until he saw her stumbling in the darkness. She never complained once.

At last, they came upon a creek. "Follow this," he

murmured as they emerged from the woods into a field. "Make sure you walk in the gravel, in case they look for a trail in the morning."

She nodded and turned down the gentle slope of the creek bank. A little while later, he saw the dark, skeletal outline of a tree snag at the water's edge. Here, the creek ran so shallow, he could pick out sand bars. "Cross here."

"How much farther is this place?" she murmured, sounding weary.

He softened, and tugged the painting from under her arm to carry it for her. "We're almost there, I promise. It's well-hidden. We'll be safe for the night."

She gave a brief smile and stepped into the creek bed. Her shoulders drooped, and he knew she was near exhaustion. Had those dungheaps given her any food? Water? Rest? Rage burned low in his belly. If they so much as laid a hand on her again, they'd come back missing fingers. He eased past her and took her hand, guiding her across where the going was easiest. As furious as he was, nothing calmed him or cleared his head as much as touching her.

They came to a gully where the creek picked up pace again, and turned southward. Hakon recognized subtle landmarks and led them through another field, then past rock formations that twisted into eerie shapes in the darkness.

At last, they wound into a thick stand of trees, then came to a tiny miner's cabin on the edge of an overgrown meadow. One of the shutters had torn half off its hinges. The grass around the building had grown wild and tangled up to the bottom of the windowsills. "No one's lived here in years. Once in a while, I've used it as a stopover on trail hikes from Bowen Mountain. It's not great, but—"

"It's the Taj Mahal," she said, hurrying forward.

He smiled as she sped to open the door. Inside, the one-room cabin reeked with stale air, but was otherwise good enough for a night's rest. He opened a window to let fresh air in, then squinted in the starlight spilling into the cabin.

The old mattress still had some life in it, and the crude table and stools were sturdy enough. He pushed aside the bed frame, then pulled up the floorboards underneath. "Occasionally, I'm a bloody genius." Grinning, he tugged a wooden box from the hole under the floorboards, then put the bark painting in the hole and replaced the boards.

"What's that?" Faith asked, seeing his find.

After pulling the bed back over the secret hole, he set the box on the table and unlocked it with a key from his key ring. "Emergency stash." Army blankets, tinned food, and a bottle of whiskey emerged from the crate piece by piece.

She looked over his shoulder. "Emergency, is it?" Even through her tiredness, he caught the gleam of amusement in her eyes as she saw the whiskey.

He scooped a handful of candles from the bottom of the box, then laid them on the blankets. "That's right. I could use a stiff drink after this night, couldn't you?"

"You bet I can." She hooked the bottle, then plopped down on the edge of the table to take a long gulp. She set the bottle down with a deep, blissful sigh that sent a bullet of longing tearing through him, no matter how tired he was.

He looked down at himself, then realized just how

grimy he'd gotten. Mud, water, and bat guano covered his jeans. During their escape, he hadn't given his appearance a second thought. He needed a bath. And maybe a sandblaster.

No way in hell was he leaving her side.

He picked up the army blankets. "Come with me. I've got an idea."

Chapter Thirteen

Ever watch a fly get stuck in a spider web? No matter how much it wiggles and fights to get free, it only gets stuck worse. Boy, can I sympathize.
— *Faith's Journals, age twenty-eight*

Faith followed Hakon through the woods, carrying one of the army blankets under her arm. They'd been walking for a full five minutes, and curiosity riddled her with every step. "Where on earth are we going?" she asked, pushing aside a low-hanging branch.

He stopped so abruptly that she bumped into him, then he stepped aside, grinning. "To the bathtub."

Puzzled, she squinted into the darkness beyond.

A hot spring bubbled in the gully below, steaming in the chilly air. A rock wall rose straight up out of the water on one side, cutting sharp shadows against the night sky. "Oh, Hakon. You have no idea how much I—"

She cut short, feeling heat rush to her cheeks.

She didn't love him. She couldn't afford to love him. He'd have no intention of returning it even if she did.

Scrambling to cover her near-slip, she blurted, "How much I need a scouring. I hope you tucked a wire brush somewhere in this bundle." She made a show of shaking out her blanket and looking around for something wrapped within to fall to the ground.

He chuckled, and her skin tingled at the welcome sound after so many days of worry and fear. "I thought something similar earlier," he said. "We look like refugees from a trash heap." He shook his blanket out on the grass, then stripped off his shirt and removed his boots. He stepped out of his pants next, then kicked them farther up the slope.

Faith noticed something papery tumble out of the back pocket, and into the grass. She bent to pick up the yellowed envelope. "What's this?"

Naked, he halted and looked back over his shoulder. Her heart skipped at the glorious, masculine beauty of him, but then she noticed how his posture stiffened. "It's nothing. Just leave it there."

Flash. In her mind's eye, Faith saw a redheaded woman standing in a garage full of cardboard boxes. The woman was holding this very envelope and staring at it with astonishment. Even diluted in a vision, the woman's desire and pull toward Hakon seared Faith's heart.

The woman wanted him back.

At once, Faith knew the redhead was Lilah. Hakon had turned away, and she sensed he was avoiding her stare.

He had to have seen Lilah to get this envelope. Talked to her.

Suspicion and worry battled together within her. Would he give Lilah the chance to make amends for their broken marriage? Faith bit her lip, desperate to know what the envelope contained. She'd hoped—days ago—that he might come to believe they belonged together, and had always belonged together, though hundreds of years had sundered them. *Stupid fool,* she scolded herself. He had a life here, and had told her in no uncertain terms that he meant it to be a single one.

She wondered how she'd ever find the words now to tell him she was Aesa.

No. She couldn't, not now. Maybe not ever. Guilt and heartache flooded her. He'd never believe it, anyway, never believe in a love that could last through the ages. She still wasn't sure *she* even believed it. And he'd certainly never believe in her, after she changed her "story" yet again. She'd only seem jealous and desperate to keep him.

Another manipulating woman in his life. He'd hate her. No way would she set herself up for that kind of fall.

Forcing her eyes shut to hide her anguish, Faith dropped the envelope to the ground.

"Coming?" she heard him say.

"Yeah. In a minute." She pulled herself together, took a deep breath, and then began peeling off her clothes. The prospect of bathing naked with him drew her like a moth to flame. Nothing could stop her from taking that chance while it was given.

Silence, then. She'd keep her silence about Aesa, take what he offered while she remained in Australia, and be with him while she could.

And then go home.

She waded into the pool and sank waist-deep. Warm water, fizzing with bubbles, lapped around her. She leaned back to dunk her head, then came up dripping. A sigh started in her toes and surged up through her body. "This is heaven."

Hakon waded toward her, rinsing his arms of the day's dirt. Water swirled away as he came forward. "I can think of a few ways to make it more heavenly."

She closed the distance between them and laid her hands on his chest. The heat of his skin drew lazy spirals down her nerve endings. "Thank you for saving my life...again."

A smile quirked at the corner of his mouth. "Don't mention it." His fingers threaded into her wet hair, then he cupped the back of her head in one large, warm paw. Drawing her close, he planted a deep, soul-searching kiss on her lips.

Faith ceased to think about Lilah, or Sebastian, or anything other than Hakon's nearness. Nothing else mattered but being with him while she could.

His tongue traced the edges of her lips, and then thrust into her mouth. He tugged her closer, growling low in his throat. She gave an answering moan and kneaded the firm muscle of his pecs.

"Woman, you don't give a man much chance to be slow about a seduction," he rumbled, snaking his arms around her and cupping her buttocks.

Pressing her body against him, she gasped out, "Who said you needed to be slow?"

He growled again and lifted her. Water sloshed, cascading down her skin in tickling trails. Faith wrapped her legs around his waist and sighed as he drew her against his hard length. He nosed her hair aside to nip at her neck. Reaching around his back, she stroked the damp skin over his spine with her fingertips.

She could hide her feelings from him when they weren't like this, touching and kissing and blending their bodies together. But now, when he held her so close, she knew there could be no holding back. She could no longer deny that she loved him, had loved him for a thousand years, and nothing would do but to show him that...even if she couldn't speak the words. With a long, silvery shiver, she let her powers flow.

His breath steamed against her sensitive skin in the cooling night air. Reveling in the masculine shape and smell of him, she let her mind drift back through the dream-memories. She remembered loving him as Aesa, in the salty surf of their home on Hvitmar. He'd held her just as he held her now, with his mouth hot on her throat and the wind teasing her skin into gooseflesh.

He lifted her higher in his arms, then his lips closed over one taut nipple. Spirals of heat spread through her body, echoing the same joy Aesa had felt so long ago at his touch. And then the sensations melded into one, so that she didn't know which was past and which was present. Faith wound her fingers into his mane and held her to him, willing him with her body to understand how much she needed him.

When he lowered her and pressed his rigid manhood against her center, she moaned and arched her hips against him. He slipped inside her with a flush of hot spring water, and delicious shivers raced down to her toes. She nuzzled into his neck, boneless with ecstasy.

With a groan, he clutched her to him, driving deep. She gasped and tightened her legs around him, burning with the need to feel him still deeper. "Hakon, oh, Hakon."

He slanted his mouth over hers. The hot-satin thrust of his tongue mirrored the rocking of his hips against hers. She moaned, long and low, and raked her nails over his skin.

Turning in the water, he waded toward the rock wall. Faith felt it bump against her back, and gasped at the contact with the rough, cool stone.

"God, what you do to me," he said against her lips. When he drove into her, she bit off a cry of pleasure. He withdrew almost entirely, then plunged again. And again, and again. She soared higher with each stroke. When she raised her chin, his teeth grazed the tender skin of her throat.

She opened her eyes to the dark-velvet sky as Hakon pressed her ever closer to the brink. The stars glowed, close enough to touch. "Don't stop," she pleaded, reeling.

He raised her hands and pinned them against the wall with his own, trapping her between the cool rock and his blazing body. Another thrust. Another, another, faster and faster until nothing made sense but the urgency of their passion. Heart slamming, she gasped his name and shattered. A hoarse cry tore up from her throat and rang in the air, and then his groan joined it.

Panting, he rested his forehead against her shoulder, and stood there for a few moments. Then he lowered her hands, urging her arms around his neck. With her skin tingling, she embraced him. He caught her lips with his own, kissing her, nibbling at her lips. "You're bloody amazing, you know that?"

"Mmmmm." She nuzzled his ear, then went limber and loose-jointed. He caught her before she sank into the water. "Points for you, too."

His chuckle vibrated against her skin. He lifted her once more, holding her close. The damp hair of his chest tickled against her breasts.

Holding her in his arms, he waded to the bank, then lowered her to the blanket spread on the grass and knelt beside her. "That was nice. The water, and all," she said, trailing a fingertip down his chest.

"Anytime you want to take another bath, just ask." He grinned, then kissed her.

She stretched out, relishing the breath of cool air on her skin, and turned her face once more to the sky. Then she spotted a familiar bright triangle of stars near a small, circular cluster. "Hakon."

"Hmmm?"

Pointing, she asked, "What's that group of stars there?"

"Do I look like an astronomer?" He squinted briefly into the heavens, then busied himself laying kisses one by one along her midriff.

She shivered with pleasure even as she tugged him away from her belly. "It's on the map, Hakon. The bark map."

He stiffened under her hands. "I thought we were done chasing stuff all over the mountains."

"What about Sebastian? What if he reaches the end of the maps before we do, and gets that wooden carving?"

Hakon sat up. "There's just no end to your fun and games, is there?"

"I need to get that thing so *he* doesn't," she insisted.

"Look, I've already reached my quota for number of ways to risk my hide in a single year. Most of them, due to you. Burn the map, Sebastian loses his link to his little tinker toy, and we go home happy."

Scowling, she pushed upright. "I *am* the map. I've

read it with my gift. The path from step one to *X*-marks-the-spot is all in my head. He'll come after *me* to find the carving, if he can't get it on his own."

Hakon rose to his feet, then stalked up the bank and snatched his pants. "How do you know he's even aware of this super-special, map-reading gift of yours?"

"Why wouldn't he be?" Faith stood and pulled the blanket up around her shoulders. "Do you think Elliott Flintrop would have sent Sebastian all the way here to find a gifted boy without also researching me and my sister? He'd have known we'd be looking for Reilly, too. He's not an idiot."

"Glad to see you think so highly of the man who sent his hit squad after you."

"Damn it, Hakon, I'm serious."

"So am I. I'm done sticking my neck on the block." He thrust his legs into his jeans, then scooped up the extra blanket. "Let's get the hell out of here."

She gathered up her tattered shirt and grimy pants, then slipped them on, wishing she could return to McGowan's Inn so she could beg Miriam for a change of clothes.

But there were more important things to worry about right now.

With a quick glance at Hakon, she said, "I'm not asking you to come with me."

"You're not going alone, either." Before she could reply, he added, "I'll bloody tie you down if you try it."

"Don't you get it? This carving is a potential weapon on a huge scale. It allows the user mass mind control. Can you imagine the damage it could do?" He started away without waiting for her, but she jogged to his side and kept stride with him. "Even if he didn't want it for himself. If he sold an artifact like that, the first people to buy it would be hostile governments or terrorists."

"Do you ever get tired of saving the world?"

"Do you ever get tired of pushing it away?" she shot back.

He glared at her, his eyes flashing in the darkness. "What's that supposed to mean?"

"Almost from the first minute we met, all you wanted was to take your money and get out. You're so sick of people—"

"Sick of women who keep changing their stories," he snapped.

"—and you act like all you want is to be miles away from anywhere, when all you're doing is running from—" She broke off, face burning.

"From what?"

Faith jerked her blanket around herself and hurried ahead of him, trying not to show her hurt. *From me, you big stupid jerk.*

She heard ringing silence for a moment, then footsteps and rustling brush as he trotted up the trail after her. "Fine," he spat. "Once we get to McGowan's, you can pay me what you owe me, and we're done. You do what you want with the map."

His words stabbed her. Where was the Hakon who risked his life to do the right thing, to see it through even if it was a punishing task? Where was that honorable man who'd stood by Aesa, who'd given everything to defend her, even after her death?

They weren't the same man. Maybe it was time she stopped trying to reconcile the two. Maybe it was time she stopped dreaming that *this Hakon* could be anything like that one.

Turning around, Faith pleaded one last time. "Don't you care what happens to the people he'll hurt with this thing?"

"I'm not the one who wants to go out looking for trouble getting it, and then running from him once I have it."

"I'm not *looking* for trouble, you idiot. I'm going out there to protect others *from* it." She scowled at him.

"Must be great to be such a superhero. Call me when you get your fan club."

Faith seethed, blinking back angry tears. "I would rather use my gifts to help others than sit by and do nothing while innocent people get hurt. It's why I came here in the first place. To stop Elliott and Sebastian from hurting Reilly. And you know what the worst part is?"

"What's that?" Hakon crossed his arms.

"*Anyone* could sit by and do nothing. And *anyone* could stand up and stop people like Sebastian from wrecking the world for the rest of us. The problem is, most of them just don't." She marched away, not caring whether he followed or not.

Yep, she'd been wrong. She didn't love him. She loved a memory.

****

All the way back to the miner's cabin, Hakon fumed. What was she thinking, diving headfirst into more danger when she'd just escaped from it? When they got inside and barred the door shut, he snapped, "Take the bed."

"I'm not tired." Faith held the other blanket around her like a shield.

"You're going to be. We have a long walk back to Miriam's in the morning."

She glared daggers at him, then turned away and sank onto the worn mattress without another word.

He stalked to the crate on the table and then pawed through it, unearthing a tinned ham. He glanced at her. She sat gazing out the open window, shoulders sagging. Some of his anger slipped away. "Are you hungry?" he asked.

She didn't look, but lifted her head. "I could eat."

Sure, she could. Sebastian and his blokes had probably starved her. "I think we'll be safe with a low fire." After stoking one in the cabin's ancient grate, he found a pie tin, popped open the ham, then plopped it into the dish. While their makeshift dinner heated, he sat on a stool and stared into the red-gold flames.

Damn them. Damn Sebastian, and his crew, and Lilah, and everyone else who insisted on pulling him away from the solitude he'd kept for months. He'd been happy up here in the mountains, somehow able to isolate himself even when leading a mob of city dwellers on a weekend hike.

Until Faith.

He stole another glance at her. The contours of her face flickered with a soft glow. Looking closer, he saw a lick of flame twirling in her palm. She waved her fingers. The flame spun faster, and she followed it with her gaze. "What are you doing?"

"Thinking." A moment later, the flame snuffed out and she stood. She knelt beside the bed, then began pushing it across the floor.

"Now what?"

Faith pulled up the floorboards under the bed, then

extracted the bark map. She stood again, and pulled the bed back to its original position. With the blanket hanging shawl-fashion around her shoulders, she crossed the floor, cradling the painting in her hands. "I hate to burn this beautiful thing." She sat on the empty stool, then laid the map on her knees.

In spite of himself, Hakon asked, "What possessed those guys to create something for mind control in the first place?"

"As far as I can tell, they intended the carving for good purposes. It was used to join the members of their tribe together in rituals, so that they could speak to the land as one voice. Offer prayers, ask for rain, seek food." She trailed her fingertips along the map's surface. "They had no concept of it being used to do harm."

Hakon dropped his gaze to the painting. By the firelight, he saw a cluster of stars in the painting's stylized sky. Below that lay a belt of trees, and a variety of animals in a clearing. In the clearing ran a large, white band. "What's that supposed to be?"

"A river, I think." With a sigh, she reached forward, then dropped the bark map into the grate.

Stunned, Hakon watched the flames catch and consume the map. He'd told her to burn it, himself, but he couldn't help wondering just how valuable the painting might have been to a museum. He felt no relief that she'd severed one of the links to the carving.

I am the map, she'd said. What if Sebastian did come for her anyway?

They spoke little while they ate. He picked at his food without really wanting it, but she devoured hers with a speed that confirmed she hadn't eaten since

Sebastian took her. He handed her the rest of his share. "You take it."

She didn't argue, accepting the pie tin and attacking the food as if it were ambrosia.

Guilt prickled in his belly. He wished he'd stopped them from taking her in the first place. The blanket fell open around her body, and he caught the glow of naked skin in the opening of her shirt. A couple of the buttons were missing. He had to stop himself from brushing her hair back and kissing her, wanting to reassure her—and himself—that she was safe. "You sure you're not hurt?" he ventured.

Her gaze came up to meet his, and then flashed away again. "Yeah." Finished with the food, she set the plate on the table.

He tilted his head toward the bed. "You should try to sleep," he said gruffly. "I'll stay up."

She nodded, then went back to the bed and lay down facing the wall. Hakon settled onto his stool with the rest of the whiskey, and stared into the glowing coals that remained of their fire.

He couldn't have slept if he wanted to. Though the fire had been small and burnt to nothing by now, he worried more than he'd let on about Sebastian noticing it and following them. He would risk a few hours for Faith's sake, so she could rest and regain stamina. She needed food, and sleep, and a one-way ticket the hell out of the mountains.

Staring across the room at her prone figure, he frowned. She'd be safer at home, with friends and family around her, but the thought of her leaving soured his mood that much further. What might happen to her without him there to help her?

Don't be ridiculous, he chided himself. *She's lived this long without you. She'll be fine.*

He crossed his arms and leaned back against the edge of the table. Bloody hell, that was uncomfortable. At least he'd stay awake. For a while, only the snap of cooling embers and the chirp of night insects disturbed the silence.

The table's edge dug into his back until his ribs began to ache. He glanced to the bed again, and saw Faith's shoulders trembling. Was she shivering?

Sitting up, he pulled the spare blanket off the table, then stalked toward the bed. He shook the second blanket out over her.

She gave a gasp, quickly bitten off, and he leaned over her body. A single tearstain glistened on her cheek in the dying firelight. "What's the matter?"

She hunched into a ball and shook her head, closing her eyes. Her shoulders shivered harder.

Warmth settled under his breastbone, sweeping away his frustrations. He sat beside her and stroked her still-damp hair. "Faith, you're all right now. It's going to be okay."

She stifled a sob. Tears trickled from under her lashes.

Something inside him snapped. A staggering well of emotion burst forth and flooded him. Crashing. Tearing. Consuming all his frustration and fear of the past days, until all that remained was a pain echoing that on her face.

Stunned, he tugged Faith into his lap. "Don't cry now," he murmured, his voice rasping. He folded her into his arms, grateful when he found that holding her seemed to lessen the ache that flowed from her tears and into him. "You're going to be okay, don't cry." He kissed her hair and stroked her back, then pulled the blankets up over them both.

At last, her shaking subsided into the long, rhythmic breaths of slumber. Hakon continued to stroke her hair, listening to the hiss of the fire as it died out, and the sound of the wind through the trees outside.

And still, he didn't sleep.

Chapter Fourteen

> *My father used to say that doing what's right is always difficult, and rarely ever as satisfying as doing the easy thing. It's a wonder we aren't all savages.*
> —*Faith's Journals, age twenty-six*

Faith sprang awake with a gasp. Troubling dreams of chaos and ruin dissolved into the thin light of early morning.

"I was about to wake you," said Hakon from the other side of the room.

She looked up.

He stood at the table, wrapping one of the army blankets into a bundle. Lifting the pack to his shoulder, he asked, "Sleep all right?"

"Not really," she admitted, avoiding his eyes.

What an idiot she'd been, crying in front of him last night. Not about her ordeal in the mine, but about him, and what she'd decided. She could never tell him she was Aesa. Every moment she spent with him felt like reaching for heaven, but always remaining just out of touch with it. Their lovemaking at the spring last night would be their last time. She couldn't bring herself to touch him that way again, and then have to let go and return home.

And home she would go, right after putting a stop

to Sebastian's plans with the carving.

"There's a bit of jerky, if you want it," Hakon said as he approached the bed, boots thumping across the floor.

She shook her head and stood. "I'm not hungry right now. Do you need me to carry anything?"

"No. Crate's empty. Everything that's left is in this bundle." One-handed, he shut the window, then went to the door. "Better get going before Sebastian and his mates show up."

She followed him outside, grateful for the other blanket wrapped around her shoulders. A damp mist had risen in the woods, chilling her.

As they walked through the golden haze, she thought of the images she'd seen when she read the bark map using her gift. She recalled an ancient Aborigine man, probably a tribal elder, fashioning a miniature wooden bird. The tiny statue had hardly looked menacing. In her mind's eye, she'd seen it used to sing to the spirits of the earth for blessings on the tribe. Their combined voices resonated, swelling up through the wooden bird's tiny, open mouth and into the sky. A beautiful song, full of life and joy that she'd felt to the very roots of her soul.

What a travesty she had to destroy the carving.

"Faith?"

"Hmm?" she mumbled, dodging a tree stump as it emerged from the mist in her path.

"I said, can you tell where Sebastian might be?"

"Not unless I can contact a ghost or touch something of his, like a footprint or a belonging. He isn't gifted, so even if we're right on top of him, I might not sense him. I can't even sense the gifted with total accuracy." A new chill zipped down her back, stronger than any the mist had yet caused. "Did you see footprints?"

"No. But we'd better walk faster, anyway. We'll use the back routes to the inn."

They spoke little for the rest of the hike. Faith strained her senses for any sign of pursuit, but their journey remained suspiciously uneventful. She worried more with every step.

When they reached the garden behind McGowan's Inn, Hakon urged her to wait behind a stand of ornamental trees. "If I yell 'run,' I want you to do it," he murmured. "Go straight back into the fields until you reach the river, and don't stop until you get there. If I can meet you by dark, I will."

She suppressed a shiver, eyeing the inn as if Sebastian's men might pounce from around the corners. "Wait." With her power, she reached into the air for ghostly vibrations that might warn her of a hostile presence. Nothing answered her. "I don't sense anything, but be careful, Hakon."

"Always." With a wink, he laid the army-blanket bundle at her feet, touched her shoulder, and then walked away. Rubbing her chilled arms, she watched his stealthy approach from her hiding place. He checked around the outside of the building before entering its back door.

She waited what seemed hours. Every moment that passed, her heart beat faster, and she wondered if he'd met with trouble. *To hell with this waiting.* She stood, grabbed Hakon's bundle, and then stalked toward the inn.

The back door opened, and she froze in mid-stride.

Hakon ducked his head out. "Get in here, quick."

Nerves jangling, she dropped the bundle and rushed inside.

Toby sat in a kitchen chair with an ice pack pressed to his eye. His light-brown forelock stood up in spikes clotted with darkened blood. More blood oozed from a gash down the side of his face.

Faith gasped and hurried to him. "What happened?"

Toby took the ice pack away, revealing an ugly, swollen black eye. "They took Mum and Lilah."

Lilah? Even through her worry for Miriam, Faith's heart sank.

"When? Which way?" Hakon asked.

"A little over an hour ago. I phoned the police, and they've already been and gone..." Toby looked up at Hakon with a pleading expression in one good eye. "Jesus, Hakon, what the hell are those bastards after?"

Hakon stiffened and bunched his fists, looking like he desperately wanted to punch someone. "I'll find them, mate, don't worry. Just tell me which direction they went."

"North. The north road." Toby swore and pressed the ice pack back over his eye. "They took the Camaro, but the motorbike's in the shed."

"Wh-What about Reilly?" Faith managed, fearing that the boy might not have gotten to Sydney, after all. "Was he taken, too?"

Toby shook his head. "He wasn't here."

Relief swept through her, followed at once by guilt. She dropped her gaze to the linoleum floor. Lord, if anything happened to Lilah or Miriam, it would be entirely her fault. She forced back tears, wanting to beg

Toby's forgiveness.

Hakon turned his back and stomped down the hall to the front lobby without another word. "We'll find them, Toby, I promise," she said, then hurried down the hall.

The front door stood open, and she heard the clomp of Hakon's boots as he stormed down the front porch steps. She jogged outside and shut the door after her. He had already started across the parking lot to a small shed near the trees. "I can help," she called.

He spun around, looking angrier than she'd ever seen him. "You have helped enough. Go home, Faith! I don't want you here."

Wounded, she descended the porch steps. "I want to help. This is all my fault—"

"You're damn right, it is. You've been a disaster and a bloody liar since you got here."

She winced at that, but jogged across the parking lot. By the time she reached him, he'd thrown open the shed door and begun rolling the bike out. She touched his arm as he stalked past. "Please, listen—"

With a violent swipe of his foot, he put the kickstand down, then snatched her by the arms.

She froze in his grasp, her skin blazing with his anger even without the use of her powers.

His aqua stare iced over. "I've done more than enough listening to you, God damn it. These people are the only family I have. Toby's face is mangled, Miriam's too old to be dragged through the mountains, and God knows what they'll do to Lilah—" He cut himself off with a snarl and thrust her away, turning back to the bike.

Stumbling, Faith gathered her courage as he

straddled the bike. "Miriam might still be wearing the necklace I gave her. I can track her by it."

He stilled, his body rigid, not looking at her. When he spoke, his voice had gained an ominous calm. "Come on, then."

She slid onto the bike. Instead of touching him, she reached behind her and gripped the bar behind her seat. He kick-started the engine, and they peeled out of the lot as though the devil himself were chasing them.

Faith's hair whipped into her eyes until they watered, but she dared not blink and risk interrupting a moment of her power flow. The precious instant between stopping her power and restarting it might be where she finally sensed Miriam's necklace. "There's not much room in a Camaro. Do you think they might have let someone go, or left one of their men behind?"

"Don't know," Hakon shouted over the whistling wind. "Anything yet?"

Frustrated, she shook her bangs out of her eyes. "Noth— Wait. This fork up ahead, take a right." She focused on a tiny, white-noise fizz of energy in her head, trying to blot out the roar of the motorbike.

He turned so quickly, the bike lurched at a dangerous angle. Faith clutched his waist until the bike righted itself again. He leaned low over the handlebars, and they sped still faster.

A few miles farther on, the road dead-ended in a gravel bed. They skidded to a stop in a spray of stones, lurching dangerously. The Camaro sat akilter in the ditch, its nose crumpled and spewing steam.

Hakon cut the bike's engine. The car's back window had been smashed, and glass glittered all over the road. "They'll have heard us coming, if they're still around," he said. "No sense trying to be quiet now, but get behind the car just in case."

She did as he instructed, but went on scanning the woods and pushing the limits of her power. Her earlier sense of the quartz necklace remained as weak as it had been before. She refused to dwell on the possible implications of that.

Cupping his hands around his mouth, Hakon shouted, "Miriam! Lilah! Coo-ee!"

Birds fell silent in the trees around them. Faith stared up the rising slopes beyond the gravel bed. Hakon called again.

Blam! A gunshot shattered the air. Faith dropped to the ground just as one of the Camaro's tires blew. A flock of birds burst into the sky, shrieking as they flew away. Air squealed from the gaping hole in the tire's sidewall.

"Just a warning, Faith. I could make it closer, if you want," Sebastian called.

Hakon crouched beside her and pushed her between his body and the car. "Come out where we can see you, you bloody son of a bitch!" he roared.

"No, I think I'm a bit smarter than that," said Sebastian. "You've been a lot of trouble to me, Faith. Come to me, and we'll call it even. You know what I want."

Shaking with rage, Faith stood up just enough to squint over Hakon's shoulder into the trees.

"What are you doing?" he snapped, grabbing at her shirt.

"Just one look. One look, and he's flame-broiled," she growled.

Hakon wrenched the tail of her shirt, and she

almost collapsed. "We don't know where he's got the women. Stay down!"

"Let go!" She jerked her shirt out of his grasp. "He needs me. He'll shoot you without thinking twice."

"You can't possibly be thinking of going up there." Anger sparked in his eyes, mingled with a flash of alarm that sharpened even as she watched. "You aren't going alone."

With her thoughts racing, she scanned the trees again, then looked back at Hakon. The agony in his stare pulled at her until she ached. She remembered the first Hakon wearing that same look in her dreams, when he'd held his dead wife in his arms. She knew she should stop comparing the two, but *that look*...so familiar...

An idea burst upon her, and hope surged. Even if he didn't remember her, some thread of him was still connected to her. It might be enough. "I won't be alone," she said. "Give me your gran's ring."

"How the hell is that going to help?"

"I'm going to wear it while I'm with them," she whispered, "and you'll follow me through it."

"I'm not the goddamn psychic!"

"No," she said, hardly able to breathe past the pounding of her heart, "but I swear you'll be able to find me while I have it. Please, Hakon, trust me. Just once more."

Looking pained, he closed his eyes. For a moment, he sat still, but then he pulled the ring from his pocket and slapped it into her hand.

The ring sizzled with energy in her palm. She gritted her teeth against the surge and heat, then closed her fist around the delicate silver piece. Touching his arm, she said, "You'll find me, I swear it. Call the police, and lead them to me. I will protect Miriam and Lilah if it's the last thing I do." She struggled to meet his gaze. "I owe you that."

She rose and turned toward the trees, calling, "How do we know the women are alive?"

Sebastian's laughter echoed down into the gravel bed. When he spoke, his voice rang with the confidence of a man who was certain he'd already won. "Oh, Faith, don't be stupid. Why would I ruin my chance at ensuring your cooperation? Come with me, solve the bark maps, and your friends will be returned unhurt."

With a final glance at Hakon over her shoulder, Faith marched toward Sebastian's voice. She slipped Aesa's ring onto her finger as she went. *Please, God, let this work. It has to work.* Hakon had to sense her somehow, if any shred of him still remembered her as Aesa the way she hoped.

She climbed the slope out of the gravel bed, feeling his gaze on her as she went. The waves of his reluctance drifted over her, and she had to force her feet to keep moving.

Sebastian waited for her at the crest of the hill. He wore a pack, and carried a gun strapped prominently to his hip. He didn't bother to draw it on her. "I know you're capable of a few pyrotechnics, sweetheart. Why don't we just keep a lid on that by remembering I've got your friends stashed away somewhere, eh?" He tilted his head over the hill. "Let's be off. The maps are waiting."

Faith walked past him with her head high, and let slip a few choice words without troubling to lower her voice.

From the corner of her eye, she saw him raise a fist as if to smash it in her face, but he sneered and lowered it again. Muscles bulged in his jaw.

Well, that was one thing in her favor. She held the secret to finding the wooden carving, so he couldn't harm her, either.

For now.

****

Hakon watched, shaking with wrath, until Faith had disappeared from sight. He rose to his feet and glared into the woods, wishing he had Faith's power to burn things with a mere look.

Bastard. He hoped Sebastian was counting every precious breath, because it wouldn't be long until Hakon strangled them out of him.

With a scream of rage, he drove his fist into the passenger door of the Camaro. The steel dented, and glass from the broken back window pattered onto the rear seat. He narrowed his eyes at his now-bleeding hand. His knuckles throbbed, and he considered hitting the door again. No. Better to break them on Sebastian's face. "You're a dead man, Hale!"

"You first, my friend," said a voice behind him.

Hakon ducked just in time to avoid another gunshot. The bullet blasted into the quarter panel of the twisted car.

Carl stood a few strides away, laughing, with a rifle trained on Hakon. "I doubt you'll be needing the bike, will you? Didn't think so." He turned the rifle toward the motorbike.

Damn it, that was his only way back to a phone! Hakon rushed the man with his fists raised.

Carl's eyes bulged, and he turned the rifle back

toward Hakon a fraction too late. Hakon slammed into him with a furious roar. Carl staggered backward, dragging Hakon with him, and Hakon seized the barrel of the gun in both hands. His bleeding fingers slipped on the barrel. Carl tore it from his grasp, and fired just as Hakon dropped out of range. He gripped Carl's shirt, hauled him closer, and then slammed a knee into the man's groin.

His opponent groaned and crumpled. Hakon ripped the gun away, then smashed the rifle butt into the man's face. Carl sank to the ground.

Spinning away, Hakon stumbled toward the bike. His mind raced ahead. *Nearest public phone.*

Something plowed into the backs of his knees. Grunting, Hakon collapsed over the top of Carl's body and onto the gravel. The rifle fell away. He rolled to his knees just as Carl swung a booted foot at his head. He dodged, grabbed the man's other ankle, and ripped him off his feet by sheer force. Carl yelped and landed on his back with a *whump*, gasping like a fish. Blood smeared his face into an unrecognizable mess.

Hakon snatched the rifle and lurched back upright. He staggered toward the smashed car, then reached through the busted back window to the tiny cargo spot behind the rear seats. Broken glass cut at his arm. He ignored it, a minor nuisance against his need to keep Faith from harm.

Thank God Lilah hadn't thought to clean everything out of the car. He extracted a length of heavy rope, then flung the rifle toward the motorbike.

Stalking back toward Carl, he barked, "On your belly. Now."

The man rolled, limp as a rag doll. Hakon trussed

him hand to foot like a wayward calf and left him there in the dirt.

Wiping away the sweat trickling into his eyes, Hakon picked up the rifle, then returned to the bike.

A few kilometers down the road, he found a public phone and called the police, giving his location and the basic circumstances. He drove back to the gravel bed to find Carl trying to crawl away. The man had made it partway up the slopes. "Where do you think you're going?" Hakon demanded, holding the rifle on him.

Carl froze where he lay, then cursed.

"That's right. You just stay put until they exchange that rope for handcuffs, mate. You've got some explaining to do, starting with kidnapping and murder, and maybe ending up with where Sebastian's going."

Minutes ticked by. Hakon squinted into the trees, aching to follow Faith. He tried to focus, to feel her presence the way she'd sworn he would, but he could sense nothing. Every time his thoughts stilled enough to listen inward, Carl shuffled and broke his concentration.

The police arrived at last. The officer who emerged from the car removed his hat and rubbed a hand through his dark-blond hair. Hakon recognized John Graham. "Bloody hell, Hakon, are you the one responsible for all this?"

"Just for the bloke in the ditch," he answered, pointing. "He'll be wanted for murder and attempted kidnapping. I'll let him give you the details."

"Does this have anything to do with Miriam's disappearance?"

"Damn right, it does. The other men—two, I think—went up into the mountains. They've got another woman, too, John. An American that I was leading on a hike. I saw which way they went."

"Don't you dare follow them, Hakon. Leave this to me and the rangers."

Hakon pressed the rifle into John's hands. "You never saw me." He turned away and loped upward into the trees.

"Hakon! Damn it! Hakon!" John's voice faded out on a growl of anger.

Searching the brush, Hakon caught the scuff marks of boot tread in the leaf litter. He stalked after them as fast as he could without losing the trail, hating Sebastian, angry with Faith for promising something she had no way of delivering. How the hell could he find her when she was the one with the supernatural gifts? His whole world had gone to hell since she'd arrived. "As soon as I find you, woman, I'm sending you right back home, and good riddance."

They couldn't have gotten far. Forty minutes, or maybe an hour's head start? The sons of bitches had to sleep some time.

By midafternoon, he'd tracked Sebastian's party past the outskirts of Kurrajong Heights and into Wollemi National Park. Without food or clean water, he knew he wouldn't last much longer. *Well,* he thought grimly, *if I catch up to them, I can always take their rations.*

At the bottom of a slot canyon, he lost the trail. He knew Faith could have managed these steep climbs, and Lilah too, if pressed, but had they dragged Miriam down here as well? He paused, staring up into the sliver of powder-blue sky that remained visible over the canyon walls. "Come on, Faith. You said I'd find you."

Nothing.

He swore softly and closed his eyes. The wind whistled down over the rock and through the profuse tree ferns lining the canyon bottom. Far off, a cockatoo shrieked. Hakon filtered out the sounds, and tried to concentrate on Faith and the ring.

Voices. He heard the low hum of someone talking, and opened his eyes in surprise, expecting to see one of the men at the end of the canyon. As soon as he looked around, the talking stopped. He turned in a circle, checking the high ridges to be sure he hadn't been mistaken. "Come on, Faith, where are you?" He closed his eyes once more, and sought the silent focus.

No matter how he tried, he couldn't regain the voices. Cursing, he opened his eyes and stalked back to the lower end of the canyon, then sat on an outcropping of rock. He rubbed blood-crusted fingers over his stubble, debating whether to go back and pick up the trail from where he'd last seen it. The longer he waited, the colder the trail would become, and he knew he'd have less and less hope of finding her.

Less hope of ever seeing that smile, or running his fingers through her pale-blond hair. Hearing the husky murmur in her voice as he touched her silky skin...

Come to me.

Hakon shot upright with his heart thumping, as if someone had whispered the words in his ear. He spun around, but saw nothing except the nodding of the ferns as the wind passed.

Impossible.

Panting, he conjured another image of Faith, this time lying on the grass beside a moonlit spring. He remembered her grin as she brushed his chest with her fingers.

Come to me. I'm here, the voice whispered. *Find me.*

He broke into a run down the canyon. Gravel spewed out from under his bootfalls, and he jumped over tangles of brush in his path. "That's it, baby, keep talking."

Chapter Fifteen

I tried reading a prehistoric bowl once, when I worked at the museum. Not smart. I passed out, and regained consciousness three days later in the hospital.
　　　—Faith's Journals, age twenty-four

"Everything is going to be okay," said Faith, though she didn't know, herself, if that were true. They'd been trekking through the mountains all day, prodded on by Sebastian's constant threats. Faith wiped sweat from her brow, then tore a strip from the bottom of her tattered oxford shirt, and handed it to Lilah.

"I don't know who you are, or who that man is," Lilah gasped out, "but I want to go home." She took the cloth and pressed it to a cut on her cheek. Insects buzzed in the afternoon heat.

"I'm sorry. I really am. I'm going to try and get us out of this, I swear," Faith whispered.

"Why am I even *in* it? Does this have something to do with Hakon and that boy? I took the kid to Syd—"

"Shh-h-h!"

"—ney like he asked. What's going on?"

Faith glanced around, fearing that Sebastian might have overheard. Lilah had taken Reilly to Sydney? Why had she come back? For Hakon?

Sebastian had stopped them for a short rest. So far,

Faith hadn't seen Earl or Miriam. Lilah didn't know their whereabouts, and Sebastian wouldn't volunteer any information when she demanded it. She couldn't even sense the necklace anymore, which could have meant they were too far away, or Miriam had removed it, or something more menacing had happened.

Please let her be all right, Faith prayed. The only good news so far was that Reilly had been delivered safely out of Sebastian's reach.

"Time's up, ladies," Sebastian said, then smiled as if they were on an enjoyable day trip. "Faith, if you'll read this map, we can be on our way."

Faith scowled at him, but got to her feet anyway. She stalked toward him and snatched the bark map out of his hands, then slapped her hand over its surface. "I don't feel a damn thing."

"Careful, lady. You're still in a precarious position to be that testy."

"Suppose I need a day to make sure I'm reading the map right."

"Suppose I find a way to speed up the process," he countered, tossing a meaningful look in Lilah's direction. "You want your friend to go back home without too much damage, don't you?"

Faith clenched her jaw and pushed aside a guilty twinge. She had no reason to like Lilah, but that was no reason to wish the woman ill, either. Faith drew herself up to her full height. "You hurt her, and you'll wish you'd never met me."

He chuckled. "The map, if you don't mind."

With a glare full of deepest loathing, she laid her hand over the map again and called on her power.

"What are you doing?" Lilah asked behind her.

Faith didn't answer. She let the map's energy flow into her fingertips. At once, she received a barrage of images overlying one another: men sitting in a circle talking, others playing instruments, and storms crossing a vast expanse of flat, red earth. Some of the images repeated from her reading of the first map. Others were new, stronger, piling on top of the old ones. The scenes shifted so quickly, so powerfully, that her legs trembled. Breath evaded her. With a moan, she dropped the map and bent double under piercing pain.

"What? What did you see?" When she looked up, Sebastian's eyes took on a predatory gleam.

"It's too much," she said, panting. "I can't—can't concentrate. This map's twenty thousand years old."

His hand clamped on the collar of her shirt, and he jerked her upright. "You *will* read it."

Reeling, Faith pushed at him. "Get off me!"

"Don't think you're fooling me," he barked in her face. "I know you can read that map, and I know you're trying to stall me."

"I. Am. Not," she ground out, trying to dispel the whirling sensation with anger. Her stomach twisted, and she groaned again as nausea plowed over her.

"Faith? Please, leave her alone," Lilah said, her voice a mere whisper underneath the roar of psychic energy still raging in Faith's head. "Faith, what's wrong?"

"You're going to solve these maps, damn it," Sebastian snarled.

"It's—too old—on top of the other one," she said, still shivering.

"What the hell is happening?" Lilah asked. Faith felt the woman's arm slide around her back, and leaned gratefully into Lilah's tall frame. Whatever their differences, at least the woman had some sense of compassion.

Sebastian shoved the redhead away, then seized Faith by her shirt collar. *"Where is it?"*

"I don't know!" Faith struggled to maintain consciousness as bright lights danced at the edges of her vision. Only Sebastian's hold on her shirt kept her on her feet. "It's too much. I swear...can't read it..."

Stay awake, Faith, said a familiar voice in her head. The background roar calmed a little, and her grip on reality returned.

David's ghost. "Oh, thank God," she whispered. She pushed Sebastian's hand away and caught her breath. "Where's Miriam?"

Sebastian answered first. "You don't get to Miriam until I get to the end of these maps."

She's alive, David said, and Faith wilted in relief. *Can't see her, only sense her.*

"Hakon?" she asked aloud.

"What *about* Hakon?" Lilah demanded.

"Everyone just be *quiet* for a minute," said Faith, putting her hands to her aching head.

Sebastian hovered in front of her, radiating greed. His eyes glittered hopefully, and she knew he was waiting for her to reveal the location of the carving.

She rubbed her forehead. *David. Where is Hakon?*
North. Closing fast.

Elation surged through her body and almost drowned out her connection with David's ghost. She didn't dare to hope Hakon remembered who she really was—or had been. Closing a protective hand over the silver ring on her finger, she asked, *Does he sense me?*

Don't know. Get to the carving. I'll lead you, David told her.

She opened her mouth in surprise and indignation. What was he thinking? *The hell I will. If Miriam's alive, I'm going to find her!*

The carving! David's fury sizzled along her nerves.

You're dead! What are you going to do with it?

Not me, the ghost answered, and a chill swept up her back. *Sebastian.*

You're out of your mind if you think I'm helping him find that thing.

You aren't helping. I am. An icy sensation settled on her shoulder.

Faith yelped and sprang away from the ghostly touch, horrified. David had gained power since she'd last spoken with him. A lot of power, no doubt fueled by anger over his murder. *Why? Why would you help him when he let you die?*

David didn't answer. A stinging cloud of wrath impelled her forward. She shied away again, but he kept coming at her. She had no choice but to retreat.

So this must be the favor he wanted in return for his help. She put a hand over her face. "Oh, God, what have I done?" Miserable, she dropped her hands to her sides.

"What's the matter? Have you picked up a trail?" Sebastian asked. He grabbed his backpack and trotted toward her, forgetting Lilah completely.

If she'd felt guilty before for endangering Miriam and Lilah, it paled beside the shame that filled her now. In her hurry to save Reilly, she'd all but promised to hand over a deadly artifact to a man who would use it to do unspeakable damage to thousands of people. Maybe millions. Who knew how much power such an object contained? Whatever evil Sebastian did with it, the blame could be laid entirely at her feet.

When Hakon found her, he'd discover what she'd done. The look on his face... She couldn't bear to have the image in her mind.

Only one thing to do, then: she had to find the carving and clean up her own mess before Hakon found her. Swallowing hard, she slipped the silver ring from her finger and put it in her pocket. "Let's go," she mumbled, stepping away from David's chilling touch once more.

The ghost didn't speak, forcing her along down a narrow game trail. *You just wait until I find a way to pay you back for this, David, you son of a—*

A painful charge of energy burst at her back, and she leapt forward. David propelled her onward without mercy. Sebastian followed, pushing Lilah with him. The woman yelped, and Faith heard her stumble.

They hurried down the trail and past a sluggish creek. Seething, Faith wondered how long David would be able to maintain such a barrage of energy. He had no reply to any of her protests, so she guessed he was focusing all his power to send her in the direction he wanted. *You can't keep this up,* she taunted, but again she received no answer.

"What's happening?" asked Lilah.

"We're doing what Sebastian wants," Faith said, "for the moment."

"I don't understand." Lilah panted behind her, footsteps crunching as she jogged along.

Static raged on Faith's left, and she turned away from it into a stand of eucalyptus, where she found a new trail. "Trust me, Lilah, you don't want to."

For a while, she heard nothing but the sounds of Sebastian and Lilah following wherever she led, and felt only the constant attack of David's drive. At this rate, by the time they located the carving, she feared she'd collapse. There would be no one left to stop Sebastian from using the artifact in whatever destructive way he saw fit. Faith suspected the object's first victim would be Lilah...or herself.

At least Hakon wouldn't be there to see her failure.

****

Lost.

He'd just felt her a moment ago, he could have sworn it.

Hakon closed his eyes and tried to pick up the filmy thread of Faith's voice in his thoughts. Nothing surfaced. The thread had been broken.

Alarmed, he jogged back to the group of boulders where he'd last sensed her. *If you really had sensed her, and aren't just going off your nut,* he scolded himself. He flopped down in a patch of grass to catch his breath.

Maybe he just wanted to believe he'd heard her calling for him, out of guilt. He'd let her go in the first place, when he'd sworn to himself he wouldn't let her be hurt again. "Like a damned ring is going to find her for me, if I can't do it myself," he snapped.

But hadn't he felt her presence anyway, whenever she was near him but not visible? When they'd arrived at the Miriam's inn, he'd lain awake all night thinking of her. She'd been asleep in the next room, but every moment she had seemed near enough to touch. At first he'd thought it merely sexual attraction—any man with a pulse would have wanted her—but the pull had reached deeper than that.

Why should he have felt so connected to her? What made her any more special than the next woman?

He got to his feet and stalked into the trees. Judging by the landmarks where he'd heard her voice— or *thought* he'd heard her—she was heading south, southwest. Slim chances, in a park this big, but he'd have to work with it.

Some time later, he came across a small waterfall. He removed his boots and waded into the pool, letting the cool downpour wash over his sweaty skin and soak his clothing. Better than overheating, although he couldn't drink the water without something to purify it. He closed his eyes against the spray and wiped his stubbled face, deciding where to go next.

Then he heard the rhythmic *thup-thup-thup* of a helicopter. Glancing up, he saw one of the ranger choppers soar into the patch of sky visible through the treetops. Hakon ducked backward into the waterfall, letting it splash over him. If they saw him now, they'd try to get him out before he found Faith. He didn't care if they found her first, but no way would he wait uselessly at the ranger station while she was missing.

As soon as the helicopter had gone, he put his boots back on and began walking again. He hovered between anger with himself for letting Faith leave, and anger at her for getting right back into trouble. *Hardest-earned trail money I ever worked for. Why again did I start doing hikes?* he thought with a snarl of self-disgust.

He came across a raspberry thicket in the afternoon, and ate as much as he could. There'd be no way of telling what other food he might find, or how long it would take him to pick up Faith's trail again. He hoped like hell she would be alive when he got there. The alternative—God, he couldn't even spend a second thinking about the alternative.

"You look a bit worse for wear, mate," said a gravelly voice.

Hakon spun around, ready to lunge at a person, but came face-to-nose with a horse instead. Startled, he backed away and looked up at its rider.

Idiot. Too distracted, again, by Faith, and the way her safety drove him out of his mind. Sebastian could've sneaked up on him in an army tank loaded with explosives.

The man in the saddle looked as weathered as the gray horse beneath him. He tipped the wide brim of his oilskin hat. "On walkabout?"

"Not exactly." Hakon spied a second horse behind the first, wearing a bridle and empty saddle.

The horseman grinned, and his moustache bristled. "Lost, then."

Hakon risked a smile in return. "Also not exactly."

Chuckling, the man waved a hand at the riderless horse behind him. "Give you a lift? I'm headed south anyway, and the colt's already got all my spares on it." Laugh lines crinkled at the corners of his pale eyes. "We can both be 'not exactly lost' for a while."

Hakon swung up into the empty saddle. "Thanks."

"Don't mention it." The man untied the second horse's reins from his own saddle, and handed them back to Hakon. "Name's Joshua Vaughan."

"Hakon Ivarsson," he answered, looping the reins over his horse's head.

"I've got a couple of rabbits, if you're hungry," the

horseman said.

"Sorry, I can't stop."

Joshua straightened and looked back over his shoulder. "You dodging the rangers? Saw them fly over."

"I'm looking for a woman."

The horseman's laughter echoed through the forest. "You're hell and gone from finding one of them out here, mate." He touched his heels to his horse's sides, and they started off.

"She and two other women have...gone missing. Have you seen anyone pass through here?"

"Missing, eh? So that's what the rangers are on about." The man lifted his hat off his head and rubbed his wild, dark-blond hair. "Ain't seen a soul, but no one'll be ducking out of doors by sundown. There's a storm blowing down from the north side of the mountains."

Great. As if he needed more complications. "Look, Joshua, I know you don't know me from Adam, but I need to borrow your horse for a day or two. I've got to find this woman before she's hurt. If anything happens to the horse, I'll settle up with you through Toby McGowan in Bowen Mountain." He left out any mention that something might happen to *him*, as well.

When the man didn't reply, he added, "I'll pay you twice what the horse is worth."

Joshua whistled, long and low, and turned around in his saddle to peer shrewdly at Hakon. "She your sweetheart, or something?"

Hakon couldn't answer. He gritted his teeth, trying to force down the crushing sensation in his chest. The horse seemed to sense his agitation, because it pranced sideways along the trail and tossed its sable-black head.

After a moment, Joshua slapped his hat back on his head, then pulled his mount to a halt. Hakon stopped behind him, holding his breath. The man's gaze traveled over Hakon's figure. He nodded at the horse. "That colt's not fully broke. He might buck you if he spooks."

Hakon patted the animal's neck. A mountain horse, for sure. He probably knew the trails better than Hakon did, green or not. "We'll manage."

Rubbing his craggy face with one gloved hand, the man asked, "McGowan, you said? His mum owns the inn there in Bowen?"

Hakon nodded, anxious to be away. His mount stamped and snorted.

"My uncle was Miriam's husband's best mate. I've been meaning to look the old girl up." Joshua sidestepped his horse to the trailside. "Get on with you, then. There's some extra rain gear in the saddlebags."

Hakon bit his tongue, not wanting to tell the man that Miriam was one of the women in danger. "Thanks. I owe you." He kicked his horse into a lope, and headed away.

He drove the colt hard, focusing on Faith and trusting the animal to find his footing on the easy trail. As the day wore on, his anxiety increased. He found neither sense nor sign of her. The wind whistled through the branches, and lead-gray cloud cover obliterated the last of the sun. Lightning flared across the sky, followed by a crash of thunder. The horse whinnied and balked under him. Wrestling with the reins, Hakon had no choice but to dismount.

He led the horse on foot from there, pausing only

to shrug into the slightly-small oilskin he found in the saddlebag and clap the extra hat over his head. Rain began to hammer down. The colt flattened its ears and jerked its head up, trying to escape the deluge.

Crash. A bolt of lightning speared a nearby tree. The trunk cracked and split in two, slamming into the ground barely a breath away. The colt screamed and reared, its hooves thrashing the air.

"Damn it!" With his ears ringing, Hakon grasped for the flailing reins.

Slam. One of the colt's forehooves struck his arm. Hakon cursed and grabbed again for the reins. Seizing them, he pulled the animal down by sheer force. Pain burned through his left forearm. "Easy, boy. Easy, now, mate," he said over the noise of wind and thunder. "I don't like it any better than you do."

The colt whinnied again, dancing sideways. Lightning flashed again, and Hakon saw the smoldering ruin of the blasted tree. "Best we get out of here," he said, climbing back into the saddle. "Sorry, but you've got four legs, and you're faster." He nudged the horse into a gentle trot, patting its neck and murmuring until it settled. The blow to his arm had been a glancing one, but it ached like the devil. By the time they'd reached a park road, the injury throbbed painfully, and both he and the horse were wet through in spite of the oilskin coat draped over them both.

"Least the footing's better," Hakon muttered as the colt trotted along in the gravel, snorting. Wind rushed through the treetops.

As they went on, lights beamed from behind him, stretching past him and his horse into the darkness beyond. A car had come up behind them. He turned in the saddle to squint at the approaching vehicle.

Then its driver hit the gas.

Cursing, Hakon jabbed his horse's sides with his heels. The colt scrambled to obey, and they shot forward.

The car's engine roared. Hakon didn't dare look behind him as they galloped headlong down the road. Rain pelted him, and he leaned low over the straining colt's neck, squinting at the sides of the road in the glare of the car's headlights. Ditches, poor footing, steep banks. Nowhere to turn. "Come on, run!" he shouted in the horse's ear. The engine revved again, sounding closer.

There! Hakon saw a low slope leading up off the road, and jerked on the horse's right rein. The colt flattened its ears and sprang to the right, flying up the slope with its breath churning.

The vehicle rocketed past them, horn blaring. Hakon spun his mount around and saw the car lurch to a sliding stop with its nose toward the opposite side of the road. The driver door opened.

"Hakon, look out!"

Miriam.

Blam! The colt shrilled again as a tree branch blasted apart overhead. Hakon's heart stuttered at the near-miss, and he fought to keep the horse under control.

In the glow of the headlights, Hakon saw the driver of the car wrestle with something, and then emerge from the car. The man peered into the trees, then stumbled closer, wiping rain out of his eyes.

Earl.

Hakon gave the colt's shoulder a silent rub and

backed the animal deeper into the trees, skirting the place where they'd come up the bank. Slowly, he urged his mount back down the slope a couple of meters away, until only a few fringes of wet shrubbery hid them.

Earl stood at the roadside, staring upward into their last hiding place. He held a rifle low at his side, and spat a gob of what must have been tobacco into the weeds.

Now. Hakon kicked the colt's sides again, and it bolted toward the man. The horse's body slammed into Earl's. The rifle fell into the weeds, and the man went flying onto his back. The horse shied and reared, striking the air over Earl's body.

Earl shouted and held one arm over his face while pushing backward with the other.

The colt came down on the man's leg with a *crack*. Earl howled in agony and clutched the broken limb. The horse hopped sideways and champed at the bit, ears twitching.

"Easy, now. Easy," Hakon said, patting the trembling horse's shoulder. "Well done, boy." He backed the horse away, dismounted, then picked up the fallen rifle.

"Hakon? Hakon, are you all right?" came Miriam's terrified voice.

"Yes. You?"

"I-I think my arm is broken," she called.

Hakon tied his horse to a tree, then approached Earl with the rifle raised. Rain spilled down off the brim of his hat, blurring the man's figure as Earl folded himself over his broken leg and whimpered. He cocked the rifle and glared down at the defeated man. "I'd call that an eye for an eye, wouldn't you, mate?"

Hakon turned away and strode toward the car, whose wipers were still whisking over the windscreen. "Miriam?" He ducked through the open driver door.

Miriam had been tied to the passenger seat. She turned a tearstained face toward Hakon. "Is he g-gone?"

Swallowing the lump in his throat, Hakon put the rifle down, then knelt on the driver's seat and reached for the knots of the rope. "Don't worry, old girl, he isn't going to be bothering anyone anytime soon. I'll get you out. What happened?"

"H-He took Lilah. He forced us to go with him. They hurt my Toby—"

"Toby's all right, I've seen him."

"I f-fell down a slope." Miriam's fragile expression crumpled. "That horrid Hale man took Lilah and Faith. He said s-something about a map. He w-wanted us to come after him..." She gave a sob that dissolved into sniffles as he untied the rest of the ropes. He went around the passenger side of the car, then pulled her out.

Cradling her arm, she pressed her tiny frame against his bigger one. He wrapped his arms around her. "Oh, my boy, my wonderful, brave boy..."

Hakon kissed the top of her head, struggling to master his own emotions. "You're all right now, love. Let's fix that arm."

He glanced at Earl, but the man hadn't moved. Good. Probably passed out, the bastard. Hakon urged Miriam into the driver's seat, then splinted and tied her arm the best he could. He pulled the ropes from the passenger seat. "Did you see a ranger station on the way through here?"

"Yes. Not far back, we passed a post."

"All right, I'm going to take this man on the horse, and lead you there. You follow in the car. Can you do that with your injured arm?"

"I think so."

Hakon tied Earl's hands together and hauled him upright. By then, the man had regained consciousness, and he yelped in pain. When Hakon approached the horse, dragging his captive alongside him, Earl pulled backward with a look of terror on his face. "Don't bother trying to get away," Hakon rumbled. He grinned and tipped his head toward the horse. "Kicked your arse good, didn't he?"

The colt snorted and pricked its ears.

The storm had leveled out into a steady downpour. Hakon swung up into the saddle again, then hauled Earl up over the horse's withers, where he drooped like a sack of flour.

Miriam had turned the car around, and as Hakon trotted his horse away, she followed.

By the time they arrived at the ranger station, Earl had passed out again. Hakon didn't know how bad the man's broken leg was, and didn't much care. Whatever grief he got as a result of his injuries was merely payback for what he'd done to Miriam.

The ranger station was well-lit. In the glow of floodlights, Hakon saw two men jogging toward them. "What happened?"

"This man attempted to kidnap the woman in the car behind me. His leg's broken, and so's her arm."

Miriam got out of the car. One of the rangers wrapped his coat around her and guided her toward the station.

The other ranger laid a hand on the colt's bridle. "Looks like you and your horse could both use a warm bed."

"There's another woman, still out there."

"Was she with you?"

Hakon's stomach lurched. He couldn't bring himself to form the word "no." "Yes," he lied.

"All right, wait here," the ranger said, taking his hand off the colt's bridle. "I'll get someone to take your horse and—"

"I've got it. Send rangers." Spinning the horse around, Hakon kicked it into a gallop back down the road.

"Hey!" the ranger called.

Hakon only pressed the colt harder. "Sorry, boy, we're not done yet."

Miriam had said Sebastian expected Earl to come after him, no doubt to spirit Sebastian out of the mountains once he found his mind-control trinket. If Earl had been heading down this road, it was good enough for him. The son of a bitch would have a nasty surprise when he discovered his cohorts had been dispatched.

You're next, mate, he thought, boiling with fury.

Chapter Sixteen

> *My favorite childhood game was hide-and-seek, even before I gained my gifts. I guess the need to find things is ingrained in the Markham family bloodline.*
> —*Faith's Journals, age nineteen*

Sara Waverly stared across her desk at the young man with wild, short black hair and honey-colored eyes. Reilly Corcoran looked as miserable as she felt. He'd just explained that her sister was missing, and Hakon, too, having gone after her. His gaze drifted to the reproduction Rosetta Stone hanging on her wall, and his shoulders bowed with guilt.

She softened a little and mustered an unruffled air, though she was anything but. "All right, here's what we're going to do—"

The ringing phone interrupted her. "Excuse me for a minute, Reilly." She picked up the handset. "Sara Waverly."

"Doctor Waverly, it's Jack Redmond at Flintrop."

Vines of dread began knotting themselves around her insides. She smoothed out a flawless elevation drawing on her desk. "What do you have for me?" she forced out.

"Whatever's happening down there in Australia, you'd better get Faith out," he said, sounding much less hushed than the last time they'd spoken. "David Beck is dead. Carl Mancuso and Earl Masterson are facing arrest, and Sebastian's vanished off our radar. Elliott's panicking."

Self-righteous fury exploded inside Sara, and she just barely kept it under control. "Of course he's panicking. His wheeling and dealing to get the gifted under his wing is backfiring on him."

"No, Sara. I mean it. The old man's ready to send you whatever resources you need to get Faith out of there and stop Sebastian."

She heard someone bark an order in the background. Jack's line clicked, then clicked again. "Miss Waverly," said an ancient-sounding male voice.

Sara recognized Elliott Flintrop at once. "*Doctor* Waverly," she said in her frostiest voice.

"Sara," the man went on as if he hadn't heard, "I'm a lot of things, but I do draw the line somewhere. Sebastian's disappeared with a set of Aborigine bark maps, which lead to a carving that, if the stories are right, can be used for worldwide mind control. He's got no abilities of his own to manipulate the carving. Your sister is the key to using it."

"Were *you* going to use it?" Sara snapped.

Elliott cleared his throat. "I was planning on selling the maps to a museum to finance..."

"Your search for the gifted," she finished, layering all the accusation she could rally into her voice. "Let me get this straight. You're sorry now because *you* might become the victim of one of your own bad ideas?"

A moment of silence followed. At last, the old man took a long, deep breath. "I haven't been in the best of health," he said finally, "and I have no family heir to whom I choose to leave my estate, so it will most likely be dissolved. I'm prepared to name you and Faith Markham the heirs to a large percentage of the Flintrop fortune, if you can stop Sebastian from using that carving."

Sara felt the blood drain from her face. Had he just said...?

"My estate totals a considerable several million dollars, Miss Waverly," Elliott went on. "Even you know the benefits of what I'm proposing. No more bowing to financial review boards for your projects, no more scraping to meet the expectations of more affluent firms..."

Insulted and outraged—mostly because he was right—she crumpled the corner of the elevation drawing in her fist. "Why would you want to be a Good Samaritan now, Elliott? Don't you think you're a bit late for that?"

The man coughed a few times. Sara heard the wet rasp in the sound, and wondered just how sick he really was. When he spoke again, his voice was as rough as sandpaper. "I'd like to finish up my affairs with a clear conscience for the things my family has done."

Trembling with fury, Sara closed her eyes. His money couldn't fix the devastation he'd caused everyone whose life he ruined. And she'd have bet it wouldn't clear his conscience, either, if he had any shred of decency at all. She ached to say the words, but they wouldn't come out. Instead, she found herself asking, "What exactly are you proposing to do?"

"I'll send two men to Sebastian's last known location, to bring him in for questioning over his part in all of this. Your sister has the ability to contain and destroy that artifact. If she can accomplish it, she'll receive half of the reward."

"Which would work perfectly, if I knew where she was," Sara ground out. "She's been missing, and I have good reason to believe she's been kidnapped."

"Ah, yes. Reilly Corcoran. You are aware of his particular ability, I presume?"

"He told me, yes."

"The answer is simple, then. Have him locate your sister, and that is where I will send my men," said Elliott.

"How's Reilly going to find her when she's on an entirely different continent?"

At that point, Reilly stood and approached the desk to lay his hands flat on the polished wood. "I can try. I want to help."

Sara raised her eyebrows at the boy. She slid a hand over the receiver. "How?"

"Give me a map. I can get a close range from reading one with my power, usually within a kilometer or two." Eagerness radiated from the set of his shoulders, and the way he leaned over her desk. Sara studied him. What an enigma Faith had sent her.

"Miss Waverly?" Elliott coughed again. "Doctor Waverly, are you there?"

Worrying at her lower lip, Sara turned her attention back to the phone. She took a deep breath. "So what you're saying, Elliott, is that in return for helping me find my sister and stopping Sebastian, you're neatly absolved from all your family's past wrongdoings?"

More coughing. "No, Doctor Waverly. But will you at least let me try?"

Surprised, Sara leaned back in her chair. That was as close to an apology as she'd ever heard from Elliott Flintrop. No pretenses, no haughty inflection in his voice, not even a shadow of self-defense in his tone. She'd have given anything to read his mind.

She glanced past Reilly to a photograph hanging on her wall. Faith beamed out of the frame, wearing a graduation cap with an honors tassel. Steeling herself against the worry that her sister might already be dead—*No, I'd know it, I swear I would*—Sara turned back to the phone. "We'll call you in half an hour with a location."

"We'll be waiting," Elliott said, and they hung up.

Sara spread out the wrinkles she'd made in the elevation drawing on her desk. "Well, Reilly, it looks like we've got a lot of work to do. Let's start by seeing how well that gift of yours works."

****

"There's no way in hell we're getting across that gorge," Faith said, standing at the precipice of a steep drop the next afternoon. She stared downward, but the bottom of the ravine was lost in a wild tangle of shrubs and stunted trees.

"If the end of those maps is across this gorge, you're going to find a way," Sebastian growled behind her.

"What is this thing we're looking for, anyway?" Lilah asked.

Before Faith could answer, Sebastian pushed Lilah toward the edge of the cliff. The woman yelped and staggered back, then stared wide-eyed at them both. "The sooner we get to it," Sebastian drawled, "the sooner you'll find out. Right, Faith?"

Faith glowered at him, wishing desperately that she could set him on fire, but Miriam was still missing. Turning her gaze down into the gorge, she said, "There is a series of thin ledges. We might be able to climb down."

"That's more like it. Ladies first," he said, stepping aside so the women could climb down ahead of him.

Faith stared across the gorge at the trees and mountains stretching away into the blue haze beyond. Doubts stole into her heart. *Should I put the ring back on?* She reached into her pocket, but stopped before her fingers could brush the twisting silver bands.

No. She needed to make good on her mistakes before facing Hakon again, or he'd never want another thing to do with her. And she didn't *want* to see him, until and unless she'd made it right.

She slid her hand out of her pocket, then started down the cliff with Lilah right behind. When she glanced back up at the precipice, she saw Sebastian scanning the sky. Was he expecting company? Had he heard something?

There was no time to wonder. The ledges thinned in spots, and she had all she could do to maintain her balance on the precarious ridges of stone. Lilah clung to the rock with clawed hands, panting and looking ready to give up and fall. "Loosen your grip a little, or you'll tire your hands out. Like this." She demonstrated, holding her hand in a firm cup. "It's going to be all right," she assured the woman.

"I h-have a life. A job. A h-home," Lilah gasped out. Her hand trembled as she reached for the next hold. Her gaze drifted upward to where Sebastian had just begun to descend the cliff. The corners of the two remaining bark maps poked out from his backpack.

Narrowing her eyes, Faith wondered why the redheaded woman would want to go back to Hakon, a self-confirmed wilderness buff, when she had everything she wanted in the city. Then she forced her thoughts back to the problem at hand. "Stay calm. We'll get through this," she murmured. "I told him I'd find the carving. I never said he'd get to use it."

Lilah's eyes met hers, widening. "What do you mean?"

Faith bit her lip and extended a foot to the next narrow perch. How to explain without divulging her gifts? "He thinks it will bring him some kind of supernatural power. I plan to destroy it as soon as I see it."

The redhead looked like she wanted to say something more, but she turned her attention away to the next ledge.

They kept climbing until Faith's limbs ached. When she reached the bottom of the gorge at last, she nearly collapsed with exhaustion.

Sebastian was still descending the cliff, hands and feet busy avoiding a fall. *Now! Do something now, while he's occupied!* she thought wildly. She scanned the ground, but there were no loose rocks small enough to pick up and use as a missile. By the time she dug any out of the earth, he'd have made it to the bottom. She'd have to use her pyrokinesis, no matter that Lilah was watching. "I'm going to stop him," she whispered.

"Wh-What? He's our only way out of here," the woman answered.

Her voice echoed in the bottom of the gorge, and Faith winced. Sound was a lot louder bouncing off that rock. "I can get us out. Stand back," she said, marching forward and letting her power flow full-force.

Lilah advanced, hands spread. "No, Faith, you'll get hurt—"

Wham! Faith's head rocked back as she slammed into an invisible wall of energy. Her knees buckled, and she sat down hard in the scrub on the gorge floor with her head spinning.

David again.

Damn it, what are you doing? she demanded. *That was my chance!*

I want him to get to that carving, responded the ghost, seething with hostile energy, *and nothing is going to get in his way.*

Cursing, Faith struggled to her feet. *This is the last time I make a deal with a ghost,* she vowed.

"Faith? Are you all right?" Lilah stepped forward and held out a hand. "What happened?"

"Nothing," she answered through her teeth. "I'm fine." She took Lilah's hand and stood up, watching regretfully as Sebastian reached the gorge floor.

So, there would be no stopping Sebastian until they reached the end of the maps. Even then, Faith wondered if David would continue to defend his one-time crewmate. She could do nothing but cooperate with Sebastian's insane plan, at least while she knew David was keeping watch over her. His power had to give out eventually. She only hoped hers would outlast it.

Sebastian pushed them onward through most of the night, stopping only when Faith swore she wouldn't be able to use her abilities without rest. "You get a few hours, and that's it," he growled as they reached a creek. He pushed her down and tied her against a tree, then blindfolded her. "Don't want you getting any crazy ideas." His laughter grated in her ears.

For the first hour, she could only fume at Sebastian, no matter how well she realized she needed sleep to prove herself any sort of match for him when the moment came.

Then, as time wore on, her thoughts drifted to Hakon. She remembered the blazing, passionate look in his eyes when they'd made love, and how wonderful it had felt to be in his arms.

So different from the furious looks he'd given her after finding that Toby had been beaten, and Miriam and Lilah kidnapped. Her heart ached as she wondered if he'd ever forgive her for the mess she'd made of his life.

How could two people who had once been so perfect for one another, and who were destined to belong together, be so completely at odds with each other? Had she been wrong all this time? Had she only been holding on because she'd believed they were meant to be together after those stupid childhood dreams?

Would someone ever love her like that?

Disheartened, she drifted off for a while, in and out of a dreamless fog. She woke later to the sound of harsh whispering.

"She said she was going to destroy it when she found it."

"She won't get the opportunity," said a second voice.

"How are you going to stop her, Sebastian? She'll just burn you to a crisp. What are you going to do, find a flameproof suit out here in the middle of nowhere?"

Sebastian and Lilah? Horror pooled in Faith's belly. How had Hakon's ex-wife become involved in all of this? Faith stayed deathly still, fearing that even the sound of her breath might alert them that she'd overheard.

The soft puff of someone scoffing reached her ears, then Sebastian drawled, "That's what guns are for, darling. We don't want her around to tell tales about our little adventure, do we?" There was a pause, and then he added, "Don't tell me you're backing out on me already."

"I just...don't think..."

"You don't *need* to think," Sebastian said in a husky, superior-sounding murmur.

Lilah didn't answer to that, but by her silence, Faith guessed the woman had yielded. Faith's mind reeled as she absorbed the full impact of her situation. As soon as she reached the end of the maps, Sebastian would try to kill her, and if she refused to solve them, David would torment her until she dropped, possibly killing her as well. And if Lilah were truly working with Sebastian to get the Aborigine carving, Faith didn't have a single ally to depend on.

Except Hakon...but she'd taken off the ring.

Calling on her power, Faith searched her surroundings for a ghost, any ghost, who might help her. She pushed to the very edges of her already-exhausted powers—she hadn't gotten nearly enough rest—but could find no spirits hovering near who might listen to her pleas for assistance.

She couldn't even reach into her pocket for Hakon's ring. Tears pricked at the backs of her eyes. What if she never saw him again? What if he never found out the truth?

Whatever happened, she knew she had to get some sleep to restore what remained of her power. She sank into a restless doze, full of deadly, clutching hands and a man's voice, far away, calling for her.

****

Hakon's horse had a sturdy build, suggesting brumby heritage, but even that hardy mountain breed had its limits. He'd stopped during the night, long enough to give the colt a rest and gather some bush tucker for his supper, but he hadn't slept, himself. There would be no respite for him while Faith was still out there, missing. He'd tried to listen for her, to concentrate on the vivid, intimate memories of her that had brought flashes of her voice, and it pained him when he sensed nothing.

It does not mean she's dead, he told himself fiercely as he stuffed the oilskin coat into the saddlebag the next morning. With grim determination, he swung up onto the horse's back.

The sound of another helicopter brought his attention skyward. He urged the horse deeper into the trees, watching the direction of the chopper's flight. It veered eastward, and his heart pitched in his chest. Had they heard something on their radios that accounted for the sudden change of direction?

Deciding to trust his gut, he prodded the colt into a jog, scanning the brush ahead as they went. He saw no broken branches or footprints, nothing to indicate that a human had passed this way. "Faith, where the hell are you? Why aren't you talking to me?" he whispered, but only the wind and the beat of his horse's hooves answered him.

The trees became denser and larger, blotting out the sky and perfuming the air with cloying oils. His mount had to squeeze through tighter and tighter gaps, and Hakon began to wonder if he'd have to give up searching on horseback.

Then they burst into sunlight. A crevasse loomed before them and the colt whinnied, lurching backward in a desperate attempt to avoid falling over the edge. The horse's forequarters went down in a sickening swoop. "Whoa, whoa!" he shouted, hauling backward on the reins. The horse neighed again, haunches bunching, hooves scraping for purchase on the precarious stone. Gravel spilled over the edge of the cliff and clicked away toward the bottom of the ravine.

"Back up, back up," Hakon said, panting. The colt twisted away from the cliff, its neck lathered with sweat. It tossed its head, and its eyes rolled until the whites showed. Hakon soothed it into a standstill, patting its shoulder while he caught his breath. "You look like I feel about now, mate," he muttered, staring over the edge of the cliff.

Now that he wasn't fighting to avoid a deadly fall, Hakon scanned along the lip of the ravine and saw a narrow track he could follow on horseback.

If he still trusted his intuition. He peered over the edge to the gorge floor. The bottom was mostly barren, peppered here and there with a few dogged patches of grass and scrub. A person could navigate it with little trouble.

From his height and without binoculars, Hakon couldn't make out any signs that Faith had gone this way.

He must be going completely mad. He had no food,

and no weapons. What in God's name would he do once he found them, ask Sebastian to hand the women back?

The colt snorted, and began trotting along the cliff edge without being prodded. Surprised, Hakon tugged on the reins. The animal shook its head and fought him, clamping the bit between its teeth. A moment later, it shrilled and began trotting faster.

Hakon glanced around, but saw nothing that might have spooked his horse. A good thing, too, because even though they had a clear path along the top of the gorge, one swift bolt would have sent them both flying right over the edge. Nothing he did could sway the colt from its chosen direction. "All right, you stubborn bloody beast. You may as well lead for a while, and we'll see where that gets us."

The colt's ears twitched in all directions, as if it were listening for something Hakon couldn't hear. Each time it paused, it started onward again with renewed vigor.

Almost as if something were driving it...or calling it.

Suspicion and hope flickered through him, but he didn't dare let either sensation take hold. Instead, he forced his gaze to the ground.

The ravine came to an end at last with a steep, rocky path leading upward out of its depths. At the eastern point, the horse stopped, and so did Hakon's heartbeat.

A woman's footprint. And another. *Two* women; the shoe tread was different on each. And there, the larger boot print of a man.

They had come this way.

Hakon thumped his horse's sides with his heels, and they cantered on, slow enough to watch for further signs, though he longed to kick the horse into full gallop.

He didn't care how the horse had led him to the tracks. He had no idea what he could do against Sebastian, unarmed. His head swam with dire images of what he might find when he got to Faith, and what Sebastian might do to her once he'd gotten his damn artifact. But not once did he doubt that nothing would be right until he had his arms around her again, where he knew she'd be safe.

From that point, the signs were easy to follow, clearly visible in loose soil or swaths cut through meadows of long grass. Sebastian must have given up expecting anyone to come after the women by now.

His mistake.

The pent-up rage of the last few days boiled under Hakon's skin. He'd kill the man with his bare hands, if that was what it took.

He spent the rest of the morning being so furious, that only when he stopped in a field to rest the colt did he notice the deafening silence. No birds, no insects, not even the normally-constant shush of mountain wind disturbed the oppressive quiet. Even his horse had gone still as a statue, pricking its ears and looking toward the east.

Hakon took off his hat and lifted his ponytail to encourage the sluggish breeze to fan the back of his neck. The air lay thick and oily, as if the eerie hush had somehow affected it. He strode toward the horse. "Not liking the looks of this either, mate," he murmured in the animal's ear.

"Hakon?"

Lilah's voice. Hakon spun around.

His ex-wife stood at the edge of the trees, several meters away. Her white blouse and jeans were stained with trail dust, and her dark-red hair was loose and tangled. She didn't move.

Absurdly, the first thought that wandered through his brain wasn't relief that he'd found her. *Where is Faith?* He stepped behind the horse, scanning the trees.

"You found me!" Lilah cried, rushing toward him. "Thank God you found me!" Her shout exploded into the silence like a firecracker, and he winced.

As she reached him, the colt snorted and shied away. A sudden, alarming feeling of dread rushed through him as he realized he stood in the middle of a field, alone, with no cover and no weapons.

Lilah threw her arms around his neck, sobbing in his ear. Her hair fluttered into his face. "Oh, Hakon, I was so scared, so awfully scared..."

Distracted, he patted her back, trying to see around her shoulder into the woods. "It's all right, Lilah. Where's Faith?" He laid his hands on her shoulders and pushed her away to look at her face.

Then he noticed her eyes were dry. His stomach dropped in an endless whoosh.

"Faith's busy at the moment, friend," came Sebastian's voice, "but since you're here after all, you may as well join the party."

Lilah stepped away, looking anywhere but at him. Hakon pierced her with an accusing glare, knowing she felt it, but she didn't meet his gaze even once. All the horrible things he'd been imagining about Faith's fate came back in force. His gut spasmed. Sick, he turned his attention to the edge of the field.

Sebastian leaned against the trunk of a large tree, arms crossed, supremely confident of his win.

Son of a bitch. Hakon closed his eyes, and prayed to whatever might hear him.

Chapter Seventeen

> *I hate astral projecting. I'm always afraid*
> *to "leave" my own body, because I worry I*
> *won't be able to return. Anyone who wants to*
> *be gifted can take that one from me.*
> —*Faith's Journals, age eighteen*

Still blindfolded, with her hands tied behind her, Faith waited for Sebastian and Lilah to return from wherever they'd gone. David's ghost had stopped tormenting her, but didn't respond to any of her questions when she asked why they'd stopped.

Had they arrived at the end of the maps?

If I could effing see, I could figure it out for myself, she thought ruefully. She'd even tried twisting enough to touch her fingertips against the earth, and gauge her location using her psychic ability. That, too, was impossible. They had tied her so tightly against a tree trunk that she found it difficult even to draw breath. Her hands tingled with stunted circulation. "Think, think," she whispered to herself.

Aha. Her boots.

She only hoped the laces had loosened over the course of their hike. Normally, she had the chance to stop and re-tie them. Not so, on this unpleasant little jaunt.

Sebastian had bound her legs loosely together,

hobble-style, so she could walk, but not run. With one foot, she pushed at her other boot. It budged. Not much, but enough to encourage her. She'd have to be quick, before they came back. She dug the toe of her other boot into the heel of the loose one and gave it a shove.

The loose boot slipped off her foot and tumbled away. She called on her power. Pinning the toe of her sock between her other boot and the ground, she slipped it off.

Ha. Bare foot. She slapped it against the ground.

Images of Aborigine men and women flooded into her mind. Groups of them, sitting in a circle. One ancient man reached into a woven basket and withdrew an object, holding it up for all to see.

The bird carving.

Pain lanced through Faith. She grunted and struggled to hold on to the vision, then struggled more to decipher the tribal elder's language. Straining to listen, she made a note of all the inflections and sounds in each word. When the elder finished speaking, the group around him began to chant. Warm radiance shone down from the clear sky and filled the circle of men and women. The elder held the bird carving higher, and the tribe's song resonated within it.

One by one, each member of the tribe stopped singing, until only the elder was left. Then he, too, stopped, and the radiance above them faded.

You have to sing it backward, came David's voice.

Faith jumped at the sudden presence in her mind. Her foot broke contact with the ground, and the Aborigine vision vanished.

Singing the ritual backward will draw the power from the spirits back into the carving, the ghost explained. *Then it can be destroyed, and the power dispersed without harm.*

That's a damn big help, considering I have no idea what he sang! And why, all of a sudden, are you helping me? she demanded. *You've done nothing but harass me—*

Footsteps broke into her silent tirade. "Nap time's over, Faith," Sebastian growled. "Are we going on, or not?"

The carving is buried here, said David. *Tell him.*

Why should I help either of you?

I was helping you, *not Sebastian,* responded the ghost. *I had no energy to explain. The carving is here. Tell him!*

That might have explained why she'd received no answer to her questions in the past two days, but Faith still didn't believe she could trust the ghost. She lifted her chin and remained silent.

I brought Hakon, the ghost said.

Faith's heart began pounding double-speed. *He's here?*

David didn't answer. "Hakon?" she called, wanting more than anything to believe the ghost had been telling the truth. She no longer cared that Hakon might discover what a mess she'd made of things, as long as he was all right. The constant fear of the past couple of days paled in comparison to that one worry.

"Hello, love," came Hakon's voice, and she nearly burst into tears of relief at the sound.

He grunted. There was a scramble and *whump,* as if someone had fallen to the ground. A warm shoulder brushed against hers. "I see they're treating you well," Hakon rumbled in her ear.

She steeled herself, when she wanted only to lean into him and breathe in the proof that they were both alive. Nothing else mattered. "How...?" she started to ask.

Sebastian interrupted, his voice sounding close at hand. "You can have your little reunion after we talk business."

"The carving is here," she blurted. "But you have to take the blindfold off, and let me use my hands so I can find it."

Sebastian laughed. "Why would I do something that stupid?"

"Do you want the damn thing, or not?"

"Oh, untie her, Sebastian," came Lilah's petulant voice.

There was a pause. "All right, fine," Sebastian said. Faith's wrist ropes jerked, and then she was free.

She rubbed her sore wrists, then pushed the blindfold off. Blinking in the sun, she looked around. They had stopped in a shallow, sheltered canyon of gray rock. She reached for her discarded boot.

"What do you think you're doing?" Sebastian demanded.

"I can't very well search for the carving if I don't have shoes on," she said. She glanced at him and saw him pointing his gun at her.

Then she looked to her right. Hakon sat tied to the same tree to which she'd been bound. She met his gaze, and her heartbeat stilled for a long, suspended moment. His unreadable, aqua-blue stare pierced her to her core. Nothing could stop the aching joy and relief that burst through her at seeing him again, at knowing he was unhurt. She longed to say a million things at once.

Starting with *I'm sorry.*

He opened his mouth to speak, but shut it again. His gaze shifted to Sebastian.

"Let's get going, sweetheart. The day's wasting," Sebastian growled.

Faith jerked her attention back to her boot, and took her time putting it on. From the corner of her eye, she saw Sebastian and Lilah talking in hushed tones. Good. She stared at the rope binding her ankles, called on her power, and burned a tiny hole in the fibers. A thin wisp of smoke drifted up into the still air, and she prayed they wouldn't notice it. She pulled her boot on and hastily tied the laces, then rose to her feet.

If Sara had any idea what she was going through right now, she'd march herself right to Australia to wring Faith's neck, pregnant or not. Good thing her sister couldn't read minds several countries away.

"You'll search under every rock in this canyon, twice if you have to," Sebastian said. "And you will cooperate, won't you? Your friend won't be leaving this place in once piece if you don't."

Sebastian handed Lilah a second gun. The woman hesitated, glancing from the weapon to Sebastian and back with an air of doubt, but stood up straighter and took it.

A chill swooped down Faith's back. Even if she could manage one of them, it was no guarantee the other wouldn't shoot her before she had the chance to disarm them.

Or they'd shoot Hakon.

Her stomach twisted. If they killed him, she'd never be able to live with herself. She risked a glance at him, and as if drawn there, his gaze met hers again.

"Don't forget," Sebastian added, "your pal Miriam is still out there, too."

Hakon's gaze intensified, and Faith caught the barest shake of his head. Not missing anymore, then. But was she alive?

"I said get going!" barked Sebastian. He leapt toward her and pressed the muzzle of the gun into her back. "Lilah, keep an eye on Hakon while we take a stroll around, will you?"

"You know you're going to be caught, Sebastian," Faith snapped. "Even if you kill us, the rangers will catch you. You can't stop all of them, and you can't just run for the rest of your life."

"It's not your job to psychoanalyze, darling. Just find the little birdie, and then you can go home."

"I don't know why you bother lying. We both know better," she spat. Reaching into the sky with her power, she called for the ghosts.

Psychic energy pounded her senses, just as she'd known it would. Biting her lip, focusing on her breathing, she tried to sort out a single ghost from the maelstrom. She caught snatches of David's voice, but it quickly drowned in the storm of spirits. Sweat beaded on her forehead, and she wiped it away. The barrage of energy almost forced her to her knees. She struggled to bear up under its weight. Too many voices, too much power.

Then she heard the Aborigine song, a thin, glistening thread of music among the chaos, beautiful and haunting. The sound seemed to filter its strength into her, and she turned toward it.

Sebastian jogged behind her like an eager hound, but she hardly had any attention to spare for him. The bird carving called to her, not in words but feelings of joy and harmony. Stumbling over brush and stone, she hurried to the end of the canyon, where the rock severed in a narrow crevice. The carving's song filtered out of the slit in the rock.

"Here?" Sebastian asked when she stopped. "Is it here?"

The song faded, and immediately, she mourned the absence of that sense of serenity. The thought of letting Sebastian abuse the carving's power for something so evil, so hateful, so contrary to its purpose, was too much to bear. "Good luck getting it out," she said with satisfaction.

He shrugged out of his backpack, and it dropped to the ground. "You'll pry it out with your bare hands if you have to, but *I want it*, one way or the other." Wrestling with the flap and ties on his pack, he extracted a hammer and chisel, then threw them to the ground in front of her. He leveled the pistol at her once again. "Move it."

Glaring daggers at him, she picked up the tools, then chipped away at the rock. The echo chimed off the canyon walls as she worked. All the while, her mind raced. How fast could she turn on him with her new weapons before either he or Lilah fired their guns? Daring a look back toward Hakon, she saw him sitting where he'd been tied, staring at the rock crevice. His stare flicked toward her, and then quickly away. Still silent, still unreadable. Probably still furious.

And rightly so. Her throat tightened. *I am so sorry.*

Lilah stood over him, stiff but focused, with the gun ready at her side. It might take a fraction of a second for her to react if Faith attacked Sebastian, but

Faith didn't want to risk it. The choking image of Hakon lying in a pool of his own blood swamped her senses. She shook her head and tried to stifle the onslaught of shivers. Even if Lilah wouldn't shoot him, Sebastian would have no qualms about doing so. The bird carving wasn't worth that risk. Nothing was.

She chipped away at the reddish rock until her arms ached with the vibrations of pounding on the chisel. The sun blazed down, and though Sebastian had a canteen on his pack, he didn't offer her anything to drink. The carving's song didn't return, as if it could have known she was digging it out only to give it to a monster who would use it to destroy lives.

Then she heard a scuffle, and Lilah yelped. Faith looked up. Hakon was on his feet, with a brawny arm locked around Lilah's throat from behind. *How...?*

Shrieking like a scalded cat, the redheaded woman clawed at his arm with no effect. Hakon wrestled the gun from her other hand, then pointed it at Sebastian. "Next time you tie ropes, don't be in such a hurry to do something else. Drop your gun."

Calmly, Sebastian cocked his gun, then pointed it at Faith's head. "Drop yours."

Hakon's arm twitched, and he looked like he might give in. Tense seconds went by.

Now. She'd never get another chance.

Faith locked her eyes on Sebastian's gun arm, and unleashed her pyrokinesis.

The man screamed as his sleeve burst into flames. When he whirled away, she jerked at the ropes binding her ankles. They snapped. She leapt to her feet and rushed Sebastian with her hammer poised to swing.

Busy slapping at his burning sleeve, he didn't see

her until she had almost reached him. Faith swung the hammer and missed. He staggered back, then fell to the ground. He rolled until the flames went out, then pointed his gun back at her.

Faith yelped and ducked just in time as the gun fired. The loose rope hanging from her ankle caught on a spur of rock. She tripped and slammed to the ground. Her head smashed against the earth. Stars burst before her eyes as she gasped for breath, dazed.

Sebastian scrambled past her and thrust his arm into the rock crevice. From the corner of her eye, Faith saw Hakon shove Lilah away and sprint toward them.

Sebastian was too quick. He raised his gun and fired a shot toward Hakon. Hakon dropped into a crouch, and the shot pelted over his head. Sebastian aimed again.

God, no, oh, God, no. Still gasping, Faith rolled over and swung the hammer toward Sebastian.

The claw caught him a glancing blow across his calf, tearing through his jeans. His gunshot went wide and ricocheted off the canyon wall.

"Bitch!" he snarled, and backhanded her across the face with the gun.

Lightning blasted behind her eyes. Faith tasted blood, and the force of his strike piled on top of the blow her head had taken against the ground. Struggling for consciousness, she twisted her leg around, then slammed her steel-toed boot into Sebastian's gut.

He croaked and yanked his arm out of the rock crevice to grip his belly. Somehow, he managed to keep hold of his gun, and as Hakon charged toward him, he raised it to fire again.

He had Hakon almost point-blank.

Everything else whooshed out of her mind except that terrifying clarity. Faith lunged toward Sebastian with a ball of flame already in her palm. "Don't!"

Sebastian froze, wide-eyed, with the flame leaping just inches from his face.

"Drop the gun, or I'll drop this on you," she said.

"No!" Lilah cried, flying toward them with panic in her eyes.

Hakon grabbed her as she raced past, and clamped an arm around the woman's middle.

Lilah struggled, but she was no match for him. Her wild-eyed stare shifted from the flame to Faith. Even in the midst of such turmoil, Faith saw the horror and revulsion on the woman's face. Writhing in Hakon's grip, she glared at Sebastian. "You promised this would work! You said we'd be rich!"

Sebastian's laughter wheezed out, even as he sat doubled over with the fire a breath away.

"The gun, Sebastian. Toss it away from you," Faith said. She pressed her gift, and the ball of flame leapt higher.

Lilah whimpered.

"Faith, watch out!" Hakon shouted, and Faith saw Sebastian's free hand dart back into the crevice. She lunged forward with her flame spitting sparks.

Sebastian's eyes went white.

A beam of blazing blue light shot straight down from the sky, and enveloped him in an explosive glow that flung Faith away from him. A shrill, piercing sound followed it, as of a bird cry that went on and on.

Pain stampeded through her. Faith cried out in agony as the sound tore her apart. She scrambled away from the painful force-field of energy, and her flame went out. Slapping her hands over her ears did nothing to block the noise. It poured through her from the inside. Tears spilled down her cheeks.

Sebastian's lips slid back from a gleaming, toothy snarl. He dropped the gun and pulled his arm from the crevice, laughing. In his hand was the bird carving.

Faintly, Faith heard Lilah yell Sebastian's name. The woman broke free of Hakon's grasp, and raced toward them.

"STOP!" Sebastian cried. His amplified bellow shook the canyon walls.

Lilah's eyes flashed white, and she halted in mid-stride. Everything went silent.

Lowering her hands from her ears, Faith glanced from Sebastian, to Lilah, to Hakon, and back again. Her heart drummed in her chest. Terror constricted her throat to a near-strangle.

"Hakon, stand still," Sebastian ordered in that same voice, a twisted, bass-drum version of itself.

Hakon's eyes flashed, too, and he froze in place.

Leering at Faith, Sebastian said, "Go pick up the second gun, Lilah."

The woman turned, stiff as a robot, and went to do Sebastian's bidding.

No. No, oh God, no! Faith lurched to her feet, frantically scraping to gather her power and ignore the maddening ache in her skull. She battered herself against the force-field, trying to reach Sebastian, but the wall of light resisted her.

The words, Faith, came David's voice in her mind. *Sing them!*

"What?" she said aloud. "I don't know them!" She demanded her power to produce flame. A spark hopped in her palm, then fizzled out. She moaned, and desperation swamped her.

Repeat the sounds backward. Do it! You can't stop him unless you do it!

Sebastian smiled, looking blissful and serene. "Shoot Hakon, Lilah."

Slow and dreamlike, the woman began to raise the gun.

Faith choked on a scream as stark panic exploded through her. The burning-clear image of the first Hakon's death flooded her mind. She saw his body fall to the earth, heard his scream of pain, could even smell the salt air of the sea. Aesa's rage and grief rushed forth, mingling with her fears, swamping them.

And then love.

Pure, blinding, everlasting. Stronger than anything she'd ever known. And she knew exactly what to do.

Shoving her hand into her pocket, she thrust her finger through Aesa's ring. "Hakon!"

His knees buckled just as the gun went off. Shaking his head, he sprang at Lilah. The woman leapt away, still holding the gun, moving much faster now.

But Hakon was awake, and fighting her.

Through tears of relief, Faith turned back to the force-field. She pounded on it, but Sebastian ignored her, already chanting something that sounded like an Aborigine dialect. "David! What do I say to stop him?"

David's voice filtered into her mind, now mixing with a dizzying array of others. *Repeat!* she heard him shout, and she winced as the cry echoed through her throbbing skull.

Faith repeated the foreign sounds, stumbling over them, saying them again and again until she felt the

271

force-field sputter under her palms.

Sebastian screamed, his face twisting in fury, and the sound warped into the shriek of a bird of prey. He spoke his chant faster. Blue light rolled into the canyon like mist.

The backward song seemed to go on and on, so slow next to Sebastian's rhythmic, hurried chant. And then the voices of the ghosts vanished.

The force-field didn't. "What happened? What did I do wrong?" she shouted.

But David's voice, too, had faded.

Faith banged on the invisible wall. She glanced to Hakon, but he was still busy with Lilah. Faith pounded on the wall again.

And then she felt the shiver of her powers returning.

At once, she called them up and, thrusting her fears aside, mustered an astral projection. She sensed her body collapsing. Her spirit rose from it and burst through the wall.

Chapter Eighteen

There's that saying, you know—if you love something, set it free, and all that? I'd much rather hang on and never, never let go. Even if the other way is the right thing to do.
—Faith's Journals, age thirty-one

Hakon ducked as Lilah fired her gun. Seething, he lunged at her again. This time, he caught her wrist and wrestled the gun away from her. With a howl of anger, she charged him once more, grasping for the weapon. He sprang aside. Whooshing past him, she slipped in a patch of gravel and collapsed. Her head struck a stone, and she went slack.

Sebastian shrieked, inhuman, enraged. Panting, Hakon looked toward him to see a bluish shell of light fizzling around him, and another, glowing-white figure circling him within it. Sparks of red flew from Sebastian's fingertips as he tucked the bird carving under his other arm.

The white figure thrust a hand toward the carving, which instantly burst into flame. Sebastian roared in fury as the shell of light shattered. The shrill sound dissolved into a human cry of pain as Sebastian dropped to the ground, rolling to put out his burning shirt.

Exhausted and aching, Hakon staggered toward

them, his gaze riveted on the figure in white. With a start, he realized it was a pale, see-through shadow of Faith. She'd astral projected. He looked down at Sebastian, and then saw Faith's body lying beside the man. Hissing, with his shirt hanging in burnt tatters, Sebastian picked up his gun and pointed it at Faith's motionless figure.

Every nerve in Hakon's body screamed in anguish. He couldn't even call it conscious thought. The sight of her prone form blasted through him, and he had to get between that gun and Faith, no matter what. He charged forward, ignoring the protest of his aching muscles, and tackled Sebastian. The gun flew from Sebastian's hand and clattered away.

They rolled end over end, grappling for each other's throats. The smell of burned skin and cloth stung Hakon's nose. His eyes watered freely, blinding him so he almost missed ducking a punch.

When they twisted close enough to the gun, Sebastian snatched it up and fired another shot. Pain flashed along Hakon's upper arm. He grunted and jammed his boot into Sebastian's belly.

Snarling, Sebastian raised the gun again—a dead-on shot—and it clicked.

Empty.

He flung the useless weapon away and dove for Hakon again. Hakon braced for the attack, but his drained muscles could no longer support him. As Sebastian plowed into him, he rocked backward. The world spun, and his head slammed against the ground. He saw the pale flash of Faith's ghost just before everything went black.

Flame. Angry voices. The desperate need to run,

clutching to his woman's hand. If he lost her, he knew he would die. They had to flee Norway and go somewhere else, anywhere they would not be known. Nothing mattered but protecting her.

Aesa. His wife, the jewel of his heart.

Hakon risked a look over his shoulder at their pursuers. The mob surged after them, waving torches and screaming Witch! Witch! *like a pack of bloodthirsty hunting dogs. They thought she'd cursed the town.* Cursed it, *after all the good she had done for them! As if such a terrible notion could ever have entered her mind. He looked at his woman.*

And saw Faith.

****

Hakon woke with a gasp. The dream evaporated into the sunlit room in which he lay. An embroidered picture of flowers in a vase hung on the wall opposite his bed, and birdsong filtered in through the open window.

McGowan's Inn—his own room. Disoriented, he rubbed his forehead. The ceiling seemed to close in over him, claustrophobic after his driving need to escape in the dream.

Dream? He never dreamed.

Or he hadn't...before.

Sitting up, he swung his legs over the side of the bed. What was he doing back at the inn?

The door creaked open, and Miriam's head popped in. When she saw that he was awake, her lips curved into a loving smile. She entered the room balancing a small tray that smelled of her enticing chicken soup and fresh-baked bread. Her other arm was in a sling. "Here you go," she whispered, sliding the tray onto his nightstand with her good hand.

He caught her elbow before she could turn away. "I want answers, Miriam. What the hell happened?"

She turned toward him, and he released her. She touched his cheek. "You need rest."

"I'll rest when I'm dead," he muttered. He rubbed a throbbing ache in the back of his head, and wondered why he *wasn't* dead. "How did I get back here?"

"The rangers flew you back. Sebastian and Lilah were—were arrested, dear," Miriam said, as if she hated to deliver him the news that his ex-wife was associated with a criminal...and was one, herself. "Are you sure you won't eat something?"

"Tell me what happened," he insisted.

Miriam drew a soft breath and lowered her tiny form to the edge of the bed. The springs in the mattress squeaked even under her small weight. "Lilah thought you and she could work things out. She found out about that letter you had stored away—and then she learned about Faith... Oh, I'm sorry it's all been such a mess, Hakon." Sorrowful empathy shone in her eyes.

"What letter?"

She pointed at the crumpled envelope on his nightstand, the same one he'd been carrying around for days without reading it.

Hakon snatched it up and withdrew a wrinkled page, then skimmed its contents. A half-finished letter from his gran, years old, telling a distant relative some wild yarn. It spoke of an Ivarsson family treasure, buried on an island called...

Hvitmar.

The island where he and Aesa had built their home after escaping from Norway. Aesa, whose face his heart had remembered for a thousand years...but he'd come to know her in the past ten days as...

He swung his gaze upward. "Where is Faith?"

Miriam busied herself arranging things on the tray, and he sensed her avoiding his gaze. "She's gone, dear."

Hakon's heart dropped to the floor. He shot to his feet, and regretted it at once when the room whirled at a drunken angle. "What do you mean, *gone*?"

Miriam met his stare, and her frown lines deepened. "She said she'd caused you enough trouble. She was in her room crying for two days. You've been asleep the whole time."

He stepped forward, then stopped just short of grabbing Miriam by the shoulder. *"Where did she go?"*

"Home, she said. She left you this." The woman reached into her apron pocket with her sound hand. She laid Aesa's ring in his palm, along with an envelope that contained his promised fee, plus the risk bonus he'd long ago decided not to take.

Guilt money. He swallowed back a wash of anger and insult and stinging hurt.

Then he looked at Aesa's ring, fingering the twisted silver bands. He glanced at the dog-eared letter from his gran, and then snatched up the telephone receiver from his nightstand, punching buttons. "Information for New York City, New York. Get me Reilly Corcoran. If you can't find him, I want the offices of Gemini, Limited."

****

Faith stared at the images clicking on the slide projector without really seeing them. The board of directors at Whitehall University's History department had clamored for a week for her to give a lecture on the recovered artifacts. Professors and students alike had crammed the auditorium to hear what she had to say. She'd become something of a local celebrity—and substantially wealthier, thanks to Elliott Flintrop's promised portion of his vast estate—but she could find no pleasure in any of it.

Reilly was supposed to help with the lecture, but he'd disappeared several days ago on an errand that he swore couldn't wait. Then Sara had gone into the hospital this morning, in labor. It had snowed. A lot. Unusual for New York. And it was coming up on Christmas, too. Everything seemed so very perfect.

Almost.

Faith longed to be at the hospital to support her sister, but a tiny, stabbing part of her hesitated. She wondered if she could bear the sight of a happy, complete family, knowing she'd never have one herself.

She sighed. Well, she should have known better. Her relationships had always ended in disaster, and this one was no exception. Worse, even. She'd lied to him. She'd almost gotten him killed. She'd lost her heart, and would never get it back.

"Doctor Markham, I asked a question."

Blinking back threatening tears, she squinted up into the dim amphitheater seats. One of the professors had stood up. "Yes?" she prompted.

"You said you considered the bark paintings to be a series of maps. You've shown us only two of them. What happened to the others?"

Faith cleared her throat and struggled to turn her attention back to the lecture. "There was a third, but it was destroyed during the recovery, as was the carving to which the maps led." Wow, she was getting really good at stretching the truth. Must have been all the practice.

Looking back down at her notes, she went on. "Australian museums are in the process of cataloguing the remaining recovered finds." And Sebastian Hale's name was now mud in archaeological circles. He'd be lucky if anyone so much as let him into a museum ever again. After he got out of the hospital, he would have to endure a review the likes of which Faith hoped never to see. Then he'd have the pleasure of seeing the inside of a jail for a long, long time.

The memory of Hakon lying sprawled out and bleeding in the canyon rushed into her mind. She paused to swallow a knot in her throat. The rangers had shown up just in time to stop Sebastian from killing him.

She turned back to the projector screen as one of the auditorium doors squeaked open. She continued. "W-We suspect that we've recovered almost ninety percent of the stolen artifacts—"

A voice rose above the murmur of her audience. "She's wrong."

Faith's heart leapt into her throat, and then stopped beating entirely. In the light spilling in from the open doorway stood a broad-shouldered silhouette that she'd have known anywhere.

Hakon flipped on the lights, then jogged down the lecture hall steps, looking better than she'd ever seen him in a black T-shirt, faded blue jeans, and leather jacket. He carried a small duffel bag over his shoulder, and Reilly entered the auditorium behind him with an armful of papers. Members of the audience sat up straight and stared around to see who had disturbed them.

Hakon hardly wasted a look on them. He reached the floor, then dropped his duffel beside the podium with a plop. His aquamarine eyes arrowed through her, impossible to read. He ducked in front of her to get to the microphone. "She's wrong."

The audience murmured. A gray-haired man in a brown coat and spectacles stood up. "Doctor Markham, who is this man?"

She glanced from Hakon to the audience and back, then shook her head, fighting to find her tongue.

With a sickening lurch, she saw the head of the History department rise from his seat. "I'm sorry, you'll have to leave. This is an important meeting, and you're—"

"—one of the reasons these artifacts are now in safe hands," Hakon finished. "And part of the reason we just found the rest of them."

"And who are you?"

"My name's Hakon Ivarsson. I'm a wilderness guide...and a pretty good authority on Norse history."

The crowd grumbled. "What does that have to do with Aborigine bark paintings?" demanded one of the professors.

Hakon stared him down, looking amused. "Not a damn thing."

People began to stand up and gather their belongings. What in God's name was he doing? Horrified, Faith made a desperate lunge toward the podium.

"*Half* of the artifacts were found in a mine in Bowen Mountain," Hakon boomed into the microphone.

Everyone in the room stilled, including Faith, whose heart thrummed so loudly into the silence that she wondered whether the gathered listeners could hear it.

Reilly came down the auditorium steps and began distributing the papers in his hands.

"The other half," Hakon continued, "was in a cargo container in Sydney, awaiting illegal shipment to an unknown recipient."

Some of the professors glanced at the paperwork Reilly gave them, and then sat down to murmur with each other.

Stunned, Faith glanced at the slides flicking past on the projector screen, now barely visible in the lighted room. Had he just said *half*? *Half* of what was already an unprecedented historical find?

Hakon turned toward Faith, and for the first time in what felt like forever, he smiled at her. Into the microphone, he said, "I'd wager Doctor Markham has earned herself a nice, long vacation." He stepped back from the microphone and waved her toward it.

With her breath resisting all her attempts to catch it, Faith stepped up to the podium.

Everyone began asking questions at once. Somehow, she managed to stumble her way through answer after answer, all the while feeling Hakon's gaze on her. The lecture ended with a considerable amount of hearty handshakes and claps on the back, praise she'd never felt before as part-owner of a struggling archaeology firm. Almost like being an equal in the field.

Students and staff lingered as the discussion ended,

forming a guarded circle around her. She rushed through their questions and thanked them all for their time, but peered over their heads in search of Hakon. He was nowhere to be found. Even his duffel bag had disappeared. She panicked and tried to break away from her new admirers, but they stalled her, wanting more time with her.

Bit by bit, the lecture hall emptied. At last, Faith saw only Reilly, gathering up some of the papers her audience had left behind. She snatched up her briefcase, then hurried toward him to grab him by the sleeve. "Reilly, where did he go? Hakon—where is he?"

The boy shrugged. "I saw him a little while ago, talking to your boss, must've been. Maybe he left, I don't know." He smiled, and it occurred to her he looked a lot less sullen these days.

"Thanks." Breathless, she raced out the auditorium doors.

"Hvert fer þú, fagra?"

Where are you going, beautiful? Faith stopped dead, recognizing the words at once in spite of her hazy recollection of the language. Heartbeat slamming, she turned around.

Hakon leaned against the wall outside the auditorium, with his duffel bag by his feet. He angled his head and studied her with those sea-blue eyes. "Didn't want to interrupt your mob of fans." A brief flash of humor tugged at his mouth, and then disappeared.

Faith went toward him, trembling, then set her briefcase on the floor. She stood an arm's length away, afraid to touch him. "I thought... I thought that... Hakon, I'm so horribly sorry for how things went..."

He shook his head. "Stop. Just stop."

Biting her lip, she forced back her tears and waited for whatever he had to say. For her heart to break...again.

His hands came up, almost touching her shoulders, then he fisted them. His eyes clouded. "I've been dreaming. For a week now, every night. Building, digging, plowing, fishing, farming. Sharing a bed with you..." His expression softened into one of aching tenderness, and his hand came up to cradle her cheek in its warmth. His voice dropped to a mere whisper. "...Aesa."

A sob caught in her throat, and she covered his hand with her own. Could he really mean...?

He cupped her face in both hands as if he'd been waiting to do so all his life. "Why didn't you tell me?"

Tears streamed down her face, and she couldn't stop them. "Would you have believed me? I've done nothing but lie to you, and I almost got you killed..."

"I'm a Viking. It's gonna take a lot more than constant danger and mayhem to kill me." His eyes sparkled with amusement.

Scrubbing at her cheeks, she pulled away. "Stop it. Stop being funny."

He stroked her cheek, brushing tears away. "We found my treasure...Reilly and I," he said with a smile. "On Hvitmar. Coins, a bracelet, a comb... You were right. And you were right about my wife."

She stared transfixed at him, feeling the blood drain from her face, terrified to hope at what he meant by that.

He reached into his pocket, then withdrew his fisted hand. He opened his palm. In it lay Aesa's ring, gleaming in the sunlit atrium. His gaze lifted to hers, soft and tropical-blue. "I'd like to renew our vows."

Faith clapped her hand over her mouth to stifle a sob. Fresh tears tracked hotly down her cheeks.

He stepped closer, sliding his fingers through her hair with one hand as he held up the ring with the other. "That piece of me you said was missing? It's you. Marry me, Faith."

Something cosmic seemed to shift back into balance as she stared into his eyes. Joy shot through her, like a beam of sunlight piercing storm clouds. "Yes," she whispered, smiling through her tears. She raised her trembling hand.

Hakon slid Aesa's ring over her fourth finger, then pulled her into a bone-crushing embrace. He kissed her, a long, deep, searching kiss that went all the way to her toes. It was just like coming home.

When he pulled away, he was grinning. "What do you say we get out of here? I have a new horse waiting for me at quarantine, who I'd like you to meet."

Faith wiped her tears away, then took his hand in hers. Together, they made their way to the atrium, then walked out the doors. Sunshine bounced off new-fallen snow that blanketed the world in wedding white.

This? Now *this* was a perfect day.

A word about the author...

Nicki Greenwood graduated SUNY Morrisville with a degree in Natural Resources. She found her passion in writing stories of romantic adventure, and combines that with her love of the environment. Her works have won several awards, including the Rebecca Eddy Memorial Contest. Her first book, *EARTH*, debuted in 2010 through The Wild Rose Press, Inc.

Nicki lives in upstate New York with her husband, son, and assorted pets. When she's not writing, she enjoys the arts, gardening, interior decorating, and trips to the local Renaissance Faire.

Visit Nicki at:

http://www.nickigreenwood.com

Thank you for purchasing
this publication of The Wild Rose Press, Inc.

If you enjoyed the story, we would appreciate
your letting others know by leaving a review.

For other wonderful stories,
please visit our on-line bookstore at
www.thewildrosepress.com.

For questions or more information
contact us at
info@thewildrosepress.com.

The Wild Rose Press, Inc.
www.thewildrosepress.com

Stay current with The Wild Rose Press, Inc.

Like us on Facebook
https://www.facebook.com/TheWildRosePress

And Follow us on Twitter

https://twitter.com/WildRosePress

www.ingramcontent.com/pod-product-compliance
Lightning Source LLC
Chambersburg PA
CBHW070836280626
47161CB00015B/686